THE PROPHECIES

RACE FOR THE HEIR

To Jojo

Enjoy more adventures with Ben, Tobias & Murgatroyd!

Kirsty

K A Riddiford

KIRSTY RIDDIFORD

THE PROPHECIES OF BALLITOR

Book One
BEN AND THE BOOK OF PROPHECIES

Book Two
RACE FOR THE HEIR

Book Three
MERIDIAN OBSIDIAN

KABooks Fantasy & Adventure

Reissued First Edition

First Published by HandE Publishers Ltd in the United Kingdom 2010.

Published by KABooks 2012
ISBN 978-1-909191-01-3
A CIP catalogue record for this book is available from
The British Library

All rights reserved. No part of this publication may be reproduced, stored in a retrieval system, or transmitted in any other form or by any means, electronic, mechanical, photocopying or otherwise without the prior permission of the copyright owners.

All the characters and events in this book are fictitious and any resemblance to actual persons, living or dead, is purely coincidental.

This book is sold subject to the condition that it shall not, by way of trade or otherwise, be lent, re-sold, hired out, or otherwise circulated without the publisher's prior consent in any form of binding or cover other than that in which it is published and without a similar condition including this condition being imposed on the subsequent purchaser.

Copyright © Kirsty Riddiford 2009
Inner Illustrations by Nina Cadman
Typeset by KaBooks
Edited by Kayleigh Hart and Natalie-Jane Revell

Printed and bound in England
by CPI Group (UK) Ltd, Croydon, CR0 4YY

www.kirstyriddifordbooks.com
wwwkamediaworks.co.uk

For the real Ben and Alex,

The Princesses Madeleine (Maddie) and Tremelia (Milly)

And, as ever, Matt and Toby

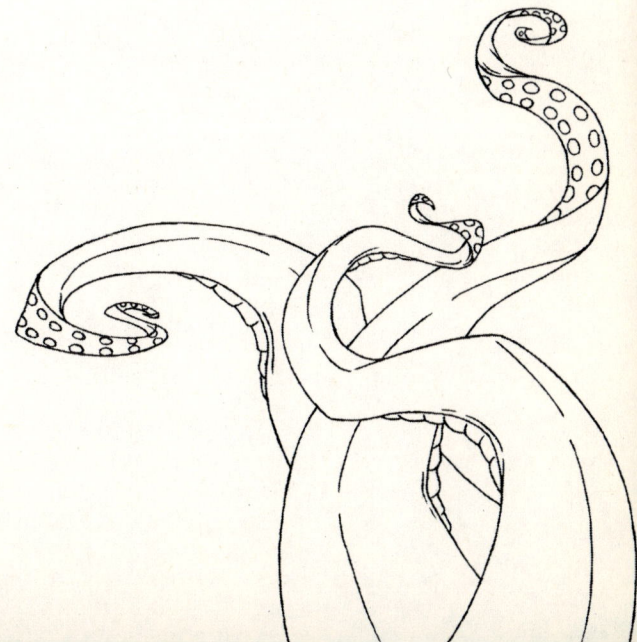

THE PROPHECIES OF BALLITOR

RACE FOR THE HEIR

books

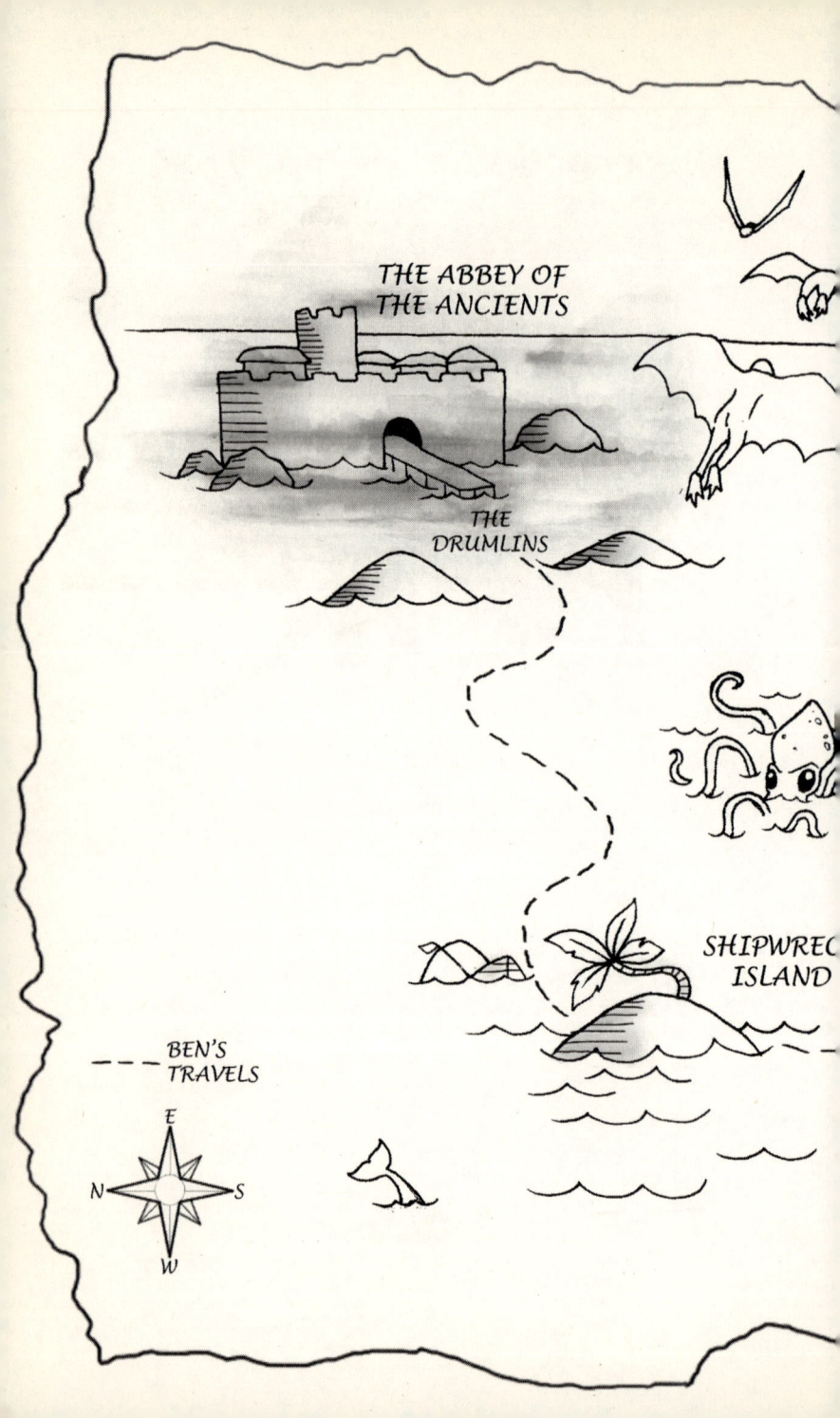

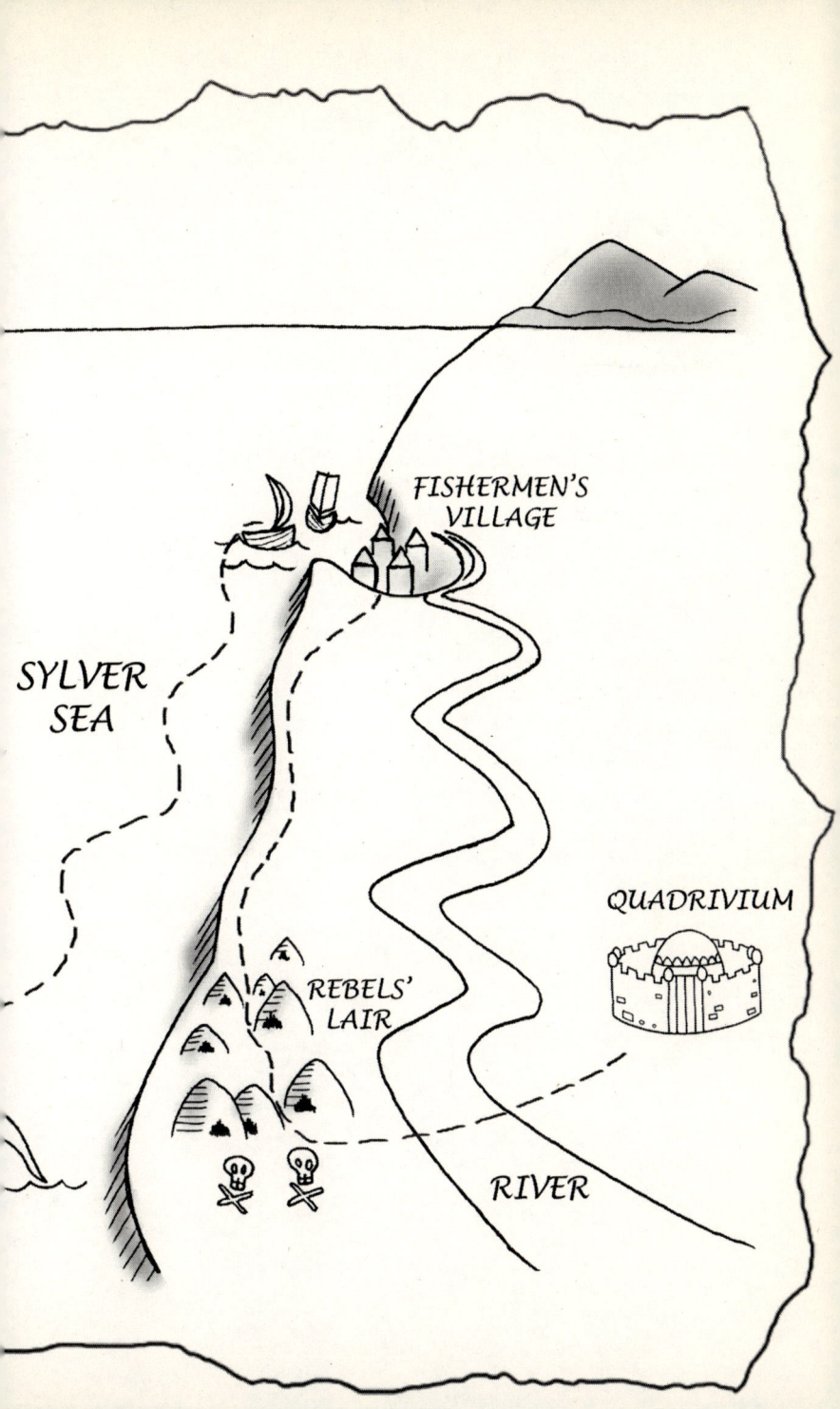

1

Nothing stirred. The young sentry rubbed his eyes and continued along the battlements towards the hut that served as a guardhouse, his breath leaving long streams of vapour that lingered in the air behind him. He stamped his feet as he walked in an attempt to coax the blood back into his frozen toes, then, just before he reached the guardhouse, he turned and began to walk back the way he had come.

The land beyond Quadrivium's walls remained as silent and deserted as ever. Derelict buildings littered the open grassland. A faint mist had appeared with the grey light of dawn and it hugged the ground, giving the impression the buildings were floating.

The sentry paused and rubbed his eyes once more. He had been looking at the same view every night for the past few weeks, but now something seemed out of place. He scanned the ruins, trying to identify what had changed. Finally, his eyes came to rest on an abandoned cottage. In the shadows of its crumbling walls, sitting absolutely still, he made out the figure of a very tall and slender cat. It was larger than any cat the sentry had ever seen, and it appeared to be observing him. He shifted nervously and glanced over his shoulder towards the guardhouse. When he looked back the cat was gone.

"Nimrod!" The whisper was very loud in the stillness of the dawn, making him jump. A face peered round the door of the hut followed by an arm which beckoned furiously to him.

Nimrod marched over. "Why are you whispering?" he said, speaking louder than necessary to cover his nervousness.

"Shhh," said the other sentry. "Come and look at this."

Nimrod allowed himself to be led through the wooden hut onto the next section of battlements that were patrolled by his best friend, Marcus, who now clutched his arm in an iron grip.

"Look over there – next to the old brick kiln," whispered Marcus.

Before his eyes had located the kiln, Nimrod had already guessed what he would see. This time he made sure he got a good look before it disappeared. The cat sat facing the wall, its head proudly raised and its paws placed neatly side by side in front of its lean body. It was far too big to be a domestic cat, thought Nimrod. He wondered briefly whether it was a wildcat, but he had never seen one this close to the city before.

He gave a start as the cat suddenly got to its feet in one fluid movement and approached the wall, moving with purpose and a powerful grace. Ignoring the two sentries watching from above, it began to pace up and down, lashing its tail from side to side as it stared up at the high wall.

"As if it's trying to find a way in," whispered Marcus. Nimrod nodded distractedly. He was trying to gauge whether the creature was a danger to the city, and whether it would be a good idea to wake their sergeant major. They had strict instructions not to disturb him unless the city was under attack, and Nimrod wasn't sure that one cat, however large, constituted such an emergency.

Marcus suddenly squeezed his arm. Nimrod glanced at his friend, but the other sentry was staring intently into the mist. Nimrod followed his gaze to see a second cat appear, as large as the first. Slowly, almost lazily, it strolled over to join the other cat and fell into step beside it. After a moment it moved away to sit on the grass. Then, from a different direction, a third cat appeared, followed shortly after by a fourth, and then a fifth. Each approached the pacing cat before moving away to join the others. Soon there were more than a dozen cats seated in a rough semi-circle facing the wall.

"It's like they're reporting back," said Nimrod thoughtfully.

"Do you think we should wake the sergeant major?" asked Marcus, voicing what his friend had been thinking.

At that moment the first ray of sun spilled over the horizon, the light picking out the spots in the golden fur of the assembled cats. The pacing cat stopped mid-stride, one paw still raised, then suddenly it turned and bounded into the mist, quickly followed by the other cats.

The two sentries looked at each other and then back at the now empty space beyond the wall. The mist began to dissipate as the light grew brighter, and the shadowy ruins took on a more solid appearance. The cats had left no trace of their visit. Although neither sentry spoke, each knew what the other was thinking: had they imagined the whole thing?

Nimrod cleared his throat. "I'd best get back to my side of the guardhouse," he said gruffly. "If old Frostie catches me on this side, there'll be troub–"

A massive explosion drowned out the end of his sentence. The two sentries were almost thrown to the ground by the force of the blast. There was the sound of falling masonry, and a plume of dust rose up beyond the guardhouse. Nimrod raced back through the hut and skidded to a halt, clutching the doorframe just in time to save himself from falling into a gaping hole.

Nothing but rubble remained of the battlements he had been patrolling just moments before.

* * *

The force of the explosion reached as far as the dungeons, which were located below the barracks in the grounds of the palace. The pale-skinned man reached out a bony hand to the wall to steady himself, grimacing as his fingers touched the damp, slimy stones.

"What was that?" asked the other man, looking up from where he was slumped on the ground. A large iron ball lay on the ground next to him, attached to his ankle by a length of chain.

"*That* was the diversion." The pale man looked pleased with himself as he wiped his soiled hand carefully on the other man's sleeve.

"At last!" said the man on the ground. He heaved a sigh of relief and tried to lever himself up into a standing position. "Will they know where we are, or do we wait for the guards to be distracted and sneak out by ourselves to join them?"

"Neither," answered the pale man, placing a hand on the other man's shoulder and pushing him back down. "It's time for me to put Plan B into effect. I must see the king immediately."

He turned to go, but was stopped by the other man's surprisingly strong arm grasping his leg. "You can't just leave me here," he pleaded, as tears began to roll down his cheeks. "What about our agreement?"

The pale man looked down in disgust at the man grovelling at his feet. "The agreement where I made you mayor of this city, where you have lived in luxury and splendour for the past ten years and more?"

The man nodded eagerly, his damp cheeks wobbling.

"That agreement expired with the failure of Plan A," said the pale man, finally pulling his leg free of the other's grasp. "Don't forget that you have been exposed as a traitor. You kidnapped the king's son and heir, and then you kidnapped the Dowager Bella – my own mother! You've made your bed, Ponsonby, now it's time for you to lie in it."

Ponsonby looked up at him in confusion. "But everything I did was for you, master. It was all part of our grand plan to rule the kingdom!"

"And the plan was flawed!" snapped the pale man. "There was too much that could go wrong – and it did. *Someone* has to bear the consequences." He turned and rapped on the thick wooden door. "Guards!"

"Wait!" cried Ponsonby desperately. "It's only a matter of time before the king finds out that *you* were behind it all! There are others who know of our association . . ." He hesitated for a second before continuing. "*I'll* tell him myself! I'll tell him everything: how you stole the Book of Prophecies and tried to use it to unite the rebels against him, how I infiltrated the council on your instructions!"

The pale man stood perfectly still facing the cell door, his back to the ex-mayor who was now almost hysterical. Finally he squared his shoulders and turned to face him. "Don't be ridiculous, Ponsonby, I wasn't going to *abandon* you," he said with a kindly tone that was so unexpected it made the other man pause for breath. "Look, I even brought you some supplies."

He unslung the bag from his shoulder and dropped it on the ground in front of the other man. A loaf of bread and a haunch of venison spilled out, and Ponsonby fell on them eagerly.

"I need to go now to execute step one of Plan B, but I'll be back." The pale man paused for a moment, watching the other tear into the meat as though he hadn't eaten in days. "I may be some time."

* * *

The pale man flung open the double doors and

entered the throne room. His confident stride faltered for a fraction of a second as he noticed the king sitting in what he already thought of as *his* throne, but he quickly recovered and moved swiftly through the ranks of assembled men. He approached the king and went down on one knee before him, noticing with pleasure that his mother, the Dowager Bella, had been reinstated to her position on the council.

"Sire," he murmured, glancing briefly at his mother through his long, pale blonde eyelashes. As he had expected, she was gazing at him lovingly. She would be a useful ally, he thought to himself.

"Rise, Damien," said the king impatiently. "Has the traitor spoken?"

The pale man was pleased that his mother had already laid the groundwork for him. It was obvious that neither she nor the king suspected him of colluding with the ex-mayor. He drew himself up to his full height and raised his voice so that everyone in the room would hear what he had to say. "Aye, sire. He confessed to summoning the rebels only moments before I arrested him – it is the sound of their cannon fire that disturbed your morning slumber. But they are merely the advance party. The treacherous vermin admitted that an entire army of rebels is on the march towards Quadrivium as I speak, intent on overthrowing your majesty!"

There was murmured dissent from the assembled men. "None of our spies have brought news of such an army," called a voice.

The pale man turned a second too late to identify the speaker. He ran his eyes over the councillors, recognising many who had been recruited by Ponsonby. He saw fear on their faces and wondered where their loyalties lay now that the mayor had been arrested. He doubted whether he could trust any of them.

Summoning his most scathing tone, he said, "And did your spies forewarn you of the rebels who are attacking Quadrivium's walls at this very moment?" As if to emphasise his words, there was a muffled explosion.

"No." It was the king who spoke, and the pale man turned back to face him, his face composed in a more respectful expression. "All available men were searching for my son," continued the king. "As you are no doubt aware, Prince Alexander was kidnapped by the traitor Ponsonby and was rescued only yesterday by your own mother, the Dowager Bella."

"I understand that your men were preoccupied, sire," said the pale man, "but I believe the kidnapping reveals an urgent need for better security for you, your family and for Quadrivium. For a start, I would suggest that you place your men under my command and let me see off this approaching army."

There was a collective intake of breath from the king's councillors before a babble of voices broke out.

"This is nonsense . . ."

"It's only a skirmish . . ."

"There's no evidence of an approaching army; it's just a few rebels causing trouble!"

"How do we know Ponsonby even speaks the truth?"

At that moment, the doors to the throne room burst open and a soldier dressed in the uniform of the king's household guards stood in the doorway. He dropped down on one knee. "Forgive me for intruding, sire, but an army approaches from the east. What are your orders?"

The king looked at Damien. "It appears your information is correct, after all, Lord Damien. What would you advise we do?"

Damien's features betrayed no emotion, but he was pleased that the king had finally used his title to which, as the queen's brother, he was entitled. He appeared to consider the question carefully before answering. "My first priority is your safety, sire. Allow me to remain by your side as your personal bodyguard throughout the forthcoming battle." There was more disgruntled muttering from the assembled men. The pale man ignored them and continued, "Assemble your troops by the east gate, every available fighting man needs to be armed and ready. And put your men under my control; I know the way the rebels fight."

A grey-haired man rose unsteadily to his feet. "Sire, the question of your safety and the command of your army is surely a decision for your council? Lord Damien does not understand our democratic process having been absent from Quadrivium for many years."

Before the king could reply, the soldier spoke up from the doorway. "There is no time for debate: the army draws ever nearer! Sire, I need your orders this very minute!"

The king looked thoughtfully at his councillors. After Mayor Ponsonby's betrayal, he was no longer sure who he could trust; whereas Damien – despite a long and unexplained absence – was his wife's brother and son of the Dowager Bella, for whom he had a lot of respect.

He turned abruptly and spoke to the soldier. "Do as Lord Damien says: prepare the men for battle, but await my command."

The man left the room in a hurry. Ignoring his councillors, the king beckoned Damien closer and lowered his voice. "So tell me, Lord Damien, what can we expect from this rebel army?"

The pale man hid his smile behind his hand. "First, sire, we must determine exactly how large a force it is. It approaches from the east, so I believe our best viewpoint would be the south-east battlements."

The king nodded slowly, and then stood. "I must dress for battle. Meet me in the guardhouse above the south-east gate at half past the hour." With a curt nod to his councillors, he strode from the room.

Damien waited with bowed head until the king had left and then turned to face the councillors. With the exception of his mother, all of them were staring at him with a mixture of hatred and envy on their faces.

* * *

Queen Katrina tiptoed into the Royal Nursery and approached the cot. Two nursemaids sat either side of the sleeping baby looking unnaturally alert, determined that the prince would not be kidnapped again, at least not on their shift. They stood and curtseyed to the queen.

"He's sleeping like a little angel, your majesty," whispered one.

"Not a peep from him all night," said the other.

The queen smiled and dismissed them with a wave of her hand. They left the nursery reluctantly and with many backward glances. As soon as they were gone, the queen picked up the sleeping baby and sat down carefully in the rocking chair beside the fire, tucking the blanket around the young prince's soft, warm body. He made a mewling sound but didn't wake. After rocking gently for a while, she undid the top two buttons of his sleep-suit and eased it back to reveal his plump shoulder with its distinctive coronet birthmark.

Her husband, the king, had exactly the same birthmark. It was the mark of royal lineage, a strange quirk of nature that branded both the present ruler and the next in line to the throne. It was said that if the king ever failed to produce an heir, a commoner would be born with the coronet birthmark and would rise to rule the kingdom. Until her son had been born, the queen suspected that many an expectant mother secretly hoped to find her own newborn marked with the coronet. But finally she had given her husband a son and heir, complete with the birthmark.

Queen Katrina bent her head and gently kissed her son's shoulder, leaving a smudge of soft tinted wax from her lips which she absently wiped away with her thumb.

She frowned. Rising, she carried the baby over to the small bathtub where a jug of water stood warming over the fire in readiness for his morning bath. She emptied some of the water into the tub, then dipped in a flannel and rubbed the baby's shoulder with increasing vigour, oblivious to his indignant cries as he was roused from his slumber.

"No," she gasped softly, hardly able to draw breath. Then suddenly an agonised wail came rushing out of her. "NOOOooo!"

2

Ben woke to the smell of frying bacon. He kept his eyes closed, listening to the sounds of activity around him, until something cold and wet was thrust into his face and he opened his eyes with a laugh.

"I'm awake, Tobias!" he cried, pushing the dog's muzzle away. The large, golden-haired dog sat back on his haunches, his mouth stretched into a wide grin. Ben propped himself up on his elbows and looked around. The sun was barely above the horizon, but the camp was already buzzing with an air of excitement. Those around him were finally returning home to Quadrivium and their families, having been rescued by Ben and his companions after spending fifteen long years trapped by an enchanted fire in the Mountains of the Outer Boundaries.

A strange looking creature, half man and half horse, trotted past and Ben jumped up. "Hi there, Samswift," he called out.

"Morning greetings, Ben," replied the centaur, slowing briefly to a walk. "Would you care to join me for a breakfast graze?"

Ben laughed. "I think I can smell something a bit more appetizing than grass, but thanks for the invite!"

He made his way through the makeshift tents and went to wash in the river. Smoke from countless cooking fires mingled with the mist rising up from the water. The river marked the outer boundary of Quadrivium's farmlands, and beyond the wheat fields he could make out the hazy dome-shaped silhouette of the palace in the distance. A spasm of nervousness clenched his stomach and he had to remind himself that he wasn't the same penniless street urchin he had been when he had left Quadrivium; he was returning a hero, bearing the ancient Book of Prophecies.

Ben was about to climb out of the river in search of breakfast when his eye was drawn to movement at the edge of the wood on the other side. He stopped and stared in surprise as Arrowbright, the young soldier who had accompanied him on his journey to find the Book of Prophecies, emerged from the trees supporting a young woman. Together they staggered down the slope towards him. Ben recognised the girl immediately, as did Tobias who was already beginning to growl, the hackles along his back bristling.

Arrowbright spotted Ben and called out to him. "Ben, quickly, come and help me with Gretilda, she's –" The rest of his words were drowned out by a sound like thunder coming from the direction of the city. Gretilda raised her head from Arrowbright's shoulder and moaned loudly.

"Hurry, Ben!" cried Arrowbright.

Jolted into action, Ben climbed out of the river and ran towards them. He looped one of Gretilda's arms around his shoulder. She slumped against him and he stumbled under her weight, but Arrowbright pulled her upright and, supporting her between them, they made their way to the riverbank and lowered her carefully to the ground. By now her moans had given way to a constant whimpering.

"What's going on?" asked Ben, cautiously putting some space between himself and the shivering girl. The last time he had seen Gretilda she had trapped Arrowbright in quicksand. The soldier had been almost completely submerged, but Ben had managed to release him using a magical strand of merman's hair. As they were making their escape she had revealed to Ben that his mother – whom he had long believed to be dead – was still alive. She had sworn to tell him what she knew only if he returned her Sacred Stone to her, which had been stolen by the pale man. It was a task that Ben had been unable to fulfil.

"He has the Stone; he's going to use it, he has the Stone; he's going to use it," muttered Gretilda over and over again through chattering teeth.

"It's all she's been able to say since I found her," said Arrowbright, looking at Ben with a worried frown.

"We *know* who has the Stone," said Ben, his cheeks burning with shame as he remembered watching the pale man disappear with it from the Mountains of the Outer Boundaries. "But what does she mean: he's going to use it?"

The shaman suddenly stopped shaking and sat up straight. She turned her head slowly until she was looking at Ben, but her eyes were unfocussed as though she were staring straight through him. Then she uttered a single word, "Teah."

Ben stared at the shaman for a long moment, then took a step forward and crouched down next to her. "What do you mean? Where is she? Where is my mother?"

"Their fates are intertwined."

"Whose fate? Tell me, whose fate is intertwined with my mother's?"

"The prince's," replied Gretilda in a clear, high voice. She opened her mouth to say more, but at that moment another roll of thunder sounded from the direction of the city. A tremor ran through the shaman's body and she began to shiver once more.

"The Stone . . . we must hurry! He's going to use it . . . he's going to use it . . ."

Once it became clear that she had nothing more to say about his mother, Ben turned away from her and looked up at Arrowbright with shining eyes. "The prince! If Gretilda's right, this must mean my mother is in Quadrivium with the prince!"

Before Arrowbright could reply, they were joined by a man dressed in a bugler's uniform that was far too small for him. Although he looked to be about the same age as Arrowbright, he had been just a child when he was trapped by the enchanted fire, and had long outgrown his clothes.

"Excuse me, sir," said the bugler, "your father is asking for you. The scouts have returned."

Although he was addressing Arrowbright, Ben noticed that the man couldn't take his eyes off Gretilda. She was a beautiful young woman, but Ben vividly recalled her ability to transform herself into an old hag as the mood took her.

Arrowbright nodded at the man. "Stay here and keep an eye on her," he ordered. "Tobias, you stay with him."

The dog watched them reproachfully as they left to hear what the scouts had to report.

* * *

"He's in Quadrivium, no doubt about it," drawled the sun leopard, pausing briefly to lick her paw before continuing. "His scent led us right to the city walls."

"Well done, Shira." The man in the faded uniform glanced up and spotted Ben and Arrowbright at the edge of the gathering. He beckoned them forward, but Shira hadn't finished.

"More troubling is the presence of the rebels," she continued.

"How many?" asked Arrowbright as he pushed through the crowd to join his father.

"Ten men: five groups of two scattered at regular intervals around the perimeter," answered the sun leopard. "Obviously not enough men to be a threat to either ourselves or Quadrivium, but they are equipped with cannons – that's the explosions you can hear. Fortunately, they have only a limited stock of cannonballs, and no other weapons that we could see, so the damage will be limited. I can't imagine what they hope to achieve by the attack."

"I'd wager it's some devious plan of the pale man," said a high-pitched voice. Ben craned his neck to locate the speaker and saw the wise, wrinkled face of the lizard who had spoken. The lizard shook its head as though to dismiss the sun leopard's news. "As you say, the rebels are too few to concern us, therefore our plan remains unchanged: we continue onwards to Quadrivium! If we depart now, we should be within the city walls by mid-morning."

"Kimon, if I may make a suggestion?"

Ben turned towards the familiar voice. A huge eagle was seated on the other side of the gathering, one of his powerful wings bandaged tightly to his side.

"Of course, Murgatroyd, the floor is yours," answered the lizard courteously.

"I am well aware that the troops are eager to return home, but *my* priority is to alert the king to the traitors in his midst before they can do any further damage. May I suggest that Arrowbright, Ben and myself take an advance party and enter Quadrivium through the nearest gate? The rest of the troops can split up and enter through the other gates in order to avoid a bottleneck."

The lizard lumbered to its feet, nodding its scaly head. "Good idea, Murgatroyd. Select your men and leave immediately. Shira can accompany you."

The crowd began to drift away to prepare for their long-awaited return home. Arrowbright and Ben joined Murgatroyd who was already giving instructions to Shira, the sun leopard. "Assemble those troops who are ready to leave and meet us by the main tent."

Shira nodded once and bounded away. Murgatroyd turned towards Arrowbright, and then stopped as he saw the look on the young soldier's face. "What is it?"

"Gretilda – she's here, in the camp."

Murgatroyd's eyes widened. "What in Tritan's name is that witch doing here?"

"She says my mother is in Quad–" began Ben.

"Shaman," corrected Arrowbright, speaking at the same time. "She's a shaman."

"I don't care what she is!" cried Murgatroyd. "She tried to sabotage our quest to find the Book of Prophecies! What does she want?"

"She wants to come with us."

Ben glanced at Arrowbright in surprise, forgetting about his mother for a moment. "I thought she couldn't leave the forest," he said, recalling what Murgatroyd had told him about a shaman's magic being drawn from a powerful force of nature. Gretilda's magic came from the thick forest that covered the area between the river and the desert. Her Sacred Stone encapsulated that power and allowed her to travel freely, but from what she said, it appeared to still be in the pale man's possession.

"She can leave the forest, but she will be powerless," said Arrowbright, "and entirely reliant on us to protect her."

Murgatroyd paced up and down a few times, shaking his head. Finally he turned to face Arrowbright. "If we take her with us, she is your responsibility. Fetch what you need and meet me by the main tent."

* * *

For such a large company they moved surprisingly quickly down the wide, grassy avenues that ran through the wheat fields. A sense of nervous excitement pervaded the troops. Many were apprehensive. They had been missing – presumed dead – for fifteen years and no one in Quadrivium knew they were coming; but each man and beast marched with their head held high, certain they would be welcomed home as heroes.

Ben walked at the head of the procession, with Tobias trotting beside him. Directly behind was one of Samswift's cousins, pulling a wooden cart. It wasn't usual work for a centaur, but an exception had been made, for inside the cart lay the Book of Prophecies. Murgatroyd rode beside the Book, his sharp claws digging into the wood of the cart as it jolted over the uneven ground. At Arrowbright's insistence, Gretilda had been lifted up onto the cart's tailgate and he walked close behind her, accompanied by the bugler who had formed an attachment to the shaman and was eager to remain by her side. Between them, Arrowbright and the bugler held aloft a faded blue banner showing the king's ancestral coat of arms.

The wheat field suddenly came to an end. Before

them lay the stretch of wasteland which encircled the city, dotted with the crumbling remains of buildings abandoned after the wall around the city had been built. Beyond the ruins was the wall itself and rising above it the golden dome of the palace, glinting in the bright morning sunlight. Ben's heart swelled with excitement as his thoughts turned to his mother somewhere within the city walls.

He was distracted from the sight by a peculiar whistling sound close overhead. Instinctively, he flung himself to the ground just as a deadly fountain of earth and rocks flew up into the air. He curled up into a ball as the debris thudded down around him, then felt Tobias's warm body cowering next to him and covered both their heads with his arms. His ears were ringing from the blast and everything sounded as though it were happening at a great distance.

When the shower of rocks finally stopped, he raised his head cautiously. Close to the wall, not far from where he lay, a huge crater had been gouged out of the earth. Shira appeared from the direction of the wheat field and approached the cart in a few swift bounds.

"All clear!" she called. "That's the last of the rebels' cannonballs – on this side of the city, at least. I'm just going to see whether those on the other side have any –" A second explosion ripped through her words. Ben saw the cart fly up into the air, catapulting Murgatroyd and the Book of Prophecies skywards. As though in slow motion, he watched the Book turn end over end, its pages fluttering open. Sunlight glinted on the bronze inlay of its cover as it turned. Instinctively, he stretched out his arms towards the falling Book. The moment he caught it, everything seemed to speed up again.

"Take cover!" roared Arrowbright, dragging Gretilda beneath the shelter of the upturned cart. Ben caught a glimpse of Shira's tail as she disappeared back into the wheat field, and then turned to see Tobias tugging at the sleeve of the bugler who was still lying in the open, stunned, his mouth agape as though to catch the clods of earth which rained down around them. The centaur lay motionless on the ground beside the cart, thick fluid the colour of sapphires pumping steadily from a wound in his side.

Ben looked in vain for Murgatroyd, and had almost given up hope when a length of white bandage fluttered to the ground in front of him. He looked up to see the eagle hovering awkwardly overhead, beating his injured wing against the air in an effort to stay aloft.

"It's not the rebels who are firing at us!" cried Murgatroyd. "It's the city guards – they must think we're the enemy! Our only hope is for me to convince them otherwise!"

Ben stood gazing after the huge eagle as he flew

unsteadily towards the city walls, until Arrowbright grabbed his arm and dragged him towards the cart.

* * *

As Murgatroyd rose slowly and painfully into the air his acute hearing picked up shouted orders coming from the direction of the battlements, followed by the unmistakeable sound of cannons being reloaded. His injured wing throbbed as he dragged himself higher into the sky. He refused to focus on the pain, and instead his senses searched for the warm currents of air on which he could glide. At last he felt the gentle ruffle of wind beneath his feathers, followed by a sudden uplift, and a second later he was looking down at the scene below from an immense height.

The tiny figures of the guards scrambled over the battlements, directing the cannons towards the approaching troops who had by now almost surrounded the city as they made their way to each of the four main gates. Murgatroyd saw a puff of smoke followed a moment later by the hollow pop of cannon fire, and men and beasts scattered, fleeing for cover.

There was no time to lose; he had to convince the guards that they were firing on their own troops. He dipped his good wing towards the battlements and began to descend rapidly. A side wind caught him and pushed him towards the heart of Quadrivium. Without thinking, he thrust out his injured wing to correct the movement and pain shot up to his shoulder. Suddenly he was spiralling out of control, the city growing larger and larger as it rushed up to meet him.

At the last moment he managed to straighten his good wing and spread his feathers wide to create a brake against the rushing wind, but the manoeuvre wheeled him round in the other direction and he found himself heading straight towards the highest point of the city: the golden dome. He took the brunt of the impact on his thickly-feathered chest and began to slide downwards. His sharp claws scrabbled for purchase, but the surface of the dome was as smooth as glass and he swiftly gathered speed. Desperately he pushed out his good wing, but succeeded only in spinning his body round so that he was sliding head first towards the square below.

The dome dropped sharply away beneath him and for a brief moment he was airborne . . . then he landed in a heap on the balcony encircling the dome and lay there, winded by the force of the impact. He didn't notice the sound of a door opening behind him until an astonished voice said, "Murgatroyd, is that you?"

Murgatroyd lifted his head, hardly daring to hope that he would see the one person who would immediately grasp the situation and, more importantly, had the authority to do something about it.

"Bella!" he sighed with relief, "I have never been more pleased to see anyone in my entire life! You have to stop the bombardment! It's us out there: me and Ben and all those who were caught up in the Great Fire of Barbearland –"

"That's impossible," interrupted Bella, a puzzled frown creasing her forehead. "Damien told us that the approaching army are reinforcements for the rebels who have been attacking the city since dawn. They're intent on taking Quadrivium! Damien's with the king right now –" Her voice was drowned out by a volley of cannon fire.

Murgatroyd waited impatiently for the explosions to cease. When he spoke again, his tone was urgent. "Bella, Damien is a traitor. It was he who stole the Book of Prophecies all those years ago, and he used it to manipulate the rebels against the king."

"No!" cried Bella, taking a step back. "Don't say such things, Murgatroyd! My son is a hero – he single-handedly captured Mayor Ponsonby! How could he possibly be a traitor?"

Murgatroyd stared at his old friend in shock. He could tell that nothing he said would persuade her that her son was the enemy. Drawing on the last of his strength, he pulled himself up and fluttered weakly to the balustrade. "I am sorry, Bella, I didn't want to be the one to tell you, but Damien was in league with Ponsonby all along. It was Damien who allowed the Great Fire of Barbearland to take place. He used the prophecy to his own advantage, but his victims didn't perish as he believed they would – they're out there right now, beyond the wall, trying to come home and being fired on by their own kin!"

Without waiting to hear her response, he launched himself into the air, knowing the instant he did so that his injured wing could not support him. Neither he nor Bella heard the door to the balcony slam shut, or the clatter of feet on the stone staircase as the eavesdropper ran from the scene.

3

The pale man strode along the battlements towards his rendezvous with the king. He was feeling confident. The rebels' dawn attack on the city had created an atmosphere of panic and uncertainty into which his claim that the approaching army were rebel reinforcements had been readily accepted as the truth. It seemed almost a shame that the rebels – who were, after all, only obeying his orders – would be destroyed by the city guards' counterattack, but the chaos of battle was necessary to cover his escape once he had executed Plan B.

A dull thud was followed by a high-pitched whine and a thunderous crash as the first of the cannonballs flew out over the city wall to explode in the ruin-strewn wasteland. The pale man smiled to himself. He had gone ahead and given the order to begin the attack. The captain of the guards had been only too pleased to comply; he had been in a state of shock ever since the troops began emerging from the surrounding fields.

As the pale man approached the south-east gate, he was pleased to see that the king had not yet arrived. He ordered the sentries manning the guardhouse to join the main force by the east gate, and sauntered out onto the battlements just in time to see a second explosion tear into an old stone cottage that stood amongst the ruins. Its front wall was blown to smithereens, and great clods of rock and earth thundered down onto the grass around it. He watched a stream of figures stumble out of the cottage and flee for the shelter of the wheat field.

The pale man smoothed the front of his immaculate white suit and felt the outline of the object that nestled within. He drew it out of his pocket and cupped it in his palm. At first glance, it appeared to be a rather ordinary rock, but he knew better, for he had stolen it from one of the old shamans. This was a Sacred Stone. Grasping it carefully between the fingers and thumb of one hand, he held it in front of his eyes and rotated it slowly. A continuous line of runes encircled the Stone, particularly noticeable in the bright sunlight which cast shadows in the shallow indentations. He tilted the Stone one way and then the other, watching the shadows lengthen around its surface. Suddenly they were obliterated by a much larger shadow that blocked out the sunlight.

"What in Tritan's name is going on?"

The pale man slipped the Stone back into his pocket and turned slowly to face the king. "Sire," he said, "the rebels were advancing rapidly. A decision had to be made, so in your absence I gave the order to attack."

The king stared at him long and hard before turning to look out over the wasteland. His eyes rested for a while on the destroyed cottage before continuing on over the huge craters gouged out of the earth until he came to a blue banner lying abandoned on the ground next to an upturned cart.

"Go and tell the men to stop firing – at once."

"Forgive me, sire, but –"

"Do it. Now." The king had not taken his eyes off the banner.

"I can't do that." The pale man slipped the Sacred Stone from his pocket and stood with it clenched behind his back.

The king turned towards him with a look of fury on his face. "Those troops are not the enemy!" he cried. "Can't you see that banner, man? It's one of ours! Stop the attack this instant and send out the medics – that's an order!"

Very slowly and deliberately, the pale man drew his hand out from behind his back and opened his palm. The runes were no longer picked out by shadows, but instead blazed brightly as though the sun itself was trapped inside the Stone and was piercing its way out through the etched markings.

"I'm afraid I'm going to have to disobey that particular order, sire," said the pale man, watching the other man's reaction carefully.

The king seemed dazzled by the light, unable to look away. The pale man took a step closer, raising the Stone on the palm of his hand as though offering up a gift. The brilliance reflected off the king's irises, turning them from dark blue to a shining white, but despite the glare he didn't look away. As the pale man brought the Stone closer to the king's eyes, the intense light from the runes became ever fiercer and brighter until finally the Stone seemed to disappear in a blinding flash.

The force of it thrust the king backwards, and he collapsed in a heap against the wall of the battlements. The pale man took a step forwards and bent over the king's crumpled body, placing the back of his hand near the king's mouth to see if he was still breathing.

Unseen by the pale man, a figure drew swiftly into the shadows of the guardhouse, and a moment later the silence was broken by the loud clatter of tin mugs falling to the floor. The pale man straightened up and stared over his shoulder at the hut. With a brief glance at the king, he turned and made his way slowly towards the open doorway.

* * *

Coloured spots swam in front of Princess Madeleine's eyes as she groped her way down the steps. Lord Damien's body had shielded her from the worst of the blinding light, but despite this her vision had still not yet returned to normal. Her rapid breathing was accompanied by a soft whimper as she moved as fast as she could without losing her footing on the steep spiral staircase.

She tried to gather her thoughts as she fled. Her Great Aunt Bella had believed all along that there was some greater mind behind Mayor Ponsonby's treacherous plots, and Madeleine's own suspicions had been aroused when Lord Damien had suddenly reappeared in Quadrivium with Ponsonby as his prisoner. At first, she had been reluctant to voice her opinions to Bella – after all, Damien was Bella's son. (Although Madeleine called Bella her great aunt and Queen Katrina her aunt, they were only related by marriage – Madeleine's mother was sister to the king.) She had finally been on her way to confront Bella when she had overheard her great aunt with an unseen visitor who had confirmed what Madeleine believed. And now she had seen it with her own eyes: not only was Lord Damien a traitor, but a murderer too.

Madeleine strained her ears for sounds of pursuit, but heard only her own footsteps and laboured breathing. She slowed to a standstill and listened carefully, holding her breath. All was silent above. She peered downwards, trying to see past the ghostly blobs of light that drifted in front of her eyes. Below her the darkness was impenetrable, but she was too frightened to retrace her steps in case she came face to face with Lord Damien; so, taking a deep breath, she continued downwards until the steps came to an abrupt end.

Resting her hand against the cold stone wall, Madeleine stretched out her foot and tested the ground in front of her. She found it to be solid, and took a small step away from the staircase. Overcoming her fear of the unknown, she slid her other foot into the darkness. The movement gave her courage and she stepped forward with a little more determination. She had taken six or seven paces when her foot struck something in her path. She leapt back and then froze, her senses alert for movement, but there was only silence. She inched forward again warily until she found the obstacle, and then, gathering all her courage, she stretched out her hand and touched it.

The object was cold and firm, with a texture like toughened leather. She prodded it gingerly, and then gave it a gentle push with one hand, but it was solid and didn't move. She reached upwards around its bulbous shape until she found the top, but it was too high to climb over. Then she stretched out her hands in both directions, but the obstacle was wider than the span of her arms. Hesitantly, she began to shuffle her way around it.

As she felt her way along, its shape began to feel vaguely familiar. It was slightly ribbed and sloped gently towards the ground before ending in a bulbous outcropping. She explored it further, trailing her fingertips down until she came to a cavity. Tentatively she felt inside. Her fingers encountered a row of hard, sharp teeth.

Madeleine began to tremble. Her breath came in jagged little pants as she stood in the pitch darkness, still clinging to what she now recognised to be the jaw of a cold, still creature. Thoughts darted around her head: what was it; what had killed it – for she was certain it was dead; were there more of the same down here; or more of whatever had killed this one?

As this last thought entered her head, she sensed movement behind her. She turned slowly, pressing herself back into the nook between the shoulder and head of the dead creature, and peered into the darkness. Something was circling. She heard a soft footfall and felt a slight disturbance of the air, and then the corpse behind her shuddered as though it had woken. A faint draught ruffled her hair from above and a strand of something warm and wet slid down her cheek.

Madeleine's survival instincts suddenly kicked in. Pushing herself away, she sprinted full pelt into the darkness, giving herself up to the freedom of sheer, unfettered panic. She lost all sense of direction but she didn't care, focussing only on the cool breeze on her face and the burn in her muscles as she ran. She heard a muffled explosion and unthinkingly turned towards it. In the distance, a pinprick of light appeared, kindling a flicker of hope in her chest. It gave her fresh reserves of energy and she raced on.

As she came closer, the light drew her gaze upwards until she had to crane her neck to look at it. Glorious daylight streamed down through a hole in the roof overhead, too high for her to reach. She slowed to a walk and stared up in dismay. She didn't notice the pile of rubble until she had walked straight into it and grazed her shinbone on a chunk of rock. She quickly dropped her gaze to the mound of stones and broken masonry, and then scrambled up it in a frenzy of eagerness until she was directly beneath the hole – but to her intense disappointment she still couldn't reach it.

Glancing back down, she saw the creature emerge from the shadows and into the circle of light. It had the same huge dimensions as the dead creature she had left behind. Lowering its massive head to the ground, it cast around for her scent. Then, as she watched, it raised its head and looked directly at her. Madeleine's legs gave way beneath her as she caught sight of its empty eye sockets above a slack, slobbering mouth. She fell to her knees, setting off a mini avalanche of rubble that came to rest at the creature's scaly paws. It dipped its head to inspect the stones, snuffling amongst them and covering them with a glistening film of saliva, then, without raising its snout, it began to climb.

Frozen with terror, Madeleine could only watch it approach. It moved slowly with a jerky gait, using its rear legs to propel its body forward and scrabbling with its front claws to find purchase amongst the loose stones. Once or twice it slid back down to the bottom and Madeleine held her breath in the hope that it would give up and go away, but all that happened was that the pile of rubble appeared to sink closer to the ground as the stones rolled outwards into the darkness, and the creature doggedly continued to climb.

Without taking her eyes off it, Madeleine felt amongst the rubble until her fingers closed around a stone with a sharp, pointed edge. She waited until the creature was so close that she could smell its foul breath, then stood up and drew back her arm. Her movement disturbed the loose rubble, causing the mound to shift, and the slab on which she stood suddenly tilted to one side. She felt herself falling backwards and drew breath to scream, but instead she gasped as her shoulders were caught in a strong grip and her balance firmly restored.

"Silence," breathed a voice in her ear. "Stay as still as you possibly can."

Obediently, she froze. Suddenly her senses were assaulted by an appalling smell as something flew past her face. There was a wet thud as it landed in the darkness beyond the circle of light. Hastily, the creature slid down the pile of rubble and disappeared after it.

"Skinned rat," explained the voice. "Now quick, climb up onto my shoulders."

Madeleine turned to face her rescuer and almost stumbled and fell for a second time. "Uncle Penthesilean!"

Penthesilean grinned at her surprise. His bushy eyebrows were dark with dust and dirt, but his teeth gleamed white.

"What are you doing down here?"

"Long story," said Penthesilean. "Cut short: Ponsonby had me arrested on a trumped-up charge. I escaped from the cell but got lost in these tunnels. But what in Tritan's name are *you* doing here?"

They both jumped as a high-pitched howl came out

of the darkness.

"Explanations later," said Penthesilean, bending down and holding out his interlaced fingers. "Come on!"

Madeleine grasped his arms and stepped lightly onto his hand. He raised her until she could step onto his broad shoulders. From there she could easily reach the edge of the hole, and she braced her arms against the sides and levered herself up and into the daylight. She turned and stretched her arms down towards Penthesilean, but the distance was too great. As she stared down at him in dismay, a movement caught her eye. He saw her flinch and glanced over his shoulder at the creature which had emerged once more from the shadows.

Desperately, Madeleine looked around, squinting in the bright sunlight. She found herself amongst the ruins of a building, which she guessed from the horseshoes lying around a blackened furnace had once belonged to a blacksmith. Her eye fell on a heap of reins lying tangled on the floor and she dragged the whole lot to the edge of the hole and looked down. The creature was halfway up the mound, moving slowly but steadily towards Penthesilean. With shaking hands, Madeleine pulled at the narrow strips of leather. She managed to free two long pieces and twisted them together, then secured one end around a heavy iron anvil and dropped the other into the hole.

Penthesilean grabbed hold of the reins just as the creature lunged towards him. He swung his legs out of range of its snapping jaws and hauled himself arm over arm up the makeshift rope. Madeleine grabbed hold of his shoulders and slowly, with great difficulty, helped him clamber out of the hole. He collapsed by her side and for a long moment they lay in silence, stunned by their narrow escape.

A strange scraping noise made Madeleine open her eyes. She raised her head. The sound came again and she spun round in time to see the anvil shift closer to the hole. The reins were pulled taut, one end still hanging down into the hole. Curious, Madeleine stood up and peered into the hole. The creature was balanced on the mound of rubble tugging at the end of the reins. Watching with morbid fascination, Madeleine didn't notice the crack in the floor. It started at the edge of the hole and spread quickly between her feet towards the anvil.

As the ground suddenly gave way beneath her, there was only time for Madeleine to give a little scream before she slipped back down into the hole, towards the creature's gaping maw.

* * *

The pale man stood at the top of the spiral staircase. His eyes darted from left to right as he debated whether to go in pursuit of whoever had been hiding in the guardhouse. He had hoped to have left the city before the king's body was discovered; the fact that someone had witnessed the murder was a complication he had not foreseen.

Finally he turned away from the steps with a furious snort. Grasping the king's shoulders, he dragged him into the guardhouse and propped him up against the door on the opposite side of the hut, then he slipped back onto the battlements, locking the other door behind him and tossing the key over the wall. He would stick to his plan, but now there was even less time to lose.

Moving swiftly along the battlements, he reached the guardhouse on the far side of the gate and raced down the steps. He exited the turret cautiously and slipped into the shadows of the warehouses opposite, then made his way to the palace by quiet back streets. He relaxed only when the guards at the palace gate let him through without a second glance, and with determined strides made his way up the flight of steps towards his sister's living quarters. He was about to knock on the door to her chambers when it suddenly flew open and the queen collided with him.

"Katrina!" he cried, grasping her hands to keep her

from falling. "Whatever is the matter?"

"It's Alexander!" The queen stared at her brother through tear-filled eyes. "He's gone!"

At that moment, the unmistakeable sound of a baby's cry rang out from the chamber behind her. The pale man gave his sister a curious look. "Who's that then?"

"It's not him – that child is an imposter! He *looks* like my darling Alexander, but the birthmark is a fake! Oh, Damien, I can't bear it!" She flung herself against her brother's chest, her whole body shuddering with sobs. The pale man shifted uncomfortably and looked round for someone to help.

"You!" he snapped as a young maidservant appeared in the doorway opposite. "Come over here and help the queen."

The girl stared wide-eyed at the queen's grief, but willingly stepped forward and helped Damien escort her back into her chambers.

"Stay with her while I fetch somebody," he ordered, before almost running out of the room. There was one person who would know where the real Prince Alexander was, but he suspected it may already be too late.

4

Madeleine swung slowly to and fro above the creature's snapping jaws. Just as the ground beneath her collapsed, Penthesilean had thrown himself forward with lightning reflexes, and grabbed her wrist. Now he lay on his belly on the ground, with his head and shoulders suspended over the gaping hole. Madeleine squealed as she felt the creature's hot breath on her ankle, and she jerked her body away, causing Penthesilean's clasp on her wrist to slip.

"Grab my other hand," he barked.

Madeleine squinted up into the light and raised her free arm towards him. Penthesilean reached down and she grabbed his wrist until she hung suspended from his arms like a trapeze artist.

"Good girl. Now I'm going to move slowly backwards until we have you out of that hole. You just hold on."

He braced his elbows against the floor and heaved. Dirt and stones showered down onto Madeleine's head as the edge of the hole crumbled against the pressure, and she screamed as she felt herself drop closer towards the creature's mouth. Penthesilean kept his grip on her wrists, but now his entire upper body hung down into the hole.

"Uncle Penthesilean . . ." began Madeleine.

"Don't move."

"But —"

"Just give me a moment," said Penthesilean, breathing heavily. The floor supporting the lower part of his body felt as though it could give way at any moment, and his hands were slippery with nervous sweat. Madeleine's wrists were starting to slide slowly from his grasp when suddenly a length of rope dropped into the hole next to him.

"Take hold of the rope," said a calm voice from above.

Cautiously, Madeleine released one of Penthesilean's wrists and grabbed hold of the rope. Penthesilean breathed a sigh of relief as some of her weight was transferred from his aching shoulders. He let go of her other wrist so that she could grab the rope with both hands, and then he felt someone hauling him out by his legs. Once his head was out of the hole, he pushed himself up and looked around. The other end of the rope was tied securely to an iron ring on the wall and a man of about his own age stood beside it. The man wrapped his arms around the rope and said to Penthesilean, "If you give me a hand, we'll have the lady out in no time."

Together they hauled on the rope until Madeleine was able to scramble out of the hole. While the stranger checked that she was unhurt, Penthesilean examined him closely. The man wore an old-fashioned uniform similar to that of the king's regiments, shabby and patched in many places. His body was lean and wiry, and his cropped hair was bleached by the sun, giving him a youthful appearance despite his lined face. Penthesilean finally realised that the man was staring back at him with a curious look on his face.

"Do I know you?" began the stranger, before stopping himself. "Forgive me, now is not the time for questions. It's not safe for us here; there's been a lull in the bombardment, but it could start again at any moment. You must come with me."

Madeleine did not resist as the stranger took her arm and led her through the doorway and out into the open.

"Do you think you can run?" he asked her, glancing over his shoulder to include Penthesilean. Madeleine and Penthesilean both nodded, and followed him in a running crouch towards the cover of the wheat field.

Faces peered out at them as they approached, and then the wheat parted and a young soldier appeared, smiling broadly.

"Penthesilean, I thought I'd never see you again!" The soldier flung his arms around Penthesilean before noticing Madeleine hovering behind. "Princess Madeleine!" he cried in surprise. Seeing the lack of recognition on her face, he continued, "My name is Arrowbright. I'm one of your uncle's men."

"*Penthesilean!*" exclaimed the man who had rescued them. "I thought I recognised you." Almost reluctantly, he offered Penthesilean his hand and introduced himself. "Matthius Brightlove."

Penthesilean could not hide his look of surprise.

"Yes, *that* Matthius Brightlove," continued the man. "Bella's husband."

Upon hearing Bella's name, Madeleine was reminded of the reason she had ended up on the wrong side of the city wall. "Bella!" she cried out loud. "She wouldn't believe the warning and now the king is dead!"

Everyone turned to stare at her.

"The king is dead?" repeated Arrowbright. "This is worse than we thought! We must tell the others right away."

He turned and ushered the newcomers through the wheat while their rescuer, Matthius Brightlove, hurried on ahead. They came to a grassy clearing filled with a crowd not just of people but animals too, animals with intelligent faces who called out to them in welcome.

Penthesilean was as bewildered as Madeleine. He grabbed Arrowbright's arm. "I don't understand – where have all these . . . *people* come from?"

Arrowbright looked at him. "It's a long story, but we achieved what we set out to do and more besides – or rather *Ben* did. He found the Book of Prophecies and released the victims of the Great Fire." He gestured to those around him, then the crowd parted and a young boy appeared, accompanied by a large, golden-haired dog.

"Penthesilean!" cried the boy, running over and embracing the old soldier. "You're alive! We didn't know what had happened to you after you helped us escape from Quadrivium."

Penthesilean took hold of Ben's shoulders and looked him in the eye. "It sounds like you did a fine job, Ben. Well done."

At that moment, Matthius Brightlove reappeared with an older man who bore a striking resemblance to Arrowbright. Beside them walked a large lizard, as long as Penthesilean was tall. Madeleine recoiled slightly as it approached.

The man bowed his head to Princess Madeleine. "My name is Bartholomew," he said, then gestured at the lizard who also bowed his head towards her, "and this is Kimon. Is what Matthius says true: that the king is dead?"

Madeleine glanced at Penthesilean who gave her a reassuring nod. "It is true," she said. "I saw him struck down with my own eyes."

"Tell us everything, from the start," said Kimon in his rasping voice.

Madeleine closed her eyes and gathered her thoughts, then began to speak. "I had gone to tell my uncle, the king, the truth: that you weren't rebel reinforcements after all – which is what Lord Damien had told the council. You see, I overheard someone telling Great Aunt Bella who you were, and I believed them because I just *knew* there was something not quite right with Lord Damien's story. But Bella couldn't believe that her son was a traitor, so I knew it was up to me to tell the king."

She opened her eyes and found everyone still staring at her. Taking a deep breath, she continued. "I saw the king heading towards the south-east gate so I followed him, but when I got there he was already arguing with Lord Damien. I hid in the guardhouse to wait for Lord Damien to leave, and I heard the king order him to stop the attack – I think he had realised it was his own men returning home – but Lord Damien refused, and then he pulled something out of his pocket, some kind of weapon. I didn't get a good look at it, but there was a bright flash of light . . . and the next moment the king was dead."

There was a collective gasp from the listeners and Madeleine looked at them almost apologetically. "I didn't know what else to do, so I ran away as fast as I could. I wanted to find someone and tell them what had happened, but it was so dark and I went too far down the steps . . ."

"And that's how you came to be in the dungeons," murmured Penthesilean. "You poor child."

There was silence while everyone absorbed Madeleine's story. It was broken by a loud groan and everyone turned to see Matthius standing with his head in his hands.

"What is it, Matthius?" asked Penthesilean.

"The pale man, Lord Damien, don't you see? He's Bella's son – *our* son!" He looked at Penthesilean. "What about my daughter, Katrina? Did she grow up to be a traitor too?"

"No," said Penthesilean. "Your daughter grew up to be queen."

Matthius looked at him in disbelief, and sat down heavily on the grass, shaking his head. "*Queen?*"

Penthesilean laid his hand awkwardly on the other man's shoulder. Many years before, they had been rivals for Bella's affection. Matthius Brightlove had ultimately won her heart, but they had only been married a few years when he had disappeared in the Great Fire of Barbearland, leaving Bella to bring up their two young children – Damien and Katrina.

Finally Matthius composed himself enough to speak. "If everything you tell me is true, not only has my son murdered his king, but his own brother-in-law."

* * *

Lord Damien found the parade ground in front of the barracks deserted. This didn't surprise him; all the soldiers were still gathered by the east gate to fight the approaching army. He smiled grimly as he heard an explosion from the direction of the city walls. The attack continued unabated.

He strode towards the gaol which was on the other side of the barracks. The door was unlocked and he breezed into the empty room, then stopped dead as his eyes fell on the empty hook where he had expected to find the keys to the cells. He had seen the guard hang them there after escorting him from the ex-mayor's cell only that morning. Then he noticed the door leading to the cells was standing ajar. Pushing it open, he made his way silently down the short flight of steps and approached Ponsonby's cell. In one quick movement, he flung open the door and then froze, his mouth falling open at the sight that met his eyes.

Ponsonby lay in the middle of the floor with the haunch of venison Damien had given him still clutched tightly in one fist. His back was arched, and he moaned and writhed from side to side. Saliva foamed at his mouth, and bits of it flecked his chin as he struggled to speak, his eyes bulging with the effort.

However, it wasn't the sight of the ex-mayor that had shocked Damien, but the small figure hunched over him, her back to the door. Sensing his presence, she turned and looked up at him with as much astonishment as he looked back at her.

He took a step forward into the cell. "Mother, what on earth are you doing here?"

At the sound of Damien's voice, Ponsonby's eyes widened, and with great difficulty he raised himself up and pointed his finger at the pale man – who grew briefly paler still – before falling back and finally lying still.

"It looks like poison," said Bella, closing the dead man's eyes before getting to her feet and wiping her hands on her skirts. Mistaking the look of horror on her son's face, she continued hurriedly, "It wasn't me – he was already like this when I got here!" She gestured to the haunch of venison. "Someone smuggled *that* in to him. I would wager any money it's poisoned. He must've eaten it so fast he didn't have time to notice that it didn't taste right – either that, or he didn't care." She gave Damien a sideways look before throwing his own question back at him. "What are *you* doing here?"

Damien gave a heavy sigh. "I have some bad news, Mother. The baby you found in the monastery wasn't Prince Alexander after all – it was a doppelgänger!"

"I know," said Bella grimly. "I heard Katrina's screams all the way from the dome. I came directly here to try to persuade Ponsonby to tell me where he had hidden the true prince, but it seems I was too late – he was already in his death throes."

An image of Murgatroyd came unbidden into her mind, the huge eagle perched unsteadily – obviously badly injured – on the dome's balcony, telling her that her long-lost son was a traitor and had been in league with Ponsonby all along. His words had been temporarily driven from her mind by her daughter's frantic screams, but she now found herself studying her son's face carefully.

Damien stalked back and forth across the room, oblivious to his mother's scrutiny. "May Tritan's waters rise up and swallow his descendants for what this bumbling fool has done!"

"Damien, stop that!" ordered Bella. He stopped mid-stride, unused to receiving orders. She took a deep breath and decided to trust him. "All is not lost.

The monks helped Ponsonby hide the baby; one of them must know where Alexander is."

"Then we must get that information from them immediately!" said Damien, already at the door.

"No." Bella shook her head. "This needs to be done properly. We tell the king and let his men interrogate the monks."

Damien felt the grains of time slipping through his fingers. With his back to his mother, he stared unseeingly through the open doorway. Finally he forced an anxious expression onto his face and turned to face her. "Mother, you have to let me do this to prove my loyalty to the king! I need to earn his trust. Let me be the one to find his son while he defends Quadrivium from the rebels. Let me –"

"It's not the rebels," interrupted Bella. She had discerned this much of Murgatroyd's words to be true by studying the approaching troops from the dome.

Damien sensed more cracks appearing in his plan. "What?"

"The information Ponsonby gave you was false; it's our own men returning. I was on my way to tell the king when I heard the news about Prince Alexander." She darted towards the door. "We have to alert him before any more casualties arise from this terrible misunderstanding!"

"No!" cried Damien, blocking her path. "Don't you

see, Mother? This makes it even more important that *I* be the one to find the heir. If I was wrong about the approaching army then the king has even less reason to trust me! My reputation is in your hands. This could be the only chance I have to redeem myself, otherwise I may as well never have returned."

He was pleased to see the hesitation in her eyes.

"I don't know . . ." she began. The silence between them grew as she stared up at him, trying to quell the uneasy feeling in her breast.

Damien suddenly noticed that the cannons had stopped. "Listen!" he cried, cupping his ear. "The guards must have realised it's not the rebels after all!" Seeing the relief on her face, he pushed home his advantage. "Now that there's no immediate need to find the king, why don't we go to the monastery and see what the monks can tell us?"

Bella was so relieved that the bombardment had stopped that she allowed herself to be carried along by her son's eagerness. "All right, but when we find out where the monks are hiding Alexander, we take the information straight to the king."

"Of course, Mother," said Damien.

* * *

Nimrod tried not to flinch as his eardrums came

under attack once more.

"The rebels are almost at the gates of Quadrivium and you give the order to cease fire! What were you thinking of, cadet?" The sergeant major's face was only inches from Nimrod's own, and he could feel the heat radiating from the man's purple-veined cheeks. "If the captain had wanted you to give the orders he would have made you a brigadier – but he didn't! What are you?"

Nimrod opened his mouth, but before he could speak the sergeant major answered his own question. "You're a cadet: the lowest of the low! You're not fit to decide when to tie your own shoelaces, and you're certainly not fit to give orders! So tell me: what were you thinking?"

He paused for breath and Nimrod seized his chance. "The banner, sir . . ."

"You've put the entire population of Quadrivium at risk . . ." He hesitated as Nimrod's words finally registered. "Banner? What banner? Don't be foolish, boy, rebels don't carry banners!" Glaring suspiciously at the other sentries who were watching in silence, he turned to look in the direction indicated by Nimrod. His eyes widened as he spotted the torn blue banner lying on the ground some distance from the wall.

"That's one of ours," he said slowly. "How in Tritan's name did they manage to get hold of . . ." His words petered out as a group of people appeared from the field of wheat and advanced cautiously towards the wall, one of them waving a white flag.

A smaller figure detached itself from the group and ran ahead. As it came closer, they heard a shout, "Nimrod, Marcus, open the gates!"

"Maddie?" whispered Marcus in disbelief as he recognised his sister.

Nimrod was quicker to react. Darting past the bemused sergeant major, he entered the guardhouse and shouted down the speaking tube, "Open the gates!"

A disembodied voice barked back, "Who is this?"

Nimrod repeated the order. "Just open the gates! Do it now!"

Below, he heard the creak and thud of the gate's bolts being drawn. A moment later the heavy wooden gates were pushed open. Nimrod raced down the turret steps, followed by Marcus and the sergeant major. He reached the bottom just in time to catch Madeleine as she tumbled through the open gate.

"The king . . ." she gasped, "the king is dead!"

"What? How?" cried the sergeant major, looking out at the wasteland as though expecting to see the king's body lying there.

"Not out there," said Madeleine, grabbing the man's arm. "It happened here – on the battlements."

The sergeant major simply stared at her. Marcus took hold of his sister's shoulders and gently turned her to face him. "Who did it, Maddie? Who killed the king?"

"It was Lord Damien," said Penthesilean as he stepped through the open gate followed by Arrowbright and Gretilda. The bugler still hovered at Gretilda's side, ready to offer her his arm, while Ben lingered at the back, half hidden behind the others, with Tobias at his heels. His face was well known to many of the guards and he didn't want to draw attention to himself, but it was the sight of Penthesilean that roused the sergeant major.

"What in Tritan's name are *you* doing here?" he cried, staring at the old soldier. "How did you escape from your cell? You're still under arrest –"

"Don't be ridiculous!" interrupted Nimrod, turning on his sergeant major. "Brigadier Penthesilean was arrested on charges trumped up by Mayor Ponsonby – who is now under arrest himself – and those charges related to the kidnapping of Prince Alexander, who has since been found." He turned away in disgust and began issuing orders. "Marcus, take some medics and head to the south-east gate. See if there is anything you can do for the king." He turned back to Madeleine. "Madeleine, did you see what weapon Lord Damien used?"

Arrowbright stepped forward and answered for her. "We believe he used a Sacred Stone stolen from this shaman." He gestured at Gretilda. "The Stone is extremely dangerous and Gretilda is the only one with any chance of taking it from him."

Nimrod nodded. "Then she'd better take some men and track him down." He beckoned to some of the sentries who had gathered round to see what was going on.

"She can't enter Quadrivium!" interrupted the sergeant major. "Practitioners of witchcraft are banned from entering the city."

Gretilda sidestepped him and was already hurrying into the city with the bugler close behind.

"Stop her!" cried the sergeant major. A few of the sentries trotted after the shaman, but instead of restraining her they formed a protective cordon and fell into step behind her. The sergeant major's face turned a darker shade of red.

Madeleine started after the shaman. "We must tell the queen what has happened!" she piped up over her shoulder.

"Nimrod, pass along the order for the other gates to be opened," said Penthesilean as he hurried through the gate after Madeleine, followed by the others.

"Right away, sir, and I'll tell the men to be on the lookout for Lord Damien," said Nimrod, moving in the opposite direction, back towards the battlements.

"This is ridiculous and I don't believe any of it!" shouted the sergeant major, trotting at Nimrod's heels like a terrier. "What possible reason could Lord Damien have for murdering the king?"

Gretilda and her escort had almost reached the entrance to one of the narrow lanes that led up the hill towards the palace, but at the sergeant major's words she stopped suddenly, causing the bugler and the sentries to stumble into her. She turned slowly to stare at him, and then began to shudder. Wrapping her arms around her chest, she doubled over as if in pain. Everyone stared at her. Eventually she stopped shaking and drew herself up to her full height until she seemed taller than everyone else present. In a voice as clear as a bell she spoke. "The king is dead. Long live the king."

Gretilda's words were greeted with silence. Then Penthesilean's eyes widened as he realised their significance. "Lord Damien is after the *prince!* Long live the king: Prince Alexander, heir to the throne! Lord Damien has killed the king so that he can rule Quadrivium through Alexander!"

* * *

Damien's eyes darted from side to side as he

followed his mother across the courtyard towards the monastery. It was a forbidding place built of dark grey stone, but it wasn't the architecture that was the cause of his anxiety; he was painfully aware that time was running out for the successful execution of his plan.

A loud thudding sound beside him made him jump. He looked round and realised that his mother was beating her small fists against the doors of the monastery.

"Open up," cried Bella, staring up at the towering doors as though daring them to defy her.

A small hatch opened at the same height as Bella's head. "State your business."

Bella lowered her chin until her fierce gaze found the speaker. "I am the Dowager Bella. Open this door at once."

The hatch was slammed shut and they heard the sound of a bolt being drawn. A moment later, the huge door opened inward. All they could see of the monk who had opened it was the top of his shiny, bald head as he backed away. Ignoring him, they hurried past and into the heart of the monastery.

The corridors were empty, although they could hear the sound of chanting somewhere in the distance. Damien followed Bella as she made her way confidently down the gloomy passages until she came to a wooden door set in a stone archway. Without pausing, she reached forward and pulled at the iron handle, but the door would not budge. Impatiently, Damien forced his way past her and pushed the door open.

They were met with a blast of heat. On the far side of the room a robed figure stood by an imposing fireplace, silhouetted by a roaring fire. Oblivious to their presence, he picked up a pile of documents and threw them into the flames, pushing the papers deeper into the fire with a poker. As he turned to grab more documents they saw his face, illuminated by the glow from the fire.

"Brother William," breathed Bella, taking a step forward. But Damien got there first. Striding across the room, he grabbed the man's wrist. Startled, the monk dropped the poker which landed on Damien's boot. The white-hot iron sizzled as it burned through the leather, but Damien simply kicked it away.

"Where is the prince?" he hissed into the monk's face.

"I don't know . . . isn't he with the queen?" stammered Brother William, unable to meet the pale man's eyes.

Bella stepped into the light and the monk's eyes widened as he noticed her. "We know about the switch," she said. "Why don't you tell us where the real prince is?"

The monk glanced at the pile of documents, but

said nothing. Damien bent to pick up the poker.

"No," said Bella with a quick shake of her head. Reluctantly, Damien left the poker where it lay. "Do you know who I am?" she asked the trembling monk. He nodded. "Then you know that as the queen's mother and a member of the king's council I have the power to grant you clemency, so why don't you tell us where Prince Alexander is and I'll make sure you are treated leniently?"

Still the monk refused to speak.

Bella sighed. "Brother William, I know that you have been acting on Mayor Ponsonby's orders, but he's dead – poisoned in his cell – so why don't you just tell us where the prince is?"

At the news of Ponsonby's death, the monk let out a sigh that sounded like one of relief. Before Bella had finished speaking, he dropped to his knees and rummaged amongst the documents. "There's a map here somewhere," he muttered, "co-ordinates, directions, everything you will need." He found the document he was looking for and held it triumphantly above his head.

Bella watched him, perplexed. "A map? You mean to say the prince is not in Quadrivium?"

"What, here in the city?" frowned Brother William. "No, no, he was taken somewhere he would be safe until –"

Damien grabbed the map from the monk's hand. "We have what we need, Mother! Let's go; time is of the essence!" He took Bella's arm and, ignoring her protestations, bundled her out of the room and down the corridor.

"What is the matter with you, Damien? He was about to tell us what Ponsonby's plan was!"

Damien finally slowed and looked down at his mother. "You're right, Mother. Why don't you wait here for me and I'll go back and see what more he has to say."

Before she could protest, he left her in the corridor and hurried back to Brother William's study. He found the old monk slumped in an armchair by the fire, staring into the flames. He sat up straight when Damien came through the door.

"What –" he began, but got no further.

Taking the Sacred Stone from his pocket, Damien advanced on the monk.

5

The palace was teeming with courtiers rushing in all directions. Pushing through the crowds, Princess Madeleine led the way up the grand staircase towards the queen's chambers, followed by Ben and Tobias. Penthesilean and Arrowbright brought up the rear, both shocked that not a single person challenged them; the palace was in turmoil.

Suddenly a stout, middle-aged woman flung herself in their path. "Madeleine, where have you been? What a time to disappear! It's such dreadful news!"

"Mother!" cried Madeleine. "You've heard? How is the queen taking it?"

"She's devastated, of course!" sobbed Madeleine's mother, her enormous bosom heaving. "She'd only just got her darling boy back and now it turns out he isn't the prince after all!"

They all stared at her in surprise.

"Madam Lovejoy," said Penthesilean, stepping forward. "Please explain."

Madeleine's mother looked at him for a long moment before recognition dawned. "Penthesilean! Why, you're filthy! Where have you been that you haven't heard the news? Prince Alexander is not the prince!" She saw the confusion on his face and continued. "The child everyone thought was the prince, *isn't*; someone has swapped him for a lookalike! The queen is beside herself and no one can find my brother! Have *you* seen the king? . . . Ugh! Is that a dog?"

While Madame Lovejoy was distracted by Tobias who was snuffling at the hem of her skirt, Penthesilean turned to the others. "Ponsonby must have known there was a chance the prince would be discovered, so he used another baby as a decoy! We have to find him and make him tell us where he's taken the real prince."

"Ponsonby was taken to the cells next to the barracks," said Madeleine. "I overheard Nimrod and Marcus discussing it."

Madam Lovejoy looked up suspiciously. "What are you whispering about, Madeleine?"

Penthesilean said quickly to Arrowbright, "Take Ben and see what you can find out from Ponsonby. Madeleine, you and I must tell the queen what has happened. Tritan knows this isn't the best time for her to learn of the king's death, but it's better she hears it from us than from anyone else." He turned to Madeleine's mother and took her arm. "Madame Lovejoy, we must see the queen immediately!"

Between them, Penthesilean and Madeleine led the large lady down the corridor towards the queen's chambers, while Arrowbright, Ben and Tobias retraced their steps out of the palace. They crossed the main square over which towered the great golden dome, and made their way towards the barracks. After the hustle and bustle of the palace, the narrow streets off the main square seemed strangely deserted. Shops were shuttered and the doors and windows of houses were barred, although they could detect signs of movement within.

"They still think they're under attack," muttered Arrowbright. "Lord Damien must have been very convincing."

They crossed the parade ground in front of the barracks without seeing another soul, and finally reached the gaol. The door swung open at Arrowbright's touch. It was eerily quiet inside. While Ben and Arrowbright hovered in the doorway, waiting for their eyes to adjust to the dim light, Tobias slipped through their legs, padded over to a door on the far side of the room and disappeared through it.

"Stay behind me," Arrowbright warned Ben.

They crossed the room to the open doorway and found a flight of steps leading downwards. The sound of Tobias's claws could be heard clattering on the stone floor somewhere below. They descended slowly to a short corridor lined with closed doors, except for the door at the far end which stood ajar. They made their way cautiously towards it and Arrowbright put his head round the doorframe. He gasped and tried to hold Ben back, but the boy pushed passed him and immediately saw what Arrowbright had been trying to shield him from. Spreadeagled on the floor, face up in the middle of the cell, was the unmistakeable figure of Ponsonby.

Ben prodded the mayor's body with his foot. "He's dead, but it can't have been for long; he's still warm." He looked up at Arrowbright, but the soldier was watching Tobias who was snarling at a chunk of meat still clasped in Ponsonby's fist. Arrowbright bent down and sniffed it.

"He's been poisoned," he said, straightening up.

"So what do we do now?" asked Ben. "The only person who knows where the real prince is, is dead. But we have to *find* him, Arrowbright! Gretilda said that the fates of the prince and my mother were entwined!"

They were startled by a voice behind them. "There *is* someone else who might know where Alexander is."

They turned to see Madeleine coldly observing Ponsonby's body from the doorway. "I left Penthesilean with Aunt Katrina – I thought I'd be more use with you," she explained. "And I can tell you that Ponsonby wasn't acting alone when he kidnapped the prince. The monks helped him hide the baby we thought was Alexander, so there's a good chance they might know where the real prince is hidden."

* * *

Bella glanced suspiciously at Damien as he brushed ash from his hands.

"Did you dig something out of the fireplace?" she asked. "Did Brother William hold something back that could help locate the prince?"

"Not exactly," replied Damien, remembering the look on the monk's face just before he had been vapourised in a flash of bright light. The Sacred Stone had proved significantly more potent in the confined space of the monk's study than in the open air. Even Damien had been surprised by the complete annihilation of paper, wood, flesh and blood, and he was confident that no evidence remained to provide any clue to the prince's whereabouts.

"Never mind," said Bella, "the map he gave us should be sufficient for the king and his men to locate

Alexander." She brandished the map as she spoke. Damien reached out to take it from her, but she turned away and hurried towards the closed doors of the monastery.

Damien started after his mother, but just as she reached the doors there was a loud knocking and a voice cried out, "Open up!" He darted into the shadows as a monk scurried forward and unbolted the door. It swung open and a soldier stepped over the threshold.

"I need some monks to accompany me to the palace immediately!" he cried.

"What is going on?" asked Bella, moving towards him.

The soldier hesitated as he recognised the queen's mother. "Ma'am, I'm very sorry to have to tell you, but the king is dead – murdered! I've been sent to fetch the monks to perform the last rites."

Damien watched in frustration as Bella, still holding the map, was surrounded by monks who had been drawn to the open doorway by the news of the king's death. They clamoured for details until finally the soldier held up his hands and spoke over them, "I don't know anything more; my orders are simply to return with some monks. Who will come?"

The hall rapidly emptied as the monks filed out after the soldier. Eventually only Bella was left. She turned slowly to see Damien standing behind her. "Did you hear?" she said, bewildered. "The king has been murdered."

"We must leave Quadrivium immediately," answered Damien. He shifted impatiently from foot to foot. In his head, he could hear the sound of boots marching up the cobbled streets, the sound of the troops he had caused to be trapped by the Great Fire of Barbearland returning home to Quadrivium.

Bella stared up at him aghast. "What are you saying? We must go to your sister at once. Katrina will be devastated; she's lost not only her child, but now her husband too!"

Damien forced himself to remain calm. He placed his hands on his mother's shoulders and stared down into her eyes. "Don't you see, Mother? It's too dangerous for me to remain in Quadrivium. I was with the king on the battlements. I was the last person to see him alive. The council are bound to pin his death on me!"

Bella shook her head. "No, no, I will speak up for you, so will your sister. Running away is not the answer."

Damien took a deep breath and framed his next words carefully. "Mother, I have many enemies in the city. The only chance I have to prove my loyalty is to find Alexander and restore him to his rightful place as King of Quadrivium." He took her hands in his and gently pried her fingers from the map. "First Ponsonby, and now the king – both murdered within the city walls. We can't be sure who the murderer is or where they will strike next. I must leave Quadrivium and find the heir to the throne before anyone else loses their life."

With the map now safely in his grasp, he let his words hang in the air between them and risked a glance through the open doorway. From the opposite side of the square a column of soldiers had appeared. Even from this distance he could see that their uniforms were old and faded. He turned back to his mother. "I must leave now." He clenched his fist around the map. "Are you with me?"

Without waiting for her answer Damien stalked through the open doorway, pausing only to grab a cloak from a hook by the door. Hurriedly shrugging it on over his distinctive white suit, he crossed the crowded square. He walked with a stoop to disguise his height and directed his gaze at the cobbled ground, careful not to catch anyone's eye. Not once did he look back. There was no need; he could sense his mother's presence and distinguish her hesitant footsteps in the crowd behind him.

Reaching the far side of the square, he ducked into a narrow side street and pressed his back against the wall. Soldiers were still marching up the hill from the city gates, all heading in the direction of the palace, but their numbers were gradually dwindling. He glanced back to see where his mother was, and drew in his breath. The crowd of soldiers in the square had parted briefly to reveal a small group of figures moving against the flow. He instantly recognised Ben's bright blonde hair. Darting forwards, he caught hold of his mother's arm and dragged her into the shadows.

"Damien, let go!" she cried. A few of the passing soldiers glanced curiously in their direction, but no one stopped.

Damien released his grip and did his best to look contrite. "Sorry, Mother," he said. "I wasn't sure you'd seen where I'd gone."

Bella faced him with her hands on her hips. "I was right behind you, Damien. I couldn't just let you walk away like that, I couldn't let you disappear again. But you need to listen to me: no one is going to accuse you of murdering the king!"

Damien nodded vaguely as he focussed his attention over the top of her head at the figures in the square. He narrowed his eyes as he watched them head for the monastery, and then stifled a gasp as he spotted the shaman. At that very moment, Gretilda turned her head sharply in Damien's direction and he ducked his head.

"Mother," he snapped, "I know that you truly believe I have my sister's protection, but she is upset and there are many who will poison her mind against me. If I return with the prince then no one will doubt me; therefore I have no choice but to leave Quadrivium. I hope that you will come with me." With that, he turned and began to walk away.

Bella stood for a moment, indecisive. She cast a long look back towards the square – a moment too late to see the door to the monastery swing shut behind Ben and the others – then turned and began to follow her son.

* * *

Arrowbright heard the distant sound of marching feet as he led Ben, Madeleine and Tobias across the parade ground. The noise got louder as they approached the palace and finally they caught sight of the soldiers. The main square in front of the palace was already more than half full and more men and beasts were arriving every minute.

One by one, doors edged open and the people of Quadrivium began to emerge. The unfamiliar sight of leopards, bears and lizards walking amongst the soldiers made them wary at first, but when a cry of recognition went up at the sight of a long-lost son word soon spread that these were indeed the king's own troops who had been thought lost in the Great Fire of Barbearland, and people swarmed on to the streets to welcome the returning heroes.

"I remember the days when beasts lived side by side with men," Ben overheard an old man telling a group of young housewives. "It weren't so long ago – you've just forgotten how it was, that's all. It'll come back to you soon enough."

They joined the throng and Arrowbright caught the arm of one of the soldiers as he marched past. "Where are you headed?"

"We've been asked to gather beneath the dome for a special welcome by the queen," answered the man, before catching sight of Ben. "Is that the Deliverer?" Before Arrowbright could reply the man was swept onwards by the crowds behind him.

The monastery lay on the opposite side of the square from the dome, and they had to force their way against the flow. They could see its bell-tower above the heads of the crowd, but their progress was delayed by the number of soldiers who wanted to thank Ben for bringing them safely home. Arrowbright finally caught a glimpse of the monastery doors through the press of bodies and pushed his way towards it, followed by Ben, Madeleine and Tobias. They emerged suddenly through the crowd to find Gretilda, with the bugler still in tow, already there and staring up at the huge doors.

The bugler almost collapsed with relief at the sight of Ben and Arrowbright. "Thank Tritan you're here," he cried. "Gretilda says the Stone has been used again, somewhere inside the monastery. What if the pale man's still in there?"

Ben looked at Gretilda. The shaman was visibly agitated, staring first at the door and then over her shoulder at the crowds that thronged the square. She seemed to be in an agony of indecision.

"We'd better hurry," said Arrowbright. He tested the door to the monastery and, finding it unlocked, pushed it open. The others stumbled in after him. The moment the door closed behind them, the noise from the square was absorbed by the stone walls and they were enveloped in a heavy silence.

"Can I help you?" They jumped as a hunchbacked old monk stepped out of the alcove beside the doorway. He glanced at each of them in turn, taking a long, hard look at Gretilda, who was as tense as a wild animal, before his gaze settled on Madeleine. His eyes widened. "Princess Madeleine?" She nodded. "I am so sorry about your uncle – the king, I mean," he said, his voice wavering slightly. "I would have liked to have said the last rites over his body, but someone had to stay behind –"

"Is that where everyone else is – with the king?" interrupted Arrowbright.

The monk nodded. "All except myself and Brother William, whom I believe is still in his study. He doesn't like to be disturbed – I'm not even sure he knows about the king's death." He mistook the glance that passed between the visitors. "Oh! Do you think I should tell him? Yes, yes, you're right; he's going to be angry with me for keeping him in the dark. I must tell him immediately!"

"Would you like us to go with you?" asked Madeleine.

The monk looked at her gratefully. "Would you? He has a bit of a temper, but he wouldn't dare show it if you're with me."

The monk set off down one of the corridors that led from the main hall, and the others hurried after him. Eventually they came to a large, wooden door. The monk raised his hand and tapped nervously. "Brother William, it's Brother Thomas. May I come in?"

There was no response. Before the monk could knock again, Gretilda sprang forward and pushed open the door. A bright light flared from within the room as though someone had struck a match, and then immediately went out. Without a word, the shaman opened the door further so the others could see in.

The room was completely empty. There was no

furniture, no carpet, no books or bookshelves; nothing apart from a covering of white dust that lay thickly on the bare stone floor.

"What has happened here?" said the monk, brushing past Gretilda. His feet stirred up the dust which curled like smoke around his legs. "Where are Brother William's books? . . . Oh my!"

Brother Thomas's face had suddenly gone as white as the dust blanketing the room. He stood motionless, staring down at something on the floor near the empty fireplace. Arrowbright stepped carefully over to the monk, Gretilda close behind him. Scattered haphazardly on the hearth at the monk's feet was a heap of white sticks. Arrowbright was about to pick one up when Gretilda stopped him with a few words. "You mustn't touch him."

"What do you mean: *him?*" The moment the words had left his mouth, Arrowbright realised that what he was looking at were bones. "You mean to say that this is Brother William?"

"What's left of him," said Gretilda in an expressionless voice. "His soul has departed." She turned abruptly and left the room. Arrowbright was about to follow her out when he noticed a scrap of paper amongst the bones. Careful not to touch them, he poked and prodded until the paper was free. It was bleached the same dead white as everything else in the room, but its edges were rough as though it had been torn from a larger document. On it was written a single word: '*drumlins*'. Arrowbright made his way out of the room and showed it to the others.

"*Drumlins* – what does that mean?" asked Ben, turning the paper over in his hands.

"It's the name of a sacred resting place," answered Brother Thomas, following them out and closing the door behind him. White-faced and trembling, he leant against it for support and they waited for him to continue. After a long moment he looked up at them. "The Abbey of the Ancients is located amongst the drumlins. It's where our abbots go when it's time for them to pass on to the next world."

"Where is it?" asked Arrowbright. "I don't recall seeing it on any map."

"You won't find it on an ordinary map," said the monk. "Its existence is a closely guarded secret." He glanced up at them almost apologetically. "*I'm* not even supposed to know about it, but I can't help overhearing things – Brother William and Brother Bernard like to talk. Apart from the abbot himself, they are the only ones who know about the abbey and its location."

"The perfect place to hide the prince," said Ben softly. All except Gretilda and the bugler turned to stare at him. The shaman was slumped against the wall with her hands covering her face, while the bugler hovered over her, ineffectively patting her shoulder.

"Ben's right, and it looks like Lord Damien has been here before us," said Arrowbright, glancing at Gretilda. "He must have used the Sacred Stone to silence Brother William."

"What about Brother Bernard?" said Ben, turning to the monk. "You said he knows about the abbey. Where is he?"

"He left Quadrivium over a week ago – I saw him off myself and I don't expect him back anytime soon; he took many days' worth of supplies."

"And I bet he took Prince Alexander with him too," said Ben. "We must follow him – to the drumlins!"

"But you'll never find the drumlins without a map or a guide," said the monk, sadly shaking his head.

"What about the abbot?" asked Ben. "You said he knew the way."

Brother Thomas gave a heavy sigh. "I can take you to him, but I'm afraid he won't be much help. You see, the abbot has not said a word for over ten years."

6

Bella had to run to catch up with her son. "Wait, Damien!"

He stopped and turned to face her. "I can't argue with you anymore, Mother. I'm leaving Quadrivium right now and I'm going to find Prince Alexander and return him to his rightful place – with or without your help."

"I've decided to come with you," said Bella, making up her mind on the spot. "But I need to get some clothes first from my chamber – I can't travel like this." She gestured at her long gown.

Damien shook his head. "You saw those crowds – by the time you've reached the palace and packed a bag we'll have lost too much time. The sooner we set out, the sooner we find Prince Alexander."

Still looking down at her gown, Bella brushed a smear of dirt from her skirt. Then she raised her head and looked at her son. "We have to go through the laundry district to get to the city gate," she said. "I sent my riding clothes to the washerwoman over a week ago, I can pick them up on our way through. They'll be perfect for travelling."

Damien tapped his foot impatiently. "Yes, all right, Mother. Now, come *on!*"

Apart from a few late arrivals who were more interested in reaching the palace than in examining fellow passers-by, the streets were quiet. Damien set a rapid pace down the steep, winding lanes, occasionally casting darting glances behind them. Bella observed the tension in his shoulders, and remained silent.

The distinctive smell of newly-washed clothes filled the air long before they reached the warren of streets that made up the laundry district. Hurrying down a flight of steps, they finally emerged onto a wide thoroughfare with hundreds of washing lines loaded with billowing sheets, suspended between the tall, narrow houses.

"This way," said Bella, dragging Damien down a side street. After a couple of twists and turns, the street came to an abrupt dead end. When he saw there was no way out, Damien took a few quick steps back the way they had come.

Bella stopped by a small wooden door and knocked three times. "This is the place," she said. "Are you coming in?"

Damien shook his head, still moving away. "I'll wait for you on the main thoroughfare."

Bella nodded, and then turned towards the door as it opened. A large woman with a red face and wet hands opened the door. Ignoring Bella, she stuck her head around the doorframe and stared down the street, but Damien had already disappeared. Finally she looked at Bella.

"Good day, ma'am," she said slowly. "I'm surprised to see you here . . . Have you brought someone with you?"

Bella brushed passed the woman and entered the house. "Hello Gertie," she said. "As a matter of fact, my son was with me – he's waiting for me on the main street. We're in a bit of a hurry. I'm here for my laundry, not for a reading – not today. Is it ready? I would have sent my maid for it, but – well, anyway, I'm here now."

Gertie nodded slowly. "Your clothes are ready." She disappeared behind a curtain and re-emerged a moment later with a bag of clean laundry. She stood awkwardly in front of Bella with the bag clasped to her bosom. "Ma'am, can I speak frankly?"

Bella held her hand out for the bag which Gertie reluctantly passed to her. She selected some garments, then slipped behind the curtain. "Do you mind if I change while we talk?"

The washerwoman stood in silence, twisting her large hands awkwardly in front of her.

Bella poked her head out from behind the curtain. "Well?"

"You mustn't go with him," said Gertie, her words coming out in a rush.

"Who – Damien?"

"He's *bad!* He's been working against everything you've been working for these past years . . ." The washerwoman's voice petered out as she saw the look on Bella's face.

"How dare you?" said Bella. "My son finally returns to Quadrivium after all these years and single-handedly arrests the traitor, Ponsonby – but now he thinks he has to prove his loyalty because he was the *last one to see the king alive* . . ." She paused, her own words ringing in her ears.

Gertie took advantage of her silence. "I'm not saying any of this to cause trouble, ma'am, but I saw his image in the soapsuds. It took me a while to realise who it was, but now I'm sure."

Bella retreated back behind the curtain. When she emerged, she was dressed in a tailored riding jacket and tight-fitting breeches. Her satin slippers looked incongruous with the outfit, but there was nothing she could do about that.

"I'm leaving now, Gertie," she said. "We've been good friends over the years, you and I, but you have overstepped the mark and I very much doubt if we will see each other again."

Without another word, she opened the door and stepped out into the street. Behind her, Gertie sank to her knees and covered her face with her hands.

* * *

Gretilda hadn't said a word since they had left Brother William's study. Ignoring the others, she set off like a bloodhound with the scent of its quarry in its nostrils, heading straight for the entrance hall of the monastery. The others followed close behind.

"Go with her," said Arrowbright to the bugler as Gretilda pulled open one of the heavy monastery doors and disappeared without a backward glance. "Send word immediately if you find Lord Damien."

The bugler's reply was lost to them as he followed the shaman into the noisy, crowded square. Brother Thomas closed the door behind him, and then led the rest of the group to an archway hidden in a shadowy alcove in a corner of the entrance hall.

"Follow me," he whispered, even though there was no one else there to hear him. They followed the monk in single file through the archway and up a winding stone staircase. Shafts of light came from narrow window slits in the thick stone walls through which Ben caught glimpses of the square below.

Brother Thomas spoke in a soft voice as they climbed. "I should warn you, he's not used to visitors. He hasn't been out of this room since he entered it over ten years ago, nor has he seen anyone other than a few fellow monks in that time, and he hasn't spoken a word to anyone . . ."

Impatiently, Tobias pushed past the monk and bounded on ahead. They could hear him scratching at something and rounded the corner to find him pawing at a wooden door, his tail wagging furiously. The monk knocked softly on the door and turned the doorknob without waiting for an answer. Bright sunlight flooded the gloomy staircase as Tobias forced his nose into the gap and entered the room.

"Arturius!"

Brother Thomas stepped back in shock and would have tumbled down the stairs if it hadn't been for Arrowbright. Gathering his wits, the monk moved forward and peered through the doorway. "Father Abbot, did you speak?"

The only response was the rapid thud of Tobias's tail on the floor. Ben, Arrowbright and Madeleine looked over the monk's shoulder into the room. It was small and sparsely-furnished, but filled with light from large windows set in the sloping ceiling, providing an uninterrupted view of the sky. Seated in a straight-backed chair in the middle of the room was a very old man. Tobias sat in front of him with his head on his lap. The man's hand rested on the dog's head and they gazed intently into each other's eyes. After a long moment the man looked up and grinned toothlessly at the visitors who were staring at him from the doorway.

"I'm ready to go home now," he said.

* * *

Gretilda moved like a shadow through the crowd of soldiers surging across the main square towards the dome. Her appearance turned many heads, but she was gone before anyone could catch her attention. The bugler tried to keep up, but it wasn't long before he lost sight of her.

"Have you seen a beautiful young woman headed this way?" he asked as he battled his way through the crowds. The only answer he received was laughter and a few mocking replies. He looked frantically in all directions, but there was no sign of the shaman.

"Danny! Hey, Danny!" A soldier pushed his way through the crowd and swept the bugler into a bear hug. "Where did you disappear to? We thought we'd left you behind!"

"Beautiful woman," repeated the bugler, "wearing a grey dress and headed this way. Have you seen her?"

"Yeah," said the soldier.

"Really?"

"It would have been difficult to miss her – what a stunner! She went that way." The soldier gestured over his shoulder. Without stopping to thank him, Danny was off.

The crowd thinned towards the edge of the square and he spotted Gretilda just in time to see her duck down a side street. He ran after her. There were fewer people off the main square, and this time he was able to keep her in sight. She trotted along the cobblestones, occasionally turning her head from left to right as though trying to catch a scent or a sound. Not once did she hesitate. She took the twists and turns of the narrow streets in her stride, maintaining a constant pace even when she had to dodge people in her path.

With Danny hurrying after her, they reached the laundry district where the sheets hung like sails above their heads, and continued down the main street. Danny was beginning to tire when Gretilda finally slowed to a walk. As he watched, she approached the entrance to a narrow side street where a large, red-faced woman stood as though waiting for her. Gretilda stopped, facing the woman. Danny was close enough to tell that no words were exchanged, but it seemed that something had been communicated for a moment later Gretilda was off again.

Danny raced after her. As he passed the washerwoman he thought he saw a startled expression cross her face, but he didn't have time to stop, even when a strangled, "No, dear! Wait –" reached his ears. He was determined not to lose Gretilda again.

The streets became narrower and warehouses loomed up on both sides, blocking out the sunlight. Danny caught glimpses of the city wall between the buildings as he ran after the shaman. She slowed as she neared the end of a street and came to a standstill. He was about to call out to her when she took a step out of the shadows and into bright sunlight. He could see the city wall behind her. She took another step out into the open, and then another, and then stopped, looking at something out of his line of sight.

Danny reached the end of the street and leaned against the wall of the warehouse to catch his breath. Gretilda was only a few paces away and he tried to call her name, but he was panting too hard, so instead he stepped out of the shady street and into the sunlight and reached out to take her arm.

A split-second before he touched her, Gretilda threw herself to the ground. The bolt of white light hit Danny's outstretched hand and shot up his arm to his chest. He stood rooted to the ground as the shimmering light travelled down his torso to his legs, before disappearing through his feet and into the earth. The last thing he saw before his legs finally buckled was the back of Lord Damien's white suit as he raced up the steps to the battlements and vaulted over the wall.

7

"I don't understand it," said Brother Thomas, "I've never heard him speak before! I've never even heard of anyone who's heard him speak."

Arrowbright and Madeleine looked across at the abbot who was fondly stroking Tobias's ears. Ben sat on the floor nearby, studiously ignoring the old man and the dog. "His name's not Arturius," they heard him mutter under his breath.

"But you heard what he said," said Arrowbright to Brother Thomas. "He wants to go home – he *must* mean the abbey in the drumlins."

The monk shook his head. "It's impossible. The departing abbot must be accompanied by an escort of the most senior monks, in this case, Brother William and Brother Bernard . . ."

Arrowbright raised his eyebrows.

"I know, I know," said the monk, "both are . . .

indisposed, but I still don't think it's appropriate for –"

"Hello? Arrowbright? Ben?" Penthesilean's faint voice drifted up from below.

Arrowbright stuck his head out of the door and called down the staircase, "We're up here!"

They listened to Penthesilean's footsteps on the stairs. Finally he appeared in the doorway. "I've been looking everywhere for you!" he said, resting his hand on the doorframe. "I found Ponsonby in his cell, but he wasn't much help – I expect you already know that he's dead. Luckily, I bumped into some soldiers in the square who'd seen you come in here . . ." He trailed off as his eyes fell on the abbot. "Who is this?"

"Someone we hope can lead us to the prince," said Arrowbright.

Penthesilean looked the old man up and down. "The queen will be pleased to hear that; she desperately needs some good news."

"How is she?" asked Madeleine anxiously.

"She's coping well, and handling herself like a queen," said Penthesilean. "She intends to address the troops shortly, but first she has called a meeting of the king's councillors to discuss the recent events and she wants us all to attend – including you, Ben."

Ben looked up. "Me! Why me?"

"Bartholomew presented her with the Book of Prophecies, as we had discussed, but the prophecies are hidden and the pages remain blank. The queen has had the Book examined by a specialist, but even he has admitted defeat. It seems you are the only one who can decipher the future. Come, we must go. They will have started without us."

Arrowbright turned and spoke to Brother Thomas. "We'll be back as soon as we can. Don't let the abbot out of your sight! Ben, we have to go."

Ben was looking at Tobias. "Come on, boy!" he called.

When Tobias didn't respond, Arrowbright took Ben's arm. "It's best if Tobias stays here. He can make sure the abbot comes to no harm until we're ready to leave."

Reluctantly, Ben allowed Arrowbright to lead him out of the room. Together, they descended the staircase and caught up with Penthesilean and Princess Madeleine who were waiting for them in the entrance hall. Penthesilean opened the huge front door and led them out into the crowd of soldiers still milling in the square.

Arrowbright fell into step beside Penthesilean as they made their way through the horde. "How much does the queen know?" he asked quietly.

"She knows that her own brother, Lord Damien, is responsible for the king's death," answered Penthesilean, "and that he has been orchestrating a rebellion amongst the rebels ever since he disappeared from Quadrivium. A warrant has been issued for his immediate arrest and there's a handsome reward for anyone who captures him – dead or alive."

"Well, let's hope he's found before he leaves the city," said Arrowbright. "We believe he has all the information he needs to track down the prince."

As they entered the gates of the palace, he gave Penthesilean a quick rundown of what they had discovered in Brother William's library. "All the evidence was destroyed, except for one tiny clue." He held up the piece of paper with the word '*drumlins*' scribbled on it. "We believe this is where the monks have taken the prince."

By now they had reached the door to the throne room and Penthesilean paused with his hand on the doorknob. He had listened to Arrowbright in silence, but now he spoke. "We should keep this information between ourselves for now, until we know who we can trust." With that, Penthesilean pushed open the door and entered the throne room.

As he had expected, the council meeting had already started. Ben, Arrowbright and Princess Madeleine slipped into the room after him and stood unnoticed at the back, watching and listening. Over the heads of the councillors, Ben could see the queen seated on her throne looking pale and distracted. He cast his eye over the crowd and caught sight of Bartholomew, Arrowbright's father, standing near the front next to Matthius Brightlove. He wondered what Bella's reaction had been on seeing her long-lost husband, and he looked around the chamber for her, but even though he stood on his tiptoes he could not see her anywhere. Instead, his attention was captured by a tall, silver-haired man who was holding court at the front of the room. The man wore a robe of crimson velvet with full sleeves that hung from his arms like banners as he raised his hands in the air.

"The Book has all the answers we need!" he cried in a booming voice. "I just need a little more time –"

"Time is something we do not have, Cardinal Bolt!"

Ben looked to see where the interruption had come from. A soldier in a smart green uniform with gold insignia on the shoulders made his way through the councillors and turned to address the gathering. "We must act now to track down the king's murderer and bring him to justice – and the search for Prince Alexander must resume at once!"

The queen sat up straighter in her throne. "What did you say? Has the search for Alexander been called off?"

The cardinal half-turned towards her. "It has, ma'am."

"But when? Why? And on whose orders?"

The cardinal now turned fully towards her, his tone softening. "I withdrew the order, ma'am, as soon as I heard of the king's death. It's vital for the safety of the kingdom that not just *anyone* finds Alexander. As you know, whoever has custody of the heir will automatically become regent until the prince is old enough to rule the kingdom himself. We need time to organise official search parties of trustworthy individuals –"

"Are you implying my men aren't trustworthy?" asked the soldier angrily.

"– and I need time to examine the Book of Prophecies to determine the prince's whereabouts," continued the cardinal smoothly, ignoring the interruption.

"But you've already admitted you can't read the Book!" cried the soldier. "And we are wasting valuable time! The fact is that Lord Damien fooled us all into believing we were under attack to provide a distraction so that he could kill the king, and he could very well have Alexander in his custody right this minute while we waste time talking. The sooner Lord Damien is under lock and key, the better!"

"The warrant for Lord Damien's arrest has been withdrawn," interjected a stout, grey-haired councillor. Ben's mouth fell open in shock and dismay. He looked up at Penthesilean to see his reaction. The old soldier's thick, white eyebrows were drawn together in a deep frown, but he remained silent as he waited to hear what more the councillor had to say. "Following his majesty's untimely death, the queen no longer has the authority to issue warrants," continued the man. "The council has taken charge, at least until the prince has been found and a suitable regent appointed. Anyway, we have no evidence that Lord Damien is involved in any of this."

"But we *know* that Lord Damien killed the king," said Bartholomew, stepping forward. "Princess Madeleine was a witness to the murder!"

"Are we to accept the word of an impressionable young girl?" said another of the councillors.

The noise in the room escalated as everyone began to speak at once. As the queen stood up to call for calm, she caught sight of Penthesilean at the back of the room. She beckoned for him to come forward, and gradually the voices died down as Penthesilean pushed Ben to the front of the room.

"Be careful what you say," he reminded Ben, murmuring into his ear. They stopped a few paces from the queen and Ben bowed low before her. When he looked up, instead of the queen it was the cardinal who stood before him.

"You are the boy with the power to read the Book of Prophecies," he said. It was a statement rather than a question, and before Ben could respond the cardinal had reached out and placed his heavily jewelled hand on Ben's shoulder. "Come with me."

He led Ben to an elaborate bronze lectern that stood to one side of the raised platform. Its sloping top was fashioned like an eagle's outstretched wings, reminding Ben that there had still been no sign of Murgatroyd since they had entered the city.

With his hand still on Ben's shoulder, the cardinal turned and addressed the chamber. "If the boy can truly read the prophecies in this great book, then we can find all the answers we need – right here and now." A flurry of consternation greeted his words and the cardinal cast a stern glance at the councillors. The muttering eventually subsided, but Ben could feel their stares boring into him and the hair on the back of his neck began to prickle.

Once there was silence, the cardinal continued. "We need to determine, once and for all, whether Lord Damien is responsible for the king's death," – there was another ripple of murmuring from the assembled men, which died down as soon as the cardinal shot another glance round the room – "and we need to know where he is right now. Finally, and perhaps most importantly of all, we need to know what has happened to Prince Alexander."

Ben allowed himself to be led on to the platform towards the lectern. On it rested the Book of

Prophecies. A wave of calm washed over him the moment he laid his hands on its familiar bronze and leather cover. He no longer felt intimidated by the councillors, but strong and purposeful. Eager now, he opened the Book and turned the pages of thick yellow parchment until he came to the illustration of the battle between the pale man's rebel army and the victims of the Great Fire.

Feeling a presence at his shoulder, he looked up to find the cardinal's face an inch from his own. He quickly looked down again and turned the page. The last time he had cast his eyes on this next page he had seen nothing but a plain white sheet – very different in colour and texture from the yellow parchment of the previous pages, and completely blank. At first, the sheet was exactly as he remembered it, but gradually an image began to appear, rising up slowly through the paper as though floating up from the bottom of a deep pond. Ben's eyes darted across the page, taking in the pale man in his sinister white suit standing on the city battlements before the proud figure of the king. In the background, blue ink began to seep up through the parchment until it took on the shape of a banner. When Ben's eyes flicked back to the pale man, his arm was raised and everything before him, including the king, had vanished – it was as though an eraser had been swept across the page. Ben flinched from the sight and instantly the cardinal was at his side, his hand gripping Ben's elbow and breaking his concentration.

"What do you see?" he hissed eagerly.

Ben reluctantly began to describe the image, and immediately questions broke out.

"So you can't be absolutely certain that Lord Damien actually *killed* the king?" asked one of the councillors who was seated beside Bartholomew.

"Was there a weapon?" asked another. "The Royal Physician said he couldn't find a single injury to the king's body."

Ben squinted at the page. The erased section was bleached a dead white and hurt his eyeballs. It was almost a relief to look instead at the illustration of the pale man, whose spotless white suit seemed vibrant by comparison. His hand was held upwards and clenched like a claw around a rock. Ben was saved from having to describe the Sacred Stone to the councillors by the cardinal, who suddenly reached across him and turned the page.

"Is there more?" he asked greedily. "Tell me, what do you see? Where is Lord Damien now? Where is the prince?"

Ben took a deep breath and looked down. The next page was also blank, and he waited patiently to see if a picture would emerge. After a while, he noticed movement and realised that what he was seeing were thick, white clouds swirling across the page. As he watched and waited, the clouds thinned and the scene slowly began to materialise. Ben started to speak.

"I see a man in monk's robes – his face is in shadow, but he's in a boat, and I think there's something in the boat with him. It looks like . . . I think it *might* be . . . yes, it is – it's a baby."

The queen got to her feet. "Alexander!"

Ben continued to gaze down at the picture, waiting for more details to emerge. He felt the presence of the queen close beside him and the cardinal hovering on his other side, but he ignored them both and focussed on the page. A dark silhouette in the shape of a bird appeared in the top corner. It was moving swiftly, growing larger with every second as though headed straight for the boat in the foreground. As it grew, one of its wings obliterated the figure of the man, and then the boat, until the bird was covering half the page – and still it grew. Ben had the feeling it was coming for him, straight out of the Book. Suddenly a ray of light pierced the mist, illuminating the bird's features. Ben gasped in horror and took a step backwards.

The moment his hands left the Book it snapped itself shut with a sound like a thunderclap.

* * *

A small rowing boat made its way through the thick sea mist. It was manned by a single figure in a dark robe, with the hood pulled low over his face. He handled the oars clumsily as he manoeuvred the boat through the hidden channels, counting each stroke softly under his breath. In the bottom of the boat lay a small bundle, swaddled tightly in a cocoon of travel-stained muslin. Every few minutes it would stir, emitting a soft snuffling noise. Each time this happened, the figure would pause, tense and alert, oars raised. Only once the bundle was still once more would he continue.

The silence was punctuated by the soft, watery plop-and-gurgle of the oars. The mist, which shrouded the boat, muffled all other sounds and covered everything with freezing droplets of moisture. At one point, the mist cleared and, by the cold light of the moon, the man caught a glimpse of nearby rocky islets. The sight appeared to give him confidence and he renewed his efforts with the oars.

Suddenly a long, piercing shriek penetrated the mist. The man flinched, dropping the oars which slipped unnoticed into the water and disappeared beneath the surface. The baby awoke and began to cry with great, lusty howls. Ignoring it this time, the man fumbled under his seat with trembling hands. He drew out a small round shield which he thrust aloft, holding it shakily with both arms.

He was just in time. A dark shape, much larger than the boat, dropped from the sky. It veered off with a furious scream as it encountered the barrier. Shaking uncontrollably, the man peered round the edge of the shield. Three grotesque, birdlike figures circled over the boat. The baby had stopped crying and was staring up at them. Their ragged wings beat the air with a soft and steady thump, and the sound was ominous in the sudden silence. As the creatures swooped lower, the man caught sight of frail human torsos, deathly pale against their dark wings. Their thin arms dangled uselessly at their sides and their withered legs fused into their tail feathers. Vicious talons protruded from their lower bellies, outstretched as if to pluck him from the boat, and atop bare, milky-white throats, feathered heads twisted to keep him in their sights.

The man cowered beneath his shield as one of the creatures opened its long, thin beak and uttered a shrill cry. Immediately the other birds drew in their wings and flew at the boat, their rapier beaks aimed straight for the man as he tried to cover both himself and the child with the inadequate shield.

The instant before the creatures hit, a clanging bell sounded through the mist. With a subtle shift of their wings, the birds changed direction, crashing into the sea and creating huge geysers of water that thundered down into the boat, swamping it instantly. The man flung down his shield and grabbed the swaddled baby as it almost bobbed over the side.

He stood with the child in his arms as the boat sank beneath him, the water rapidly reaching his knees. Then, unexpectedly, he heard the sound of the boat's hull scraping against rock. He stepped out of the submerged boat and staggered forward as two pairs of hands reached out of the mist and took the baby from him. As another pair of hands grasped his wrists and hauled him onto the island, Brother Bernard raised his eyes to look for the first time on the Abbey of the Ancients.

8

Ben sat on the wide stone window seat and looked out onto the square below. It was lit with flaming torches in readiness for the celebratory feast that the queen had laid on for the returned army. Trestle tables groaned beneath the weight of dozens of jugs of ale and platters of wild hog, apples stuffed into their gaping mouths as though to muffle their screams. Ben felt some affinity with the hogs; even now he could feel a scream of frustration welling up inside him.

There was a knock on his door and Penthesilean stuck his head into Ben's room. "I saw your lamp was still lit – can't you sleep? Bed not big enough for you?"

Ben cast a glance at the huge feather bed and grimaced. "What are we still doing here, Penthesilean? We should have left *hours* ago!"

"It's complicated," said Penthesilean, entering Ben's room and perching on the side of his bed. "The council have invoked an ancient clause allowing them to take control of the kingdom until the heir is found, and they are insisting that a special team be selected to find the prince, which takes time to organise." He paused and drew a small, leather drawstring bag from beneath his cloak. He placed it on the bed beside him and it sank into the soft eiderdown, creating a small crater. "In the meantime, however, the queen has honoured the reward which Bella promised you for returning the Book of Prophecies to the palace."

Ben glanced at the bag and then looked back at Penthesilean. "We're wasting time, we should leave tonight."

Penthesilean sighed. "It would be foolish to depart without the correct authority."

"But why does everything take *so long*?"

"Well, for a start, nothing can happen until after the king's funeral," explained Penthesilean patiently. "His lying-in-state has already been reduced from the traditional week to only two days –"

"And in the meantime, the pale man will have reached the drumlins and snatched the heir to the throne!"

Penthesilean's bushy white eyebrows drew together into a frown. "Lord Damien travels without a guide," he said, "while we have the abbot to show us the way."

Ben turned his back on Penthesilean and looked

out of the window. "I wish we were leaving tonight, and I wish I could consult the Book without Cardinal Bolt peering over my shoulder the whole time. You said yourself that we don't know who we can trust – what if someone gets to the abbot before he can lead us to the drumlins?"

"I wouldn't worry about the abbot, Ben," said Penthesilean, getting to his feet. "No one else knows this, but Brother Thomas and Arrowbright have moved him to the monk's quarters beneath the palace. Tobias is with him too." He paused in the doorway. "You should try to get some rest now. Once we've left Quadrivium, you'll be unlikely to sleep on a bed like this for a while."

Ben didn't look round as the old soldier left the room, closing the door behind him. Music and laughter began to drift up from the square below. Someone was playing a banjo, and he watched as a group of soldiers approached some giggling local girls standing at the edge of the square. The tempo of the music increased and the soldiers grabbed the girls' waists and danced them into the middle of the square.

After a while, Ben's eye was drawn to the shadows beneath the trees where the food was laid out. As he watched, an entire roast hog inched its way across the table and disappeared over the edge. None of the soldiers appeared to have noticed. Despite his mood, a grin crept over Ben's face and, when a small figure briefly showed itself above the table to grab a jug of ale, he laughed out loud.

Opening the window, he leaned out and looked down. His room was on the second floor of the palace, but there was a narrow ledge that ran the length of the wall just below his window. Ben threw his leg over the sill and then paused and looked back at his bed. Quickly, he hopped back into the room and grabbed the drawstring bag. It was heavier than he had expected and the coins inside chinked against each other as he lifted it. Resisting the urge to open the bag and count the reward, instead he stuck it up his jumper and tucked the bottom of his jumper firmly into his trousers. Then he returned to the window and climbed out.

He stood for a moment on the ledge, surveying the square. No one was looking in his direction. All eyes were on the dancing girls. Ben ran nimbly along the ledge until he came to a tall tree that grew close to the wall, then he jumped out and caught hold of a branch and quickly swung himself down to the ground.

Skirting the soldiers, he scampered over to the trestle tables and lifted a corner of the thick white tablecloth. "Gotcha!" he cried. But he was surprised to find the space beneath the table deserted except for a jug lying on its side.

Someone grabbed the back of his shirt and hauled him upright. "What do you think you're doing?" roared a man, breathing ale into Ben's face.

"Jambery, put him down!" said a voice behind him. "It's Ben, you idiot!"

The man's demeanour changed immediately. "Ben," he cried, "my hero! You saved us from the fire! Have some of my ale! Come and meet the others!"

He grabbed Ben's arm and dragged him into the crowd of soldiers. Ben was immediately surrounded by friendly faces. Everyone wanted to greet him, and he found himself passed between the soldiers, receiving hearty slaps on the back and given swigs of ale straight from the jugs. The banjo player struck up again, and Jambery caught hold of Ben's hands and whirled him round in time to the music. The next moment, Ben was lifted up and hoisted onto someone else's shoulders. He clung on for dear life as the man beneath him galloped like a mad pony around the square. The moment he was lifted down, two more soldiers jumped forward and grabbed his hands, spinning him around and around until he was dizzy and disorientated.

Gradually he became aware of the music growing fainter and the light from the torches dimmer. The two soldiers had danced with him down a quiet side street, and now they came to a stop and released his hands.

Ben sank to the ground and put his head between his knees, feeling suddenly nauseous. He took a few deep breaths of fresh air and tried to stand.

Suddenly he felt coarse cloth against his face and everything went black. The next thing he knew, his feet had left the ground as he was picked up by his arms and legs. He let his body go limp, too stunned to fight and still a little dizzy from the ale. The sounds of revelry grew even fainter as he felt himself half dragged, half carried away from the celebrations.

Finally the men stopped and dropped him on the cobbled ground. Ben stifled a groan as the bag of coins dug into his stomach, then he heard some scuffling, and a voice to his left said, "If there is anything I hate more than wearing someone else's clothes, it's wearing someone else's socks!"

"Socks *are* clothes," said another voice. "But I know what you mean; these uniforms smell like they haven't been laundered in years!"

"They probably haven't . . . What should we do with them?"

"Chuck 'em in the trees. We're close enough to the party that if anyone finds them, they'll just think someone had too much to drink and decided to strip off. The bodies won't be found for days, by which time –"

"By which time, what?" said the other man. "Let's

face it: we don't have a plan. Ponsonby made so many promises, but now he's dead will Glarebourne honour them?"

Inside the sack, Ben blinked in surprise at the sound of Ponsonby's name. He momentarily relaxed his possessive grip on the bag of coins as he realised that these weren't any ordinary thieves.

The man continued to speak. "To tell you the truth, I don't reckon Ponsonby was the one calling the shots anyway. There's no way he was the top banana. I reckon –" His voice suddenly broke off as footsteps approached.

"You have the boy?" The newcomer's voice was deep and gravelly.

"He came right out and joined the party," said the man to Ben's right. "We didn't even need to break into the palace."

"Did anyone see you?" asked the deep voice.

"Nah, we nicked a couple of uniforms and blended right in. No one would have seen anything they'd remember tomorr–" Ben heard something crash to the ground nearby and the voice broke off. After a long pause, the man said, "What was that?"

The footsteps moved away and Ben strained his eyes to see through the thick cloth. Suddenly the sack was whipped off him and he was yanked roughly to his feet. Someone grabbed him round the waist and hoisted him upwards towards more hands which pulled him quickly onto the rooftop. As Ben looked down, he saw a boy of about his own size climb into the sack and lie down on the cobbles. It had all taken no more than a few seconds.

A few paces away, the three men stood with their backs turned. One of them bent to pick something up. "Broken jug – must have fallen out of a window." He looked upwards as he spoke.

"Never mind that," said the man with the gravelly voice. Moonlight fell across his face as he turned, and Ben saw a livid scar that ran all the way down his cheek from his forehead to his jawline. "We have to get the boy off the streets. Let's go." He bent down to pick up the sack, and threw it easily over his shoulder. Without so much as a glance around, the three men disappeared down the alleyway.

As Ben turned to thank his rescuers, he was pushed from behind and almost fell off the rooftop. He regained his balance and looked round at the boy who had pushed him. "Joe! I *knew* it was you! I saw you steal a hog . . ."

Joe glared at him with a scowl that caused his dark eyebrows to meet in the middle. "I can't believe you left me behind in that school," he snarled. "You are so lucky I didn't do the same to you just now!"

Ben stared at him. "I'm sorry, Joe," he said slowly.

"I didn't have much choice. Mayor Ponsonby was after me and I had to get out of Quadrivium fast . . ." He broke off as he noticed a grin creep across Joe's face.

"I'm only kidding!" said Joe, slapping his thigh. "You should've seen your face! School isn't so bad once you get the hang of it. I can even write my own name now – look." He crouched down and began to daub his finger in the dirt of the gutter.

Ben heaved a sigh of relief. So much had happened since he and Joe had been captured by the soldiers and taken to the school. Rounding up the street children had been part of Ponsonby's plan to track Ben down, but Arrowbright and Penthesilean had managed to free him from the school with the help of Joe and the other street children, who had distracted the soldiers while Ben escaped.

Ben glanced at Joe's writing. "Not bad . . . but listen, Joe, I might need your help again. Would you do something for me?"

"This's getting to be a bit of a habit, mate," said Joe, looking up at him. "What's in it for me?"

Ben pulled the drawstring bag out from under his jumper and opened it. "All yours," he said, shaking the bag under Joe's nose. The gold coins within made a soft chinking sound. "I just need your help."

Joe listened intently while Ben explained what he needed. "We'll be ready," he said finally. "You can count on us!" He held out his hand and they shook each other's little fingers before twisting round and slapping each other's backsides in the ritual greeting, and then Ben was off, scampering across the rooftops towards the palace.

The fresh night air cleared his head. He could hear the celebrations still in full swing and took a wide detour around the main square, careful to keep out of sight of the revellers. The streets behind the palace were deserted, so he dropped down to ground level and raced across to the wall that surrounded the stables. It didn't take him long to scale and he crouched cautiously at the top for a moment, peering down into the yard. It was quiet and full of shadows; the only light came from a couple of lanterns near the gate. He let himself down the other side and dropped onto the roof of the stables, landing with a soft thud. A whinny came from within and Ben froze as he heard the sound of a door opening. Light poured out across the yard from an unseen doorway, and the elongated shadow of a man stretched out across the cobbles. A smaller shadow slipped past the man, taking on a solid form as it rounded the stable block and raced towards Ben's hiding place, coming to a stop directly below him.

There was a soft woof and in a flash Ben slipped off the roof and threw his arms around Tobias.

"Ben, is that you?" said a familiar voice. Ben turned to see Arrowbright striding towards him. "What are you doing out here? Shouldn't you be in bed?"

Ben stood up and took hold of Arrowbright's arm. "Someone tried to kidnap me," he said in a low voice as he dragged him back towards the doorway.

Arrowbright looked concerned. "Who was it?"

"I'm not sure, but one of them mentioned Ponsonby." Ben watched Arrowbright close the door behind Tobias and lock it. "Arrowbright, I think we should leave Quadrivium immediately." He continued speaking as Arrowbright led him down a narrow, winding corridor with stone floors. "Someone wants to sabotage our plan – if we wait for the council to handpick a search party, Damien is going to get to the prince before us!"

They turned a corner and found Tobias waiting in front of a closed door. Arrowbright paused with his hand on the doorknob and looked at Ben seriously. "I think you may be right. And Murgatroyd shares your concerns."

"Murgatroyd?" cried Ben. "He's alive?"

Arrowbright pushed open the door and Tobias bounded across the room to where the abbot was sat in an armchair by the fireplace. Perched on a low table beside him was Murgatroyd. The eagle's feathers stuck up in all directions and his injured wing had been rebandaged.

He saw Ben standing in the doorway. "You're letting the draught in," he snapped. "Come in and close the door, we have a lot to talk about."

Arrowbright shrugged at Ben and said softly, "Physically he's not in good shape and his temper hasn't improved any, but his mind is still sharp."

They entered the room and Ben looked around. He recognised the monks' quarters immediately. "Are we safe here?" he asked.

"For now," answered Arrowbright. "No one but Penthesilean knows where we are – oh, and Brother Thomas, who is preparing us a light supper." He gestured towards some double doors with little porthole windows. Ben sank down into a comfortable chair on the opposite side of the fireplace from the abbot, as Murgatroyd began to speak.

"There is no point in waiting until morning. I say we take the Book and leave Quadrivium immediately."

"I'm more inclined to agree with you after hearing about the attack on Ben," said Arrowbright, "but what will the queen say if we simply disappear overnight? Will she think our motives the same as Lord Damien's?"

"Penthesilean can stay behind to explain the situation," said Murgatroyd. "I'm not happy leaving the queen in the hands of that viper's nest she calls a council – who knows how many of them were recruited by Ponsonby?"

Ben glanced around, distracted by the tantalising smell of food. Brother Thomas entered the room carrying a tray piled high with pieces of roast chicken and a loaf of bread. He put the tray of food on the table next to Murgatroyd and returned to the kitchen. Once he had gone, Murgatroyd snatched a couple of drumsticks and a chicken wing from the tray and laid them out on the table.

"Right, so this is the plan," he began. "Using Tobias as a lookout, Arrowbright and I will escort the abbot out of the city. Ben, you will rendezvous with us outside the south-east gate once you have the Book."

Ben looked at him. "The Book?" he repeated.

"Of course, we can't leave it behind – we might need it."

"I last saw it in the throne room," said Ben, "but Cardinal Bolt might have moved it."

"He hasn't," said Murgatroyd.

"But how am I going to get into the throne room . . ." began Ben, and then stopped as he remembered where he was. "Even if I do manage to get in, how will I get the Book out of the palace without being seen?"

"I'm sure you'll think of something," said Murgatroyd.

* * *

A wave of claustrophobia washed over Ben as he climbed into the familiar tunnel above the ceiling in the monks' kitchen. He heard Arrowbright whisper "Good luck" before the trapdoor was swung shut behind him and everything went black. Taking a deep breath, he began to shuffle forward on hands and knees. The skeleton key, which Bella had given him just before his original excursion into this passageway, swung on a fine silver chain around his neck, chinking softly as it bumped against his mother's locket.

He hadn't gone very far when he heard footsteps approach. Lamplight spilled through the decorative grille that ran along the bottom of the corridor, creating dancing shadows across his path. He froze, despite knowing that no one could possibly see him hidden behind the wall, and then heard a familiar voice. "Keep quiet and let me do the talking."

"But we're the ones who caught him!"

"Yeah, we want some of the credit."

"Cardinal Bolt does not deal with people like you," said the gravelly voice. "You are here only to restrain the boy, and you would do well to remember your place."

The voices faded along with the light until Ben was left in darkness once more. He crawled forward with renewed determination and gradually the key around his neck began to twitch and glow. A wooden door appeared out of the gloom and as Ben drew nearer he held the stirring key firmly in his grasp. Cautiously, he placed his ear against the door. He could hear voices, but they were too muffled to make out the words, so he carefully slid the key into the lock and eased open the door.

The first voice he heard had a dangerous edge to it. "Who is this child you have brought before me?"

"This is Ben, your grace, the reader of the Book," said the gravelly voice.

Ben opened the door a little further, but all he could see was the back of a curtain. He crawled through the doorway and closed the door softly behind him, then lay on his stomach and lifted a corner of the heavy velvet fabric. The first thing he saw was the unmistakeable crimson-robed figure of Cardinal Bolt standing over the boy who had taken his place in the sack.

"What is your name, child, and who do you belong to?" asked the cardinal.

"The name's Jasper," answered the boy, staring boldly back at the tall man, "an' I don't belong to no one."

The cardinal sighed and turned to the man with the scarred face. "Can't I trust you to do this one small task for me?" he said with a curl of his lip. "Release the boy and try again tomorrow night." The man began to turn away, but the cardinal hadn't finished. "Oh, and Glarebourne?" Glarebourne turned. "Don't disappoint me this time."

"No, Cardinal Bolt," said Glarebourne and left the room, dragging Jasper with him. His two henchmen stepped out of the shadows at the back of the hall and hurried out after him.

Ben quickly dropped the curtain as the cardinal turned and stepped up onto the podium. He heard the man's footsteps approach and then stop. The room was silent for a long time, so Ben lifted the curtain again and cautiously peered out. The cardinal was staring down at the Book of Prophecies which lay open on the lectern. As Ben watched, the tall man bent over and brought his face so close to the Book that his nose almost touched the page. Then he lifted one of the pages and examined the parchment against the light from his lamp. Finally, with a deep sigh, he let the page fall back into place and closed the Book. Picking up his lamp, he stepped down from the podium and strode from the room. The double doors swung closed behind him and Ben heard a loud click as the lock was turned.

Ben waited for a few moments, then drew back the curtain and trotted over to the Book. Gathering it in his arms, he jumped off the podium and ducked behind the huge tapestries that lined the room. He felt his way along the narrow space between the rough stone wall and the tapestries until he came to a door at the end, which he knew from past experience opened into an alcove off the main corridor. He let himself out of the throne room and peered round the edge of the alcove just in time to see the cardinal reach the end of the corridor and disappear from view.

The lamps were burning low, indicating the lateness of the hour. Their flickering light was reflected in the suits of armour that lined the corridor, without reaching the dark spaces between. Tucking the Book firmly under one arm, Ben darted in and out of the shadows until he reached the end of the corridor, then stopped and listened.

"The throne room is locked and bolted," he heard the cardinal say. "Here is the key; make sure no one tries to enter." There was a mumbled response and then Ben heard a pair of heavy footsteps coming towards him. He didn't have time to run back to the alcove, so instead he hid behind the nearest suit of armour, clutching the Book to his chest.

There was a loud yawn and two guards passed by, looking neither to the left nor the right. Ben watched them continue down the corridor, then sidled out from behind the armour and rounded the corner. He found himself in the gallery that overlooked the palace's main entrance and which was lined with marble statues. A wide stone staircase led down to the grand hall where another guard was closing the large double doors to the palace. After placing a wooden bar across them, the guard drew up a chair, sat down, and promptly fell asleep.

Ben scanned the gallery. Stained glass windows lined the walls, but each was securely fastened. To find a way out on the ground floor, he would have to go past the sleeping guard and run the risk of being seen by the other guards who could return at any moment.

A sudden flash of inspiration made him look up. Overhead was a huge glass dome which allowed natural light to flood into the entrance hall during the daytime. Tucked into the larger panels of glass were smaller panes that could be opened to let in fresh air. Having been up on the roof of the palace many times before, Ben knew that these windows could only be opened from the inside, and therefore were fastened with just a simple latch. He looked around and caught sight of a thick red rope hanging down behind a nearby statue. His eyes followed it up towards the ceiling and he judged the distance between the rope and the glass dome, trying not to think about the drop to the stone floor below.

A soft cough in the corridor alerted him to the return of the guards. Without giving himself time to think, he tucked the Book under his arm and grabbed hold of the rope. He could hear the guards' footsteps coming closer and quickly swung his feet off the floor, but as the rope took his weight a bell began to ring loudly in the depths of the palace.

Ben heard the sound of running feet coming towards him. Using his legs to propel himself upwards, he climbed out of sight just as the guards reached the gallery and hurried down the main staircase.

"What was that?" they shouted to the other guard, who had woken with a start.

"I don't know! I think it's coming from the kitchens."

"Is it the alarm?"

They all took off towards the source of the clanging bell, leaving the main entrance unguarded. Ben quickly slithered down the rope and dropped to the floor. In seconds he was down the stairs and grappling with the heavy bar that lay across door. He managed to lift it free, but it slid from his arms and fell to the floor with a crash. Without waiting to see if anyone had heard, Ben opened the door and slipped through. He hesitated for a moment, but all was quiet in the square. The celebrations appeared to be over.

He was about to step out of the shadows of the doorway when a man appeared unexpectedly from a nearby alleyway. Ben drew back quickly. The man was dressed in the same shabby uniform as the other survivors of the Great Fire, but after his recent experience with Glarebourne's thugs Ben was taking no chances. He waited and watched.

The man staggered forward a few steps and then stopped and burped loudly. One by one, he began to pick up jugs that littered the ground and discard them, until he finally found a full one that he raised to his lips. After taking a long swig, he began to sing tunelessly at the top of his voice. Ben cringed and looked around. Suddenly, the singing broke off and a window banged shut. Ben looked back at the man who was now standing, drenched, in a puddle of water. Grumbling to himself, he limped out of the square.

Once Ben was sure the man had gone, he moved out from the shadows. Carrying the Book awkwardly under his arm, he crossed the square, making his way over and around the sleeping bodies of the soldiers who lay in his path. He reached the far side and entered a cobbled side-street, then broke into a trot. The street was well-lit but deserted, and led downhill towards the city wall.

As he passed a doorway, a hand suddenly shot out and grabbed his shoulder, swinging him round. Ben staggered and almost fell. He drew in his breath sharply, and then gasped as he was overcome by fumes.

"Ben, it isshh you, isn't it?" slurred the soldier. "I

jussh' wanna say thankssshhh . . ."

"No problem," said Ben, trying to prise the man's hand from his shoulder.

"No, no, no," continued the man, "you ssshaved us all . . . Here, have a drink." He thrust the jug into Ben's face.

"I, er . . ."

"Thanks, we'll have some of that." A hand appeared from behind Ben and took the jug. Ben's blood ran cold as he recognised the voice, and he turned slowly to look up into Glarebourne's scarred face. Behind him were his two henchmen.

"Hey!" said the drunk soldier. "That wasshh for Ben, not you! Give it back!" He made a grab for the jug and lost his balance, staggering into Glarebourne and pushing him back into the other two men. Ben didn't wait to see what happened. He took off, running as fast as he could with the heavy Book in his arms.

Behind him he heard Glarebourne's gravelly voice. "Get him!"

Ben darted into a dimly-lit alleyway. He didn't have much of a head start and he could already hear the pounding feet of the men close behind. As he ran, he searched desperately for a way up onto the rooftops – a drainpipe or a low wall – when suddenly a small figure darted out in front of him.

"This way, Ben!"

Joe's small, wiry build was instantly recognisable, but his dark hair was hidden beneath a peculiar headpiece that looked suspiciously like the head of a mop. Without faltering, Ben raced after him.

The alleyway joined a wider passage and suddenly there was another boy running alongside them with a similar contraption on his head. The passage split in two and Joe pulled Ben one way while the other boy went the other way. Ben heard the men hesitate briefly before the footsteps resumed, but they sounded lighter this time and he guessed that the men had split up.

The passage came to an abrupt end in a small, paved courtyard with an ancient tree growing in the centre. Ben and Joe stumbled to a halt beneath it, and a dozen or more boys dropped out of its branches and landed on the ground around them. They all wore the mop-like wigs over their own hair, and in the dim light they all looked very much alike. Ben glanced over his shoulder as Glarebourne and one of his henchmen entered the square.

"Got you now, you little pest," growled Glarebourne, advancing steadily towards Ben with his arms outstretched. But before he could reach him, the other boys closed ranks. Ben felt the Book wrenched from his grasp, and the next instant the boys were gone, all racing out of the courtyard in different directions. Joe grabbed Ben's hand and pulled him after them. There was an angry shout, and the chase resumed.

Ben could hear the men's feet pounding the cobbles behind them. He expected at any minute to feel a hand reach out and grab him. There was a flash of movement as one of the wigged boys crossed their path carrying the Book of Prophecies under his arm. Glarebourne shouted something and suddenly there was only one set of footsteps following Ben and Joe. They skidded round a corner and Joe leapfrogged over a wall and scrambled up onto the roof of the house beyond, followed closely by Ben. Another two boys popped up from behind the wall to take their place and Ben lay flat against the roof, his heart thumping as he listened to the footsteps recede.

"The Book!" he whispered urgently to Joe when he finally caught his breath. "I need the Book!"

Joe sat up. "Come on then," he said, pulling Ben to his feet.

The backstreets of Quadrivium were like a labyrinth, doubling back on themselves and with many unexpected dead ends, but Ben and Joe simply leapt across the winding streets below as they raced across the rooftops. Keeping out of sight, they followed the sound of running feet and it wasn't long before they had caught up with Glarebourne who was rapidly gaining on the boy with the Book.

Ben watched them disappear round a corner.

"Wait here," said Joe, and sure enough, a moment later, the boy reappeared, doubling back down the alleyway. Joe whistled softly through his teeth and, without breaking his stride, the boy threw the Book straight up into his waiting arms. Joe stepped away from the edge just as Glarebourne appeared in pursuit. He didn't seem to notice that the boy was no longer carrying the Book and continued after him. Ben and Joe listened until the echo of their footsteps had faded away, then Joe turned to Ben with a grin.

"Good plan, mate," he said. "You'll be long gone before he realises he has the wrong boy – *again!*"

"I couldn't have done it without you," said Ben. He took the Book from Joe and clasped it to his chest, then looked out over the rooftops towards the city wall. "Why don't you come with me, Joe?" he said impulsively.

Joe shook his head quickly. "Nah, I'm doin' alright here, 'specially with that extra loot you gave me! Anyway, I told you, school ain't so bad. I'll be able to read and write proper soon and then I can be anything I want, maybe even a teacher . . ."

Ben was about to break into laughter when he saw the look on Joe's face and realised he was serious. "Anything can happen," he said, thinking of everything that had happened to him in the past few days. He held out his little finger for Joe to shake. "Thanks again for your help."

They bumped backsides one last time, and then Ben turned and made his way over the rooftops towards his rendezvous with Murgatroyd and the others.

* * *

Bella studied her son as he bent his head over the map. His white hair was softened by the glow from the small fire he had begrudgingly allowed her.

"Damien?"

"Mmmm," he answered without looking up.

"Where have you been all this time?"

"What?"

He still didn't look up, but she could tell that she now had his full attention. "I've been worried. You vanished without a trace fifteen years ago and now suddenly you're back. Where were you?"

Finally he raised his head. She held his gaze for as long as she could bear, and then looked away. "I was worried," she repeated.

Damien carefully folded the map and tucked it into the inside pocket of his immaculate white jacket before replying. "It's a long story." Bella raised her eyebrows and he sighed. "I went looking for the Book of Prophecies and I was taken hostage by the rebels. I was forced to live with them in the mountains until . . ."

"Yes?" prompted Bella, as he trailed off.

Damien stood up. "Mother, it's late," he said as he removed his jacket. "We should get some sleep and make an early start for the coast."

He carefully turned his jacket inside out to reveal a silken, inky-black lining, and hung it from the branch of a tree. Not a sliver of the brilliant white fabric could be seen, and the shape of the jacket hovered above the ground as though someone had cut a black hole in the air. Declining Bella's offer of a saddle blanket from the bag of laundry she had collected from the washerwoman, he stretched himself out on the stony ground and closed his eyes.

Bella wrapped the blanket around her shoulders and stared into the fire, finally allowing her busy thoughts to push their way to the front of her mind. Gertie's warning about her son had brought back Murgatroyd's words: that it was Damien who had stolen the Book of Prophecies, that her son had been working with Ponsonby all along. She shied away from this line of thinking and forced her thoughts back to the present.

The two of them had left Quadrivium on foot and travelled west until they had reached the river that marked the city's outer boundary. Only once they had crossed the river had Damien finally agreed to stop and make camp for the night. Now Bella found herself questioning their hurried departure from Quadrivium and Damien's determination that they travel alone. She dearly wanted to trust her son, and it was clear that *she* was the only one *he* trusted . . . And perhaps he was right, she thought; after all, the king himself was dead. She repeated the words to herself until they lost their meaning: the king was *dead*; the *king* was dead; *the king was dead.*

Suddenly she sat bolt upright. Of course the king wasn't dead! Alexander was next in line to the throne, which meant that *he* was king now – although, until he came of age, whoever was his guardian would hold the power to the throne. She glanced quickly at Damien but his eyes were tightly shut and his breathing was slow and steady.

No, she thought, surely not.

9

Shira the sun leopard was waiting for Ben when he dropped over the city wall and into the wasteland beyond. "Follow me," she said softly, then turned and bounded into the darkness. Ben set off in the direction she had taken, past the looming shadows of the derelict ruins and into the wheat field beyond. He followed a path of trampled wheat stalks and soon heard the murmur of voices and saw the glow of firelight before emerging out of the wheat and into a clearing.

He looked around in surprise, quickly realising that not all the survivors of the Great Fire had entered the city. Gathered around a large bonfire were a variety of beasts and a small contingent of soldiers. Shira had joined the other sun leopards, each of which lay as close as they could to the fire without singeing their fur. Their eyes were closed, giving the impression they were dozing contentedly, but the occasional flick of a tail or the twitch of an ear betrayed their wakefulness. Through the leaping flames, Ben caught sight of Samswift standing absolutely still except for his tail which swished impatiently from side to side. The centaur stared directly at him, but gave no sign of recognition.

Ben moved closer to the fire and bent down to rest the Book of Prophecies on the ground. There was a rumble of growls and coughs as the creatures acknowledged his presence and Kimon, who had been deep in conversation with Arrowbright and Murgatroyd, looked up and saw Ben standing in the firelight. The lizard lumbered to his feet, his wrinkled dewlap swinging to and fro, and beckoned him over. Ben picked up the Book and went over to join them. As he sat down, he spotted the abbot lying in the shadows with Tobias beside him. Tobias looked up, thumped his tail once on the ground, and then rested his head back down on the abbot's feet.

"You did well, Ben," said Kimon, gesturing at the Book with his scaly claw. "Murgatroyd asked a lot of you and you delivered, as he knew you would."

The giant eagle nodded in agreement, then turned back to Arrowbright. "So, are we decided?" he asked, continuing their conversation which had been interrupted by Ben's arrival.

Arrowbright gave Ben a welcoming smile before

answering. "We'd be able to move more swiftly with a small force, but we don't know what problems we might encounter."

"That is true," said Kimon solemnly, "but Shira and her cousins will be able to scout out the territory and warn you of impending danger."

"And what of Samswift?" said Arrowbright. "He's asked permission to join us."

Kimon frowned. "I question his motives. Samswift craves revenge for the death of his cousin. He blames Lord Damien, even though Canterquick was killed by canon fire from Quadrivium's own guards."

There was a brief silence as they remembered the brave centaur. Murgatroyd was the first to break it. "Samswift would be a useful addition to our team," he said, "provided he consents to take the yoke." Kimon looked shocked at the suggestion, but Murgatroyd went on. "We'll need a wagon; the abbot won't be able to keep up otherwise, and then there's the Book of Prophecies . . ." He gestured with his wing at the large and cumbersome book. "Perhaps now that Ben is here," he continued, changing the subject, "it would be a good time to consult the Book?"

They all turned to look at Ben, who tried unsuccessfully to stifle a huge yawn.

"Right now the boy needs some sleep," said Kimon. He raised a claw. "Hamilton, could you show Ben where he can rest his head?"

A curly-haired ram appeared out of the darkness and butted Ben gently in the direction of the sleeping abbot. Ben put up token resistance, but the warmth of the fire was having an effect and he could barely keep his eyes open. Leaving the Book of Prophecies with Murgatroyd, he allowed the ram to push him towards the pile of soft straw where the abbot was softly snoring, Tobias at his feet. A dark cloak lay neatly folded on the straw next to them. Ben picked it up and lay down. He pulled the cloak up around his shoulders and closed his eyes, but to his surprise he found that he couldn't fall asleep.

He sensed a presence standing over him and opened his eyes. "Gretilda!"

The shaman sank down beside him and hugged her knees into her chest. "The Book is safe?" she asked softly.

He nodded. "It's with Murgatroyd." He glanced at her sideways, then asked, "Gretilda, what did you mean when you said the fates of the prince and my mother were intertwined?"

She looked at him strangely. "I *said* that?"

"Yes," replied Ben. "When you first came out of the forest."

"Did I really?" She stared into the distance and sighed, absentmindedly pulling at the frayed hem of her thin grey dress with her long fingers. Ben waited for her to say more, but she seemed to have forgotten he was there and his eyes had begun to drift closed by the time she spoke again. "The pale man still has my Stone; I wasn't strong enough to take it from him. He killed Danny, the bugler..."

Ben forced his eyes open and looked at the shaman. She pushed back her silvery-blonde hair and he saw a tear trickle down her cheek. Then she turned her head and looked at him.

"I need your help, Ben," she said quietly. "Let me come with you and I will tell you all I know about your mother. Just let me come with you, I beg you."

"Tell me now," said Ben.

She shrugged her slender shoulders. "The story is long, and there are but a few hours until dawn. Take me with you to the drumlins and I will tell you everything on the way. Take me with you and everything I know, you will be told. Take me with you..."

Her voice was low and hypnotic and Ben felt his eyelids grow heavy. He nodded wearily as his head sank downwards and he was asleep before it even hit the straw.

* * *

Ben was woken what felt like moments later by a

hand on his shoulder. He groaned and rolled away, falling off the bed of straw and onto the ground. It was hard and cold, but he was too tired to climb back onto the straw and simply lay where he had fallen.

"It's time to go, Ben," said Arrowbright in a low voice.

Reluctantly, Ben opened his eyes. It was still dark and his eyelids drifted closed again, but he gradually became aware of movement around him. Soon curiosity got the better of him, and he opened his eyes and sat up.

It looked like everyone else had been awake for some time – or perhaps they hadn't been to sleep at all, he thought. The air was full of little puffs of vapour from the sun leopards' warm breath as they padded restlessly around the dying embers of the fire. The abbot and Tobias were sitting together a few paces away, equally bright-eyed, their heads moving in unison as they watched the sun leopards pace up and down.

Ben looked for Arrowbright and saw his familiar silhouette appear out of the gloom, followed by a large, strangely-shaped figure. As it came closer, Ben realised it was Samswift pulling a wooden cart similar to the one they'd used for their first, ill-fated approach on Quadrivium. The leather straps of the harness were fastened securely across the centaur's muscular human chest, while the reins hung loosely from his shoulders.

He came to a stop and stood patiently as Arrowbright helped the abbot into the back of the cart. Tobias leapt up beside him and stood with his tail waving in the air as though eager to be off.

Ben got up hurriedly and went over to join Arrowbright. "We're leaving? Right now?"

"I let you sleep for as long as I could," said Arrowbright, "but we have a lot of time to make up."

Ben scanned the clearing. "Yes, but . . ." he began, and then found what he was looking for. Gretilda and Murgatroyd were standing a few paces away, locked in a fierce argument.

Ben ran over to them, and caught the tail end of Murgtroyd's sentence. "– I can't trust that you won't sabotage the journey!"

"What's going on?" he asked.

Gretilda turned to face him. "Murgatroyd says I can't go with you."

"Why not?"

"Because she's nothing more than a distraction," snapped Murgatroyd. "It's just like before, when she tried to deter us from our quest to find the Book of Prophecies –"

"If Gretilda isn't coming, then neither am I," interrupted Ben.

The huge eagle stared at him with his beady eyes. "You don't mean that."

Ben met his gaze and said nothing.

"Fine!" sighed Murgatroyd finally. "As long as she promises to do as she's told. Now, come along, Ben, we've wasted too much time already! You must give us a reading from the Book." Turning his back on the shaman, Murgatroyd made his way over to the cart, holding his injured wing awkwardly against his feathered chest. Arrowbright bent and lifted him into the back of the cart.

Gretilda mouthed "thank you" at Ben as he turned and went to join the others. There was a flare in the darkness as a lamp was lit, and the Book of Prophecies seemed to leap from the shadows as its bronze cover caught the light. Arrowbright lifted it carefully out of the cart and placed it on the tailgate in front of Ben.

Silently, the sun leopards drew closer, their amber eyes gleaming out of the darkness. Murgatroyd, too, edged closer to the Book and Gretilda moved silently to stand at Arrowbright's shoulder. Ben felt all their eyes upon him as he lifted the heavy bronze cover and turned the pages of thick parchment, but this time he knew himself to be amongst friends.

He took a deep breath and looked down at the page that had last revealed a creature of such unimaginable horror that the Book had slammed itself shut. The image before him now was one of tranquillity: a calm stretch of water beneath an overcast sky. The water was perfectly still – there was not so much as a ripple. It stretched in all directions as far as he could see, but obscuring the horizon were many low hills that rose up out of the water like the humped backs of huge underwater beasts.

He began to describe what he saw. "I see water . . . an ocean, but there is also land: small hills, islands perhaps . . ."

"Drumlins," said a soft voice. Everyone looked in surprise at the abbot who was huddled in the back of the cart. With a wavering arm, the old man pointed north. "Drumlins," he repeated.

Arrowbright drew a map from his pocket and flattened it out beside the Book. "To the north lies the Sylver Sea," he said, pointing to the top of his map. "There aren't any islands marked on my map, but then this area hasn't been widely explored" – he shot Murgatroyd a meaningful glance – "for good reason. Many have disappeared without trace trying to discover what lies beyond the Sylver Sea."

"Well, it's all we have to go on," said Murgatroyd shortly, "so we should get going."

Arrowbright folded the map and put it back in his pocket, then he wrapped the Book of Prophecies in a waterproof oilskin and placed it in the cart beside the abbot and a pile of provisions.

Ben looked about the clearing. "Where's Kimon?"

he asked. "And Hamilton and the others?"

"They've taken up positions near the city wall," said Arrowbright as he checked that everything in the cart was securely tied down. "They'll provide a diversion in case anyone tries to follow us."

"Come *along*," snapped Murgatroyd. "We don't have time to chat!"

Arrowbright quickly covered the Book and the provisions with a tarpaulin and helped Gretilda into the back of the cart. Ben scrambled up beside her and watched Arrowbright approach the silent Samswift and murmur something in his ear. Then the young soldier extinguished the lamp and pulled himself up onto the bench at the front of the cart, taking care not to touch the centaur's reins.

Ben dangled his feet over the tailgate as they pulled away from the camp. Behind them, to the east, the sky already showed the first pink streaks of dawn, but as he twisted round to face the front, the way ahead suddenly looked very dark.

* * *

Cardinal Bolt opened his eyes and stared at the canopy above his bed. A familiar tingle of pleasure filled his chest as he pictured the Book of Prophecies waiting for him in the throne room. He sat up and swung his legs out of the bed, feeling for his velvet slippers which he found in their customary spot on the antique rug. He slid his feet into them, then padded across the room and flung open the curtains. A shaft of early morning sunlight flooded the room, and Cardinal Bolt turned and cast a satisfied eye around his bedchamber.

The room was dominated by his four-poster bed which had been hand-carved from a single block of ebony by the best craftsmen in the kingdom. Opposite the bed was a matching dressing table on which lay his collection of ivory-backed brushes. Crossing the room, he picked one up and ran it through his thick mane of silver-grey hair, admiring his reflection in the gilt-edged mirror. Once he was satisfied with his appearance, Cardinal Bolt entered his dressing room and ran his hand along the row of crimson robes. He selected one of his favourites, made of a particularly fine velvet with extra panels in the skirts which allowed them to swirl flatteringly around his long legs as he strode the palace corridors. He smiled at the image and then dressed hurriedly, for once not waiting for his valet. After fiddling impatiently with the silk laces on his soft leather boots, he kicked them off and instead thrust his feet back into his slippers before leaving his room.

He paused for a moment in the doorway to his

sitting room and surveyed with delicious anticipation the empty glass case where the Book of Prophecies would soon rest. The Book would be in good company, he thought to himself, eyeing the rare and unusual volumes that lined his bookshelves. He drew in a deep breath through his long nose, savouring the musty scent of old books, and then swept out of his chamber and into the silent corridors of the monastery.

He met no one. The hour was still early and few of the monks were inclined to attend dawn prayers. Attendance had slipped since the abbot had confined himself to the tower, but this wasn't something the cardinal concerned himself with. Reaching the monastery door, he unbolted it and strode out across the square, relishing the bracing chill in the early morning air.

"Fine morning," he called to the palace guards as he breezed in through the open gate. The men rubbed the sleep from their eyes and looked after the cardinal in surprise. The cardinal took the steps up to the palace doors two at a time and bounded in.

"Good morning, men," he said to the guards inside the doorway, who were already on their feet, expecting the day shift. "I take it that the throne room is still secure? May I have the key?"

"You won't need it," answered one of the guards. "Her majesty is in there, conferring with Brigadier

Penthesilean."

Cardinal Bolt felt some of the day's shine slip away. "Penthesilean?"

"Yes, sir," said the other guard. "He was here first thing, most anxious to see the queen."

Cardinal Bolt spun round and ascended the staircase at a run, slowing only as he approached the open doorway of the throne room and heard Penthesilean's booming voice. "The decision was not taken lightly, and if we could have waited until morning to consult your majesty, then of course we would have; but any delay might have led to disaster for yourself and for the kingdom."

Cardinal Bolt moved closer to the door but was unable to catch the queen's reply.

"Of course, your majesty," he heard Penthesilean say. "I will remain by your side for as long as you require my services."

The cardinal heard the sound of footsteps approaching the door. A moment later he found himself staring into the piercing blue eyes of Penthesilean.

"Good morning, Cardinal Bolt," said Penthesilean, showing a distinct lack of surprise at finding the cardinal lurking in the corridor. He glanced down in amusement at the cardinal's slippers which were poking out from beneath his robe. "Were you in a hurry when you dressed this morning, by any chance?"

"Is that the cardinal?" called the queen. "Do send him in, Penthesilean."

Penthesilean held the door open for the cardinal, forcing him to duck under his outstretched arm. The cardinal scuttled into the room and bobbed his head towards the queen. Then, unable to wait any longer, his eyes gravitated to the lectern and he gasped in shock as he found it standing empty. "Ma'am, the Book . . . ?"

"The Book has been put to use," said the queen briskly. "Ben and Lieutenant Arrowbright have taken it and have departed Quadrivium to find my son."

"But the council agreed that –"

"That agreement was overtaken by events late last night," interrupted Penthesilean from the doorway. "Ben came close to being kidnapped, leading us to suspect that Lord Damien may still have collaborators within Quadrivium and possibly on the council itself. In the interests of the kingdom and his majesty, King Alexander, it was decided that a select group should leave immediately."

Cardinal Bolt's mind reeled with disappointment. "Of course," he mumbled. "No time to delay, no time at all . . . If you'll excuse me." Without waiting for the queen's permission, Cardinal Bolt turned and stumbled from the room, while Penthesilean gazed after him with a thoughtful expression.

10

Ben woke with the sun beating down on the back of his head and a stale taste in his mouth. He rolled his neck to ease out the stiffness, and looked around. They had left the wheat fields behind and were now travelling through open grassland, but looking back over his shoulder he could still see Quadrivium's skyline in the distance. He yawned and stretched his arms over his head, then jumped down to join Arrowbright who was walking in silence beside Samswift the centaur.

The soldier dropped back when he saw Ben. "Sleep well?" he asked, offering him his water flask.

Ben nodded and took a long drink, then wiped his mouth on his sleeve. "Where are the others?" he asked.

"You've just missed Shira. She reported back a few minutes ago to say the way ahead is clear. Murgatroyd's gone with her to meet up with Kimon and see if he has anything to report. They should be back soon. The abbot's still asleep, Gretilda's somewhere nearby, and Tobias . . . ah, here he is!"

The large dog bounded towards them. Ben bent down and stretched out his arms, but Tobias continued straight past him and took a flying leap into the back of the cart. The abbot woke and threw his arms delightedly around the dog while Tobias's tail thumped loudly against the side of the cart.

Ben looked away. "How long do you think it will take for us to reach the Sylver Sea?" he asked.

Arrowbright shook his head, pretending not to have noticed Ben's disappointment at the dog's behaviour. "I honestly can't say. This is the easy bit and we're making good time so far, but once we cross the river – well, that's Quadrivium's boundary, and who knows what we'll encounter." He looked down at Ben. "We have some dangerous territory to cross . . ." He broke off as there came a rustling in the grass behind them. They both turned quickly towards the sound, but it was only Gretilda.

The shaman drifted through the long grass carrying armfuls of leafy herbs. Dropping them in the back of the cart, she came to walk alongside them, linking her arms through theirs. They walked in companionable silence for a short while until Shira appeared with Murgatroyd clinging to the thick fur around her neck. Arrowbright took his arm from Gretilda's and lifted the injured eagle back into the cart. Ben noticed Murgatroyd's mood seemed much improved by his excursion with the sun leopard.

"Kimon reports no sign of activity from Quadrivium during the night," he said as he rearranged his feathers and made himself comfortable. "We decided he may as well proceed into the city and do what he can to help Penthesilean."

"What of Lord Damien?" asked Arrowbright.

"There's been no sign of him either, which concerns me slightly," admitted Murgatroyd, his feathery brow drawing together. "He's had quite a head start."

While Arrowbright and Murgatroyd continued their discussion, Gretilda drew Ben ahead of the cart where they walked for a while in silence. Ben could feel the locket, which held his only likeness of his mother, bouncing against his chest on the end of the fine silver chain. The silence lengthened until Ben began to feel awkward. He took a deep breath and opened his mouth, but at that moment Gretilda spoke.

"I saved your mother's life."

Ben stopped and stared at her in astonishment, but she carried on and he had to run to catch up with her as she continued speaking. "The whole village heard her screams; it was a terrible sound which reverberated through our forest and terrified the children, and some of the older ones too. Many thought that it was a demon come to ruin our crops and sour our milk. They were right about the demon, but it wasn't us it was after."

"She was being attacked by a *demon?* Did you kill it?" asked Ben, his eyes wide.

Gretilda glanced at him. "No," she said evenly, "if I had, you wouldn't be here now."

Ben gasped. "*I* was there?"

"*You* were the demon, Ben. Your mother was in the throes of childbirth and very weak when I finally found her in the depths of our forest. She had travelled a great distance and was utterly exhausted. She was incapable of making it to the village so I helped deliver you in the very same clearing where we met – for the second time – not so long ago."

Ben remembered that meeting clearly. While on the trail for the Book of Prophecies, he had become separated from Arrowbright and the others in the middle of a forest, with night drawing in. The shaman had appeared to him as if in a dream, first as the same beautiful young woman who walked beside him now, and then as a hideous old hag, urging him to seek her and drawing him towards her village.

He bombarded Gretilda with questions. "Where had my mother come from? What happened after I was born? Where did she go next?"

"Once I had nursed her back to health and you were

old enough to travel, she made the decision to seek sanctuary within Quadrivium's walls. Although we had made her welcome, she was skittish and couldn't settle in our village. Any stray traveller passing through would send her into a frenzy of anxiety and she would disappear for days at a time. I finally agreed to provide an escort to take her to the Royal City, and the day she left is the last I saw of her."

"Then how do you know she is still alive . . . and what did you mean about her fate being intertwined with the prince's?"

Gretilda raised her hands in front of her face with the fingers raised, and turned them this way and that. "I am a shaman, Ben, a practitioner of the old magic. I only have to encounter a mortal once to keep the threads of their existence in my hands. That is how I drew you to me in the forest; that is how I can sense the presence of he who stole my Stone, and the continued existence of your mother."

"So where is she?" asked Ben eagerly. But it was clear that Gretilda hadn't heard his question. She had suddenly stopped walking and stood as still as a statue, with her head raised. She still hadn't moved by the time the cart caught up with them.

"What is it?" asked Arrowbright. There was no response from the shaman.

Shira appeared out of the long grass and bounded

up to the group. She began to speak even before she had reached them. "We've picked up Lord Damien's trail heading due west!" she cried. "He's going the wrong way!"

Murgatroyd's eyes gleamed. "His intelligence must be faulty – this is excellent news!"

Gretilda gave a start as though waking from a trance. "He was here," she whispered. "He was here and he crossed this path . . ." She took a few unsteady steps away from the group and then stopped. "There's someone with him," she said, turning back to the others. "Someone I haven't come across before."

"Gretilda's right," said Shira. "It's the queen's mother – the Dowager Bella is travelling with Lord Damien."

Murgatroyd's feathers drooped. "I tried to tell her, to warn her about him, but she wouldn't listen."

Ben was just as shocked as Murgatroyd by the news, but his eyes were on the shaman. She had begun to move away from the group, slowly at first and then with a more determined step.

"Gretilda, wait!" he cried, running after her. "Where are you going?"

"He has my Stone," murmured Gretilda. "I must go after him."

"But you can't go, you haven't finished telling me about my mother!"

Gretilda's pace slowed.

"Ben!" Murgatroyd's tone was sharp. "Come back here!"

Ben grabbed hold of Gretilda's arm. "I stuck up for you! I told Murgatroyd you wouldn't jeopardise our quest. If you leave now and go after Lord Damien, you'll spoil everything!" Gretilda finally came to a stop, still staring straight ahead. Ben pressed on. "Once we've found Prince Alexander and returned him to the queen we'll go after Lord Damien together and get your Stone back – I promise!"

Reluctantly, the shaman allowed him to lead her back towards the group. Murgatroyd looked them up and down. "Is everything alright?" he asked Ben suspiciously.

"Everything's fine, Murgatroyd," answered Ben. Not wanting to meet the eagle's gaze, he looked ahead and his eye caught a glimmer of sunshine on water. "Is that the river?"

It was a timely distraction. Murgatroyd shifted his gaze from Ben and turned to look. "At last," he said. "Shira, go and find a suitable place for us to cross."

The sun leopard bounded away and returned almost immediately. She led them to a wide bend in the river where the shallow water flowed slowly and the sand was firm enough to support Samswift's hooves and the weight of the cart. Still in his harness, the centaur made his way to the water's edge. Taking a bone cup from the saddlebag slung over his back, he leant down and dipped it in the water, then raised it to his lips and drank deeply.

"We'll stop here for our noonday meal," announced Murgatroyd. He fixed Gretilda and Ben with his gaze. "Everyone stay together, I don't want *anyone* wandering off."

Once they had eaten and refilled their water flasks, Arrowbright fished his map from his pocket and flattened it out on the sand. "We're here," he said to the others, pointing to a snaking blue line on the map. "The shortest distance to the coast is due north –"

The abbot nodded. "North," he said, grinning and pointing. "North."

"– but these markings here concern me," continued Arrowbright. Ben leaned forward to see what he was talking about. Dotted between the river and the sea were many tiny skull and crossbones. "They indicate danger. It might explain why Lord Damien was heading west; it's a longer route to the coast, but it avoids this area here."

Murgatroyd paced to and fro. "If that's true, and Damien's still on the right track after all, we have no time to lose – we *have* to take the shortest route."

The abbot was still nodding enthusiastically, but Arrowbright looked hesitant.

"Why don't I see what the Book has to say?" suggested Ben.

Murgatroyd shifted impatiently from claw to claw while Arrowbright fetched the Book of Prophecies from the cart. Opening the bronze cover, Ben flicked hurriedly through the pages until he came to what looked like an exact duplicate of Arrowbright's map. He drew the map towards him and compared it to the Book. The bend in the river was clearly marked on both maps, as was the Sylver Sea to the north. The only difference was that the Book of Prophecies showed no skull and crossbones.

"It appears to be safe," he said slowly, closing the Book and handing the map back to Arrowbright. "I agree with Murgatroyd; I think we should take the shortest route to the coast."

Once the decision had been made, it didn't take them long to pack up the cart and cross the river. At first, the landscape on the other side was similar to the gently undulating hills of waist-high grass through which they had already passed, but as the afternoon wore on it began to change. The ground rose steadily and the grass became short and scrubby, gradually thinning out until they were walking on loose gravel which was unsteady underfoot.

As the path grew steeper, it became increasingly difficult to walk, but no one wanted to climb into the cart and put extra pressure on Samswift's bowed shoulders. Only the frail abbot, whose bones were as light as dust, and Murgatroyd with his injured wing, rode in the cart with the Book of Prophecies. Ben walked silently alongside the cart, with Gretilda on the other side and Arrowbright bringing up the rear. Shira had left a couple of young male sun leopards with the group while she and the rest of her cousins had split up – some to go on ahead and check out the territory, some to follow Lord Damien's trail. The coats of the young leopards were a solid gold, without the darker spots that would emerge as they matured. They loped self-importantly ahead of the cart, sure-footed on the steep and slippery slope.

After what seemed like hours, the ground finally began to level out. Ben looked up and gave a cry, "The sea! I can see the sea!"

Everyone turned to stare in the direction he was pointing. In the distance was the unmistakeable sight of sunlight dancing on water. They picked up the pace, directing their gaze towards the sea which appeared closer with each step they took. But as the ground levelled out, the terrain became increasingly inhospitable. The path wound its way through rocks and large boulders until they were walking through an eerie landscape of huge, chalky tombstones that towered overhead, intermittently blocking their view of the glittering sea.

Conversation died away and the travellers listened intently to the sound of their footsteps and the crunch of the cart's wooden wheels on the stony ground. Ben found himself adjusting his stride so that his steps matched the centaur's steady pace. He identified Gretilda's light footfall, the soft padding of the sun leopards, and Arrowbright's firm tread, but he suddenly fell out of step with Samswift when he heard another footstep. It appeared to be coming from their right, but with every sound echoing off the rocks around them, he couldn't be sure.

Arrowbright appeared beside him. Ben caught the soldier's eye and knew that he had heard the other footsteps too. The two young sun leopards stopped mid-stride and the cart rolled to a stop behind them.

"Lord Damien?" Ben asked softly.

"No." It was Gretilda who had answered. Everyone looked at her.

"How can you be sure?" asked Arrowbright, studying her face intently.

"I would feel his presence, and that of my Stone. It is not he."

Only the abbot sat unperturbed in the cart as the rest of them looked nervously over their shoulders at the towering boulders.

"Shira?" suggested Ben weakly.

"We wouldn't hear her even if she was walking right next to us," said Murgatroyd. He raised his injured wing as though desperate to take to the air.

The silence seemed to mock them as they strained their ears. The footsteps had come to a halt the moment they had stopped. Suddenly a rock fell to the ground at Ben's feet and shattered into a thousand chalky fragments. It was so unexpected that none of them had noticed from which direction it had come.

Arrowbright bent down and picked up a red rag from amongst the shards of rock. With a grim expression, he held it out to Murgatroyd who examined it with his beady black eyes before swivelling round to peer intently at the boulders. Ben followed his gaze, but the glare from the bright sunlight bouncing off the pale rocks made it difficult to see.

"Ben, take the Book of Prophecies and get beneath the cart," said Murgatroyd in a low voice.

"What's going on?" asked Ben, not moving.

"Gretilda, you too," continued Murgatroyd, "and the abbot."

Arrowbright helped the abbot from the cart and ushered him beneath it, then turned to Ben. "The rebels have us surrounded," he said grimly, "and they've just issued a declaration of war."

11

Bella shaded her eyes and looked up at the cliffs which stretched along the coast as far as she could see. In places, they dropped straight down into the waves with no beach, not even a line of rocks, to separate the two. Seawater ran over her bare feet and she felt the pebbles on which she stood shift as the water ran between them, as though threatening to pull her into the sea.

She stumbled back up the beach to where she had left her bag in a patch of shade cast by a large rock. She was hot and tired. They had spent the morning travelling in silence. Damien had set a fast pace and had once again refused to answer any of her questions, deflecting them with a deftness which had seemed satisfactory at the time, but looking back she now realised he had failed to answer a single one.

She gazed down the beach in the direction her

son had gone. After leading her at breakneck pace down the treacherous path from the cliff top, he had suddenly become concerned for her welfare, insisting she remain on the beach and rest while he found the fishing village that was marked on Brother William's map to see if he could buy a boat. There was still no sign of him, apart from a perfectly straight line of shoeprints in the sand, which had resisted the tide's attempts to wash them away. She remembered how, as a boy, he had always refused to remove his shoes and socks on the beach, and it appeared that this side of his character, at least, had not changed in the years he had been away.

She sat down in the shade beside her bag and closed her eyes, listening to the sound of the surf. Suddenly her eyes flew open and she raised her head. Above the sound of the waves crashing onto the beach, she thought she had heard shouting. She shaded her eyes once more and looked up at the cliffs. A sudden flash of red caught her eye, then it disappeared and all was silent again, but for the sound of the waves and the lonely cry of a seagull.

* * *

Ben looked out from between Samswift's hooves. He couldn't see anything but the chalky gravel that dug sharply into his knees and elbows as he knelt beneath the cart.

Gretilda winced as Ben shifted his position. "You're on my fingers!" she hissed. Ben tried to edge up to give her more room, but with Tobias and the abbot competing for space, there was no more room to give. All seemed quiet, so he wriggled out from beneath the cart and stood up.

"Ben, get back under the cart!" hissed Murgatroyd as he spotted Ben's blonde head.

Before Ben could obey, Arrowbright held up his hand for silence. Ben looked over at him and went cold with shock. A giant of a man, naked from the waist up, had suddenly appeared on the path in front of them. His dark cheeks were streaked with red paint as though raked by the claws of a wildcat, and in one hand he held the longest spear that Ben had ever seen. The man stood perfectly still, staring straight at them. Then, very slowly, he raised the spear and brought it swiftly to the ground, smashing the gravel into dust.

Suddenly the air around them was filled with shrieks and wild cries. Ben looked up to see similarly half-naked, painted men scampering like monkeys over the boulders towards them. Each carried a spear which they banged against the rocks in unison, filling the air with a chalky white dust. The beat gathered momentum until it was just a constant noise.

Slowly and menacingly, the huge man approached the cart. When he was only a single pace away, he held up his hand. Immediately the banging spears stopped. In the sudden silence, Ben could hear waves crashing onto the beach below. Still without saying a word, the man raised his spear and pointed the tip at Ben's chest. Arrowbright lifted his arm to push the spear away, but the man jerked the spear to Ben's throat and stared threateningly at the soldier. Raising his hands, Arrowbright took a step back.

Ben stood absolutely still. The tip of the spear felt ice cold against his neck, and goosebumps broke out on his arms and legs despite the heat of the day. Slowly, the man traced the spear back down to Ben's chest, then, with a sudden sideways movement, he tore open Ben's shirt.

There was a loud intake of breath from the watching rebels, and the the air was filled once more with the sound of beating spears. The man stared at the locket that hung on its long chain around Ben's neck, then reached forward and grabbed hold of it. "Thief!" he roared, tugging at the locket.

Ben twisted away. "Leave it! It's mine!" He winced as the chain dug into his neck, but didn't break. The man's face darkened and he pulled harder, but still the chain didn't break.

Around them the rebels began to chant, "Thief!

Thief! Thief!"

"No!" cried Ben. "It's mine – my mother gave it to me!"

"Thief! Thief! Thief!"

"Stop!"

The booming voice was instantly obeyed. The rebels stopped chanting and banging their spears, and everyone's attention shifted away from Ben. Cautiously he turned to see what they were staring at. Behind him, still harnessed to the cart, stood Samswift. The centaur had raised himself up to his full height until his head was on a level with that of the huge man. For the first time since they had left the camp, he began to speak.

"Mighty Decidius, until recently you and I were comrades in adversity, both of us nearly destroyed by the Great Fire of Barbearland, both of us saved by this boy standing before you." Ben swallowed as the man's eyes swivelled towards him and then back to the centaur, who continued. "Please, let the child pass in peace."

Decidius turned back to Ben, who noticed for the first time that the man's eyes were a bright sky-blue.

"Is this true?" asked Decidius. "*Are* you the one who saved us from the Great Fire?" Ben nodded. "And you say your mother gave you the locket?" Again, Ben nodded.

The man examined Ben's face intently as though searching for a sign. He stretched out his hand towards Ben, who drew back involuntarily. Decidius stopped. "May I?" he asked, pointing at the locket.

Cautiously, Ben bent his neck and allowed Decidius to draw the chain over his head. For a moment the man dangled the locket between them, then he lifted it to his face and stared at it with his blue eyes. Ben sensed the rebels draw closer.

"I didn't believe it," said Decidius in a voice little more than a whisper. "When they told me the Deliverer was Teah's son, I didn't believe it – but this is the very same locket I gave to her before I went away. I would recognise it anywhere."

Tears began to run freely down his face, mingling with the red war paint. Ben looked away in embarrassment, but he was desperate to know more. "How do you know my mother?" he asked.

"Teah is my daughter."

The blood rushed in Ben's ears. He stumbled and suddenly found huge, muscular arms wrapped around him.

"My grandson! The Deliverer!" cried the rebel leader, clutching Ben to his chest in a tight and slightly sweaty embrace. A cheer went up from the rebel horde and hundreds of spears pounded against the ground.

"You're my . . . my grandfather?" gasped Ben. "But

how can that be? You're a rebel."

Decidius finally released Ben and pulled a large red handkerchief from the pocket of his tattered trousers. "We don't call ourselves rebels," he said, rubbing the handkerchief across his eyes. He took one last look at the locket before handing it back to Ben. "We are the Maoren People, foremost amongst the mountain tribes. Your mother was, *is*, a Maoren. *You* are half Maoren."

While Ben digested this information, and his grandfather blew his nose loudly and heartily into his handkerchief, Murgatroyd finally piped up. "Does this mean we're guaranteed safe passage through your territory?"

"Of course," said Decidius, stuffing his handkerchief back into his pocket, "but where are you going? There's nothing north of here except the Sylver Sea."

While Arrowbright helped Gretilda and the abbot out from beneath the cart, Murgatroyd explained that the abbot was guiding them to the drumlins to retrieve the infant prince, who was now the King of Ballitor.

The rebel leader nodded slowly as he listened. Only once the eagle had finished, did he speak. "There is just one more thing that puzzles me. Tell me, why is the rest of your party travelling separately from you?"

He noticed their confusion and led them to the edge of the cliffs. Standing on the beach below was a small figure looking out to sea.

"Bella!" cried Ben. "And she's alone."

"Wait." Murgatroyd was staring intently out to sea. The others followed his gaze and saw a speck on the horizon. They watched it grow larger until they could make out a boat with a white sail. It was heading directly for the beach, tossed about like a toy as it encountered the rough surf, but the single figure on board managed to bring it safely onto the rocky shore. The faint sound of wood scraping against the shale reached them on the cliff top as the figure hauled it up the beach.

"Lord Damien," said Murgatroyd, spitting out the words as though they left a nasty taste in his mouth.

Ben's grandfather gave a low growl and gestured to his men with his spear. Before anyone could stop them, the rebels swarmed down the cliffs towards the beach. Hearing the commotion, the pale man looked up. He saw the rebels rushing towards him and swiftly hauled Bella into the boat, then pushed it out of the shallows and into the surf. Watching from the clifftop, Ben saw him disappear countless times beneath the waves, always resurfacing, until the boat was safely clear of the shore and at last the pale man pulled himself on board.

The rebels reached the beach and began to dive into the waves. For a moment, it looked as though they would catch the boat, but at the last minute an offshore breeze sprang up, filling the sail and whisking it out of their reach.

The sound of laughter filled Ben's ears. He tilted his head but then it was gone, replaced by the constant crash of waves and the hiss of the wind, until he was no longer sure whether or not he had imagined it.

* * *

With one hand on the tiller, Damien reached down and tossed a bucket to Bella. "Start bailing," he told his mother, "or we'll sink."

Shocked into submission by the rebels' sudden and unexpected attack, Bella took the bucket and began scooping water out of the sailboat. As fast as she could bail it out, more came splashing over the side to replenish the ankle-deep pool that sloshed around the bottom. She was so absorbed in her task that she didn't notice that her son was deliberately angling the boat into the waves so that it would continue to fill with water.

With his mother distracted, Damien looked back at the shore. The rebels were hauling themselves onto the beach where they stood shaking their spears at the boat. He ignored them and directed his gaze at the cluster of people standing on the cliff top. The massive figure of Decidius was easily recognisable even from this distance, but he wondered who the others were. Unlike the bare-chested rebels, they appeared to be fully dressed. Moving slowly, so as not to attract his mother's attention, he drew his telescope from his pocket and expanded it to its full length.

A large wave broke over the side of the boat, covering his gasp of surprise as he recognised Ben. He shot a glance at Bella, but she was still bailing water with fierce determination and didn't appear to have noticed. He raised the telescope to his eye once more. The soldier standing by Ben's side looked vaguely familiar, but it was the sight of the third figure that caused the telescope to slip from Damien's grasp. It landed with a splash in the bottom of the boat.

Bella reached out and picked it up. She looked at her son and then back at the shore.

"It's all right, mother," said Damien, snatching his telescope out of her hand and sliding it shut. "The rebels have retreated."

"That was a close call," Bella commented. "If you hadn't arrived when you did, they would have taken me prisoner."

"Perhaps."

"You saved me, Damien."

Damien gave his mother a brief smile, but his mind was on the third figure on the cliff. He had immediately recognised her as the shaman who had followed him to the walls of Quadrivium and cheated death. Her life had been saved only by the actions of the bugler, who had stepped in front of her at the last minute and received the full force of the blast from the stolen Sacred Stone.

His eyes narrowed as his thoughts turned to Ben. What was he doing on the cliff with the shaman? Had he discovered Alexander's whereabouts and, if so, did he have another map to guide him to the drumlins? But there *was* no other map; he had been so careful to destroy all the documents in Brother William's study . . .

His hand went to the bulge in his jacket pocket where the Stone rested. He stroked it possessively, only half listening to his mother's voice, "I'm sorry if I've been asking too many questions. You saved my life back there and I won't let anyone tell me you're a traitor ever again . . ."

As Damien caressed the Stone, another thought crossed his mind: could the Stone itself be acting as a magnet, drawing the shaman towards it – and with her, Ben? His hand clutched at the Stone through the fabric of his jacket and he stared into the deep, dark blue sea. Then he looked back at the shore which was already no more than a pale line on the horizon. As he watched, it soon became indistinguishable from the sky. The wind was brisk and they were rapidly drawing away from their pursuers. His grip on the Stone relaxed and he gave it a final pat before turning his attention to his mother.

"Why don't you take the tiller for a while," he said, flashing his white teeth in a sudden smile, "and I'll bail?"

* * *

Back in Quadrivium, Cardinal Bolt paced the length of his sitting room, barely noticing the beautiful objects around him. He heard the door open and paused just long enough for his eyes to register Glarebourne standing in the doorway before he resumed his pacing.

"Ben has left the city," he snapped, "and worse still, he has taken the Book of Prophecies with him."

"I know," answered Glarebourne. The cardinal spun round to face him with a questioning look. "We ran into the child after we left you last night," he explained. "He had the Book with him."

"And?"

Glarebourne hesitated before replying. "He got away," he said slowly, reluctant to elaborate. "I would have informed you immediately but the hour was late and –"

"Let me get this straight," interrupted the cardinal.

"After presenting me with the wrong boy earlier in the evening, you encountered the *right* boy – purely by chance, it would appear – and *once again* he slipped through your fingers?" Glarebourne opened his mouth to respond, but it appeared the question was rhetorical for the cardinal simply drew breath and continued without a pause. "Three grown men who, by your own admission, are skilled in the art of theft and thuggery allowed one small boy carrying a heavy book to outwit you for the second time in one night?"

This time Glarebourne didn't attempt to reply but simply stared down at his feet, feigning interest in the dirt that his shoes had deposited on the carpet.

"Do you have any idea which direction the boy went?" asked the cardinal in exasperation. Glarebourne shook his head without looking up.

"Imbecile!" The cardinal turned and rested his hands on the empty glass cabinet. He took a few deep breaths. "I *must* have that Book," he muttered to himself.

Glarebourne shuffled his feet uncomfortably and stared at the back of the cardinal's head. The silence in the room lengthened, broken only by the loud tick of a clock. Just when he couldn't stand it any more and was about to speak, there came a knock at the door.

"Cardinal Bolt?" said a voice.

The two men turned to see an old monk hovering

in the doorway.

The cardinal scowled. "What is it?"

The monk hesitated, casting a curious glance at the man with the badly scarred face who was also scowling at him.

"Well?" snapped the cardinal. "I haven't got all day!"

"I thought you should know that the abbot has departed for the drumlins," said the monk.

"He's done *what*?"

"The abbot has departed, your grace – for the drumlins, for the Abbey of the Ancients. Would you like me to make the necessary arrangements for the selection ceremony?"

"Selection ceremony?" The cardinal stared at the monk as though he were speaking a different language.

"Yes, your grace – to select a new abbot." The monk mistook the look on the cardinal's face for one of confusion, and continued. "Traditionally it's the cardinal's responsibility to announce the departure of the old abbot and to initiate the selection of his successor –"

"Why wasn't I told of this before now?" interrupted the cardinal, his voice cold with contempt.

"Forgive me, your grace, but you don't like to be disturbed before the sun has struck the dome, and the abbot left late last night, after you had retired for the evening." The monk was unnerved by a grim smile that began to spread over the cardinal's face. He edged nervously towards the door. "Should I instruct the scribes to start writing the formal announcements?" he stammered.

"Of course, carry on, carry on," said Cardinal Bolt, suddenly gracious. He waved a crimson-clad arm in the man's direction. "Please close the door behind you."

When the monk had gone, the cardinal turned to Glarebourne with a triumphant look on his face. "All is not lost!" he cried. "It's no coincidence that the abbot has left Quadrivium on the same night as the boy! He's leading them to the drumlins; that is where they expect to find the prince, and that is where *we* shall find the Book!"

Glarebourne frowned, scanning his memory for mention of the unfamiliar name.

The cardinal laughed at his expression. "Ah no, dear Glarebourne, ordinary mortals have no knowledge of the drumlins. It is forbidden for anyone except the serving abbot and a few senior monks to know the location of the Abbey of the Ancients." As he spoke, he approached the bookcase and surveyed the shelves. Finally, he lifted down a slim volume with a plain black cover. "Fortunately," he said, brandishing the book, "thanks to my tireless efforts in seeking out rare manuscripts, I have in my hand one of the few written records of the abbey's location!"

Glarebourne stretched out his hand for the book, but the cardinal lifted it out of his reach. "You really think I would trust *you* with this kind of information? Oh no, my dear fellow, this time we will go together so I can make sure the job is done properly."

With a lighter step, the cardinal turned and made his way through his bedchamber and into his dressing room. He surveyed the row of richly embroidered robes for a moment, then swiftly selected two or three garments and gathered them in his arms. Re-entering his bedchamber, he dropped the robes on the bed, and then noticed Glarebourne through the open door to his sitting room.

"What are you waiting for? Pack whatever you need and order my horse to be saddled – and one for yourself. We leave within the hour!"

12

Shira appeared just as the rebels, bitterly disappointed at having so narrowly missed capturing Lord Damien, were clambering back up the steep cliff. She slunk towards the group, keeping her head low to the ground while her cousins sat a few paces away and busied themselves washing paws and ears.

Murgatroyd turned on the sun leopard as she halted beside the cart. His frustration at watching Lord Damien sail off towards the horizon sharpened his tone. "Where in Tritan's name have you been?"

"We lost Damien's scent –" began Shira.

"And we were ambushed by the rebels!" interrupted Murgatroyd. "If it hadn't been for Samswift, and the fact that Ben turns out to be the grandson of the rebel leader, things could have turned nasty!"

Shira acknowledged Decidius's presence with a small bow of her head before turning back to Murgatroyd.

"Lord Damien has disappeared. We followed his scent south to a fishing village, but there his trail went cold. He appears to have vanished into thin air."

"Didn't you hear what I just said – we were *ambushed!*" squawked Murgatroyd. "You and your cousins were supposed to be scouting out the territory and warning us of imminent danger!"

Shira looked at Murgatroyd in surprise. "We did, but we knew Decidius wouldn't harm you," she said, as though it should have been obvious. "He was a fellow captive in the Mountains of the Outer Boundaries – Samswift knows him well. I thought it more important to follow Lord Damien's trail and see where it led, but now it seems we have lost him . . ."

"We haven't lost him," said Arrowbright, with a resigned sigh. "He's taken a boat."

"He's sailing to the drumlins," added Ben.

Shira turned and looked at the ocean as though seeing it for the first time. "He went out *there*?" she said, arching her golden eyebrows. "Onto the *water*?" The others simply nodded. Shira looked incredulous for a moment, then turned and began to lick her back paw with a sudden urgency.

Murgatroyd shook his head in disbelief, before drawing in his wings and summarising the situation to Ben and Arrowbright. "This is very bad news; with a fair wind behind him Lord Damien will reach the drumlins in no time at all."

"Then you have no time to lose," said Decidius from behind them. "You must catch up with him! There's a fishing village nearby where you should be able to borrow a boat."

While his men helped Arrowbright lift the abbot back into the cart, the rebel leader approached Samswift, who stood patiently in his harness. Decidius looked the centaur up and down. "When my spies first saw you, they thought you must have been enslaved by some evil trickery," he said finally. "None of us could believe such a noble beast would allow himself to be used for this humble work."

"Needs must," said Samswift shortly, bowing his head.

"He carries a precious burden," explained Arrowbright as he placed the Book of Prophecies into the cart beside the abbot.

Decidius gazed at the Book and made a strange gesture over his heart. Then he watched Gretilda climb into the cart. "You are a strange group," he said, eyeing the shaman with distrust. "What need has your party of one such as she?"

Gretilda gazed back at the rebel leader with her green eyes. She was still reeling from the shock of sensing Damien and her Stone so close, then suddenly whisked away once more.

"She saved my mother's life," explained Ben to his grandfather. "And she tells me that Teah still lives."

Decidius stared first at Gretilda and then down at Ben. "It has been a long, long time since I last saw your mother," he said, sadly.

Ben prised open the twin silver ovals of his locket and showed his grandfather the miniature that rested inside – the portrait of his mother that Prince Trestan, the leader of the mermen, had painted when Teah had sought refuge with his people. Decidius bowed his head over the tiny portrait and gazed at it for a long time.

His concentration was broken by the crunch of the cart's wheels on the gravel as it began to roll forward. He snapped the locket shut and handed it back to Ben. "She was a beauty, your mother." He pulled out his red handkerchief and wiped his eyes.

"Can you tell me more about her?" asked Ben, as they fell into step behind the cart. "I don't remember much."

Decidius heaved a long, grunting sigh. "She caused me a great deal of trouble," he began. Ben looked at him in surprise. "It wasn't entirely her fault," continued his grandfather. "She was the sweetest, most beautiful daughter a father could wish for, but that was the cause of the trouble; every man wanted to be her mate. There were many fights over my Teah

– many black eyes and broken jaws, I can tell you!" He guffawed loudly, then stopped as quickly as he had started. "To put a stop to the jealousy, I decided to get her safely married before I left to fight the king's men who were stealing our land. I had hoped to match her with a strong man, someone who could protect her honour and be a worthy son-in-law to me, but Teah knew her own mind and had already chosen a mate."

"My father! Who was he?"

Decidius looked down into Ben's face as though searching for something. "He wasn't even one of us," he said finally. "He was a scientist from Quadrivium – part of an expeditionary mining force, he said – but he'd become separated from the rest of his team and stumbled into my territory where he was taken prisoner. He was a puny man – tall and thin with no muscles to speak of – but he could talk! And Teah would listen to him for hours. He fascinated her in a way that nobody else could, and naturally she fascinated him too – that goes without saying."

"So what happened?" prompted Ben.

"They fell in love. Foolishly, I had accepted him into the tribe – he was a very likeable man and made himself useful with his little inventions. They asked for my permission to marry, but I refused. I told Teah to take some time to think about it, and if she was still determined to have him when I returned then I would go along with her wishes. I left the next day, expecting to be back within a few weeks, but it was to be fifteen long years before I finally returned home."

"So what happened to my mother?"

Decidius called one of his men over. "Gratham stayed behind, he can tell you what he knows."

Gratham was a young man with dark, deep-set eyes. He fell into step beside Ben and Decidius and picked up the story. "The one you call Lord Damien arrived in our village on the day of Decidius's departure, carrying the Book of Prophecies with him. The Maoren people are nomadic warriors; we have no need of books and so we paid it little regard, not knowing its true value. This 'Damien' also brought with him dire warnings of death should our warriors go forth on this particular campaign, but he was barely more than a boy at the time and no one believed him. Instead, he was chained up with the dogs and treated with contempt. But when Decidius didn't return, and the boy began to accurately predict all sorts of events – births, deaths, lightning storms – the superstitious amongst the tribe petitioned for his release and treated him like some sort of god.

"It wasn't long before he noticed Teah and began to follow her around. They were close in age and she tolerated him at first, but as his influence grew he became more arrogant, and she began avoiding him.

He was insanely jealous of the time she spent with her chosen mate – until, one day, the scientist simply disappeared."

Ben's eyes were wide as he followed every word.

"It was as though he had never existed," continued Gratham. "All his clothes, his equipment, even his strange eating utensils – they all disappeared with him. Teah was distraught. She spent most of her time wandering on the boundaries of our territory. Damien ordered her to be brought back to camp, but time and time again she managed to slip away. It was soon after he announced their betrothal that she disappeared for good."

Ben stared into space, imagining his mother's despair.

"No one ever discovered what happened to her," said Decidius sadly.

"I think I know," said Ben.

They looked at him in surprise, and he told them what he had learnt in his recent travels to find the Book of Prophecies: about how his mother had found sanctuary with the mermen, and how she had provided a diversion so the mermen could escape the Conscriptors, and how Gretilda had saved his and his mother's life when his mother was giving birth to him in the shaman's forest.

"And then Gretilda helped my mother get to

Quadrivium," he finished.

"Quadrivium!" exclaimed Decidius. "But the Maoren tribe were sworn enemies of the king. Why would she go there?"

"Perhaps she thought she'd find my father there," said Ben. He hesitated before continuing. "There's one other thing Gretilda told me . . ."

"What?"

"She said my mother's fate was intertwined with that of the prince. The problem is she can't remember saying it – I think she was in some sort of trance at the time – but she is adamant that Teah is still alive, and her connection to the prince is the only clue I have to go on."

At that moment, they crested a rise and the rocky landscape fell away to reveal a crescent-shaped bay below. It looked as though someone had taken a scoop out of the landscape with an enormous spoon, as on the other side of the bay the cliffs continued uninterrupted down the coast. Inland was a narrow valley through which a brown river meandered before emptying into a lagoon. At one point the river had broken through the sandbank that separated the lagoon from the sea, and from their high vantage point they could see a cloud of brown water mushrooming out into the blue ocean. Their gaze was drawn to a cluster of huts built on stilts over the lagoon itself.

"That is the village I was telling you about," said Decidius, pointing.

"Where are the boats?" asked Murgatroyd, narrowing his eyes as he scanned the bay.

"The fishermen will be out at sea, but they always return before dusk." Decidius took a step back. "It's probably best if I'm not seen; they fear us" – he grinned suddenly, his white teeth flashing in his dark face – "with good reason, I will admit. But they have many boats, and I feel certain you'll be able to persuade them to part with one."

He turned then to Ben and looked at him long and hard, as though etching the boy's features on his memory. "Find my daughter, Ben," he said softly. "Bring her home to me."

Then, turning quickly, he vanished with his men back into the mountainside.

13

Brother Bernard's deep sleep was penetrated by the fierce cold. Without opening his eyes, he groped for the furs that covered his bed, but instead of fur his hand met with scratchy wool. With a grunt of irritation, he propped himself up on his elbow and stared down at the thin blanket that was barely large enough to cover his body. The sight of it brought his memory flooding back, and suddenly he was wide awake.

He was lying on a narrow bed in a small, and otherwise bare, room. A pale, sickly light seeped in through a barred window high above his bed. There was no glass in the window, and tendrils of mist drifted through the open space to join the vapour of his breath.

Shivering, Brother Bernard swung his legs off the bed and flinched as his bare feet touched the cold stone floor. He was relieved to see his thick wool habit hanging from a hook beside the door, and hurried to put it on. The bottom half was still damp from where he had waded ashore the night before, but nevertheless he was glad of its warmth. He pulled the cowl up over his ears and knotted the silk cord firmly around his waist, then looked for his fur-lined boots. They were nowhere to be seen; instead, he found a pair of rope sandals placed neatly side by side on a mat by the door. He slipped his feet into them and was about to push open the door when the silence was shattered by a shrill cry.

Brother Bernard froze as his mind was filled with the nightmarish image of the birdlike creatures he had encountered the night before. He looked over his shoulder, half expecting the light from the window to be blocked by their tattered wings, and to see their withered human arms plucking listlessly at the bars, but to his immense relief he saw nothing but swirling mist. The cry came again, and this time he recognised the lusty howls of Prince Alexander.

He pushed open the door and looked up and down the unlit corridor before turning towards the sound of the crying baby. He had learned to distinguish between the different cries emitted by Alexander to convey tiredness, hunger or – the monk's least favourite – a dirty nappy. Right now, Brother Bernard guessed that Alexander was hungry – which reminded him that he was too.

He made his way along the corridor by the meagre light coming through the doorways on either side. Peering in, he saw cells identical to the one he had just left. All were empty. He continued along the corridor until eventually it opened up into a cloister. Brother Bernard found himself on a covered walkway lined with stone arches through which he could see a neatly manicured lawn. Dew lay thick on the grass, and in the silvery drops of moisture was a line of footprints. Brother Bernard followed the trail with his eyes and caught a glimpse of a cloaked figure disappearing through an archway on the opposite side. He gathered up his robes and hurried across the grass.

"Wait!" he cried, his voice echoing off the cloister's walls, but when he reached the other side the person had vanished. He stood for a moment, perplexed, and then a wooden door opened right in front of him and an elderly man in a coarse brown habit appeared. He glared at Brother Bernard and raised a finger to his lips, before beckoning him through the doorway.

Brother Bernard followed the monk into a long hall. Two rows of stone pillars ran down the centre of the room, supporting a high ceiling. The hall was sparsely furnished, with plain wooden tables and benches where a handful of monks sat eating. A couple of them glanced up as he entered, but lowered their heads quickly without making eye contact. Apart from the scrape of spoons on bowls, the room was silent.

Brother Bernard followed the elderly monk past the diners to the far end of the room where a modest fire burned in the grate. A large, cast-iron cooking pot was suspended over the fire, and Brother Bernard forgot everything else as the smell of food reached his nostrils. He hurried towards it and was taken by surprise when he heard a familiar gurgling cry. Looking round, he noticed, for the first time, a cot standing on one side of the hearth. He averted his eyes. The prince was no longer his responsibility, he told himself, picking up a wooden bowl. Breakfast, on the other hand . . .

His mouth began to water as he watched the elderly monk dip a ladle into the cooking pot. He held out his bowl and the monk dribbled a spoonful of thin gruel into it before turning back to the pot. It was a moment before Brother Bernard realised that the monk had laid down the ladle and was tending to the fire. He stared at his bowl in dismay, barely noticing the monks who had entered the hall behind him. They shuffled around him in silence as though he was just another pillar holding up the roof. When he saw that they received the same meagre rations, he gave a sigh of resignation and sat down heavily at the nearest table.

His breakfast was gone in two mouthfuls and he

was washing it down with a mug of cold, bitter-tasting tea when the door to the hall opened. A young, fresh-faced monk rushed in carrying an over-full pitcher and spilling most of its contents onto the stone floor. He slowed as he approached the cot. He placed the pitcher carefully down on the hearth beside it, then picked up one of the prince's bottles. Brother Bernard watched with amusement as the young monk tried to prise off its lid. A hiccupping cry came from the cot, gathering strength until it erupted into a continuous, full-blown wail. The monk cast panicked glances into the cot as he continued to struggle with the bottle, but the cries became increasingly louder and some of the other monks looked up disapprovingly from their bowls.

Brother Bernard finally took pity on the young monk and went to help him. With a practised twist of his wrist, he unscrewed the lid and handed the bottle back to the monk, who gave him a grateful look. He lifted the pitcher to fill the bottle, but by now his hands were shaking so badly that most of the milk missed the bottle and splashed onto the stone floor.

"Allow me," said Brother Bernard with a sigh, taking both the bottle and the pitcher from the young monk. In a few minutes, he had the bottle filled and Prince Alexander tucked into the crook of his arm, feeding happily. Feeling pleased with himself, he glanced up to find the other monks staring at him with various expressions ranging from curiosity to relief. Still no one had said a word.

* * *

Brother Bernard escaped from the refectory as soon as he could. He noticed the expressions of alarm on the other monks' faces as he had put the baby back in its cot and stood to leave, but none of them had tried to stop him.

Back in the cloister, he decided to explore the abbey with the vague idea of finding someone who could tell him what to do next. He set off down one of the passageways, looking out for the cloaked figure he had seen earlier. He wondered whether it had been someone of importance, someone who could help him get back home to Quadrivium. Deep in thought, he continued to the end of the passageway and took the short flight of steps at a quick trot, barely noticing them. He was taken off guard when the steps unexpectedly stopped at the edge of the sea. He teetered on the last step, his momentum almost carrying him forward into a tangled mass of shiny brown kelp. Its rotting, salty smell was overpowering. Brother Bernard covered his nose with a corner of his cowl and looked warily up into the open sky. It was deserted. The only thing moving was the seaweed which drifted gently on the surface of the water.

Brother Bernard gazed out over the flat, grey sea. Although the day was overcast, the air was clear and he could make out in sharp detail each of the rocky islands that rose out of the sea, blocking his view of the horizon. This was his first proper sighting of the treacherous drumlins that he had navigated the previous night. The island on which the abbey stood was surrounded by this natural defence against intruders.

Brother Bernard shivered and was about to turn and climb the steps when a sudden movement caught his eye. He paused and stared along the outer wall of the abbey, but there was no one there. He shook his head and turned to retrace his steps when his gaze fell on a rock. It was too far away for him to be sure, but there were dark patches on it that looked suspiciously like wet footprints. Now that he was paying attention, he noticed other rocks protruding at regular intervals like stepping stones through the kelp-strewn sea. He followed them to the point at which the abbey wall curved away, and narrowed his eyes. Looking carefully, he could see a break in the monotonous grey of the stone wall; it was a wooden door, set into the wall and only noticeable if one looked directly at it.

Brother Bernard looked at the stepping stones

draped with slippery, wet kelp, and frowned. Then, with a shudder, he turned his back on them and made his way up the steps and into the abbey. He returned to the cloister just as a group of elderly monks tottered out of one of the doorways. He stood back to let them pass and watched them disperse in silence, heads bowed and hands clasped beneath their robes. He cleared his throat loudly, but every one of them ignored him. As the last of the monks was about to disappear down a passageway, Brother Bernard gathered up his robes and hurried across the grass towards him.

"Wait, Brother!" he cried. His voice echoed off the stone walls, but the monk continued walking. Brother Bernard came to a stop in the centre of the quadrangle, oblivious to the drizzle that had set in, quickly coating his hair and face with moisture. He closed his eyes and thought of roaring log fires, conversation, music, and mugs of steaming tea.

He stood like this for a long time until the rain began to soak through his habit. Finally he opened his eyes and caught his breath. Standing in a corner of the cloister, framed by one of the arches, was the cloaked figure he had seen earlier. Brother Bernard took a step forward and his movement was mirrored as the figure took a step towards him, moving out of the shadows. He gasped in surprise as he saw the face of the cloaked figure. It was a woman. She stared at him with her large, grey eyes before retreating back into the shadows.

Brother Bernard began to hurry after her, but tripped on the hem of his wet robes, managing to get them tangled around his legs. By the time he had freed himself and crossed the quadrangle, the woman had disappeared – but once again she had left behind a trail of footprints. Eagerly, Brother Bernard followed them into a narrow passageway, straining his ears for the sound of her footsteps.

The passageway led to a garden enclosed by a high stone wall. Brother Bernard looked around, but there was no sign of the woman. To his left was a greenhouse which stretched the length of the garden. The glass was opaque with condensation. Brother Bernard thought he saw movement within and took a step towards it, but was stopped in his tracks by a mild voice.

"Brother, do you mind?"

Brother Bernard looked down to find that he had nearly trodden on a monk who was kneeling beside a vegetable patch filled with limp-looking leafy vegetables. "I'm so sorry," he apologised hurriedly. "I don't suppose you've seen a woman pass this way?"

The monk got to his feet, wiping his hands on the side of his habit. "You must mean the abbess?" Brother Bernard nodded eagerly and looked around, half expecting her to reappear. "You're lucky," said the monk, "she doesn't show herself to everyone. She must have led you to me so that I could help you settle in."

It began to dawn on Brother Bernard that the gardener was the first person to speak to him since he had arrived, but then the monk's words sank in. "What do you mean 'settle in'?" he asked suspiciously.

"Show you the ropes, explain how things work around here, ease you into this way of life," said the monk. "It's hard for new arrivals – getting used to the silence, the weather, the *food*." He gave a wry grin as he waved a hand at the vegetables which were drooping under the persistent rain. "It takes quite a bit of getting used to – but don't worry, you've got plenty of time."

"No, I don't – I'm in a hurry," replied Brother Bernard firmly. "And if the woman I saw is the abbess, I need to speak to her urgently about getting back to Quadrivium."

The monk looked at him pityingly. "You're here to stay now, Brother."

"You don't understand. I've done what I was asked to do, and now I want to go home."

The monk glanced over his shoulder. "Come with me," he said, turning away.

"But the abbess –"

"She's gone. Come on, let's go somewhere we can talk properly."

Reluctantly, Brother Bernard followed the monk past the greenhouse towards a cluster of apple trees growing alongside the wall. Half-hidden behind the trees was a wooden ladder propped up against the wall. The monk hitched up his robe and climbed the ladder, quickly disappearing amongst the branches of the trees. Brother Bernard sighed heavily and, with a last look at the empty garden, followed the monk. He found him perched on top of the wall looking out at the view. It was the same dull seascape Brother Bernard had seen on the other side of the island, nothing but rocky mounds in an endless, grey ocean.

The monk swept his arm in a wide arc. "Welcome to the drumlins! There's only one way in and no way out."

"What do you mean: no way out?" asked Brother Bernard, already sure he wasn't going to like the answer.

"How did you get here?"

"By boat, of course."

"And what happened to it?"

"It sank." Brother Bernard shuddered as he recalled the previous night. "I was attacked by some horrible winged creatures – they just appeared from nowhere! I was distracted and the boat hit some rocks . . ."

The monk nodded sympathetically. "The same thing happened to me, more or less," he said. "No boat has ever made it here intact. If there was a way to get off this island, do you think anyone would stay? It's all right for the abbots; they come here to die, but for those of us who bring them here . . . What is it?"

Brother Bernard was wriggling with excitement. "But I didn't come here with an abbot, I came here with Prince Alexander of Ballitor – and sooner or later someone's going to come looking for him."

The other monk shook his head sadly, "And why do you think their fate will be any different to ours?"

Brother Bernard didn't have an answer to that, and the two monks sat on the wall in silence. A bank of fog rolled in from the open sea, and they watched it smother the drumlins one by one beneath its thick, white blanket. After a while, a bell began to peal from somewhere within the abbey, and Brother Bernard turned hopefully to the other monk, "Lunch?"

"Midday prayers," answered the monk, swinging his legs back over the wall. Halfway down the ladder he leant across and plucked a shrivelled apple from a tree, then threw it to Brother Bernard. "Take this – it might help fill your stomach until supper."

Brother Bernard took a bite of the apple and almost gagged on the bitter flesh. He was about to chuck it into the sea, but stopped himself as the monk's words sank in. He scrambled down the ladder, pausing only to fill the pockets of his habit with as many of the worm-riddled apples as he could lay his hands on.

As they approached the cloister, Prince Alexander's cries could be heard, loud in the otherwise silent abbey. Brother Bernard was about to turn and head in the other direction when the young monk appeared, holding the screaming baby awkwardly in his arms. His face lit up when he spotted Brother Bernard, and he gave him a pleading look that the older monk was unable to ignore. Sighing, he approached the monk and took Prince Alexander from him. Putting the baby over his shoulder, he patted him firmly on his back until a loud burp — of which Brother Bernard himself would have been proud — erupted from the young prince.

"There," said Brother Bernard, trying to hand the baby back to the young monk. "Now all he needs is a nap."

Instead of taking the baby, the monk began to walk away. After a few paces, he turned and beckoned. Brother Bernard looked round but his gardening friend had disappeared, so, with another sigh, he shifted Prince Alexander more comfortably against his shoulder and followed the young monk.

They walked in single file down a passageway Brother Bernard had not yet explored. It led into a paved courtyard surrounded by windowless walls and an arched walkway that ran around the courtyard's perimeter. On the far side, a square tower rose up above the walls. It looked to be about three storeys tall and had a row of windows at the very top. Through the archway below the tower, Brother Bernard could see a small wooden door which the young monk was now heading towards.

Although it was early afternoon, the light was beginning to fade and the air was turning noticeably colder. Brother Bernard tucked a fold of his wool habit around the sleeping baby, then hurried across the courtyard and followed the other monk into the tower. By the light from the doorway he could see the bottom of a stone staircase. He took the stairs slowly, noticing the air growing steadily warmer as he climbed. At the top he found the young monk holding back a red velvet curtain and motioning for him to enter the room beyond.

Curious now, Brother Bernard stepped over the threshold and took his first look at the room. His jaw dropped open, and then his mouth slowly widened into a huge grin. The windows were draped with thick velvet curtains and a fire burned in the grate, casting a welcoming glow. On either side of the fireplace stood a comfortable armchair piled high with cushions. Brother Bernard took another step into the room and his eye fell on a table on which stood a large bowl filled with shiny red apples – nothing like the worm-ridden ones in his pockets. Beside the table was a cot made up with crisp white linen and fur-trimmed blankets. He quickly crossed over to it and laid down the sleeping prince, then he grabbed an apple from the bowl and sank into one of the fireside chairs, an idea beginning to take shape in his head.

Finally he looked up at the monk who was hovering expectantly in the doorway. "All right, I'll take care of the prince –" he paused and sighed heavily, as though he was doing the young monk a huge favour, "– but he's going to need fresh meat – lots of it – and a flagon of ale, which is very important for babies' digestion." He took a large bite of the apple and munched it noisily. The monk hesitated in the doorway and Brother Bernard waved his hand dismissively. "Hurry along! I'll need it all before the prince wakes up!"

With an anxious glance at the baby, the young monk nodded once and left the room. Brother Bernard smiled to himself as he heard his footsteps clattering down the stone steps, and settled in for a long snooze.

14

The path down to the lagoon was steep and rocky. The cart clattered noisily over the rough stones and Samswift's flanks were shiny with sweat as he concentrated hard to keep from losing his footing. The others walked alongside, while the abbot sat happily atop the steeply-tilted cart and pointed the way forward.

They were about a quarter of the way down when a boat appeared around the headland. Ben watched it tack slowly into the bay. As it came closer, he could see three crew members moving about on deck. They were running from one side of the boat to the other, peering into the water. As he watched, an anchor was tossed over the side, followed shortly after by some fishing nets; but not long after that, the nets were hauled back in, the anchor was shipped and the boat sailed on.

Ben continued down the path, watching curiously as the crew repeated this pattern two or three times. It was a while before one of the figures lifted his head and noticed them. The man's reaction was immediate. Getting the attention of his fellow fishermen, he pointed up at the party of travellers descending the path, then dashed across the deck and began to pull on a rope attached to the sail. The boat swung round and headed for the shore. By the time Ben and the others had reached the bottom, the fishermen had hauled their boat onto the beach and were waiting for them on the other side of the channel of water that flowed into the sea.

"Let me deal with this," said Arrowbright softly to the others. "Ben, you come with me. The rest of you stay here. Samswift, try not to look so fierce, and Murgatroyd, keep quiet. They may not have heard an eagle speak before, and we don't want to scare them off."

The fishermen's bodies were thin and malnourished, and they carried no weapons. They watched in silence, their eyes as wide as saucers, as Arrowbright and Ben approached. When they paused at the water's edge the fishermen urged them forward with insistent gestures. The water was flowing sluggishly through the shallow channel, and Ben and Arrowbright paddled quickly across and stood facing the fishermen on the sandbank.

"We want to buy a boat," said Arrowbright, slowly and clearly.

The tallest fisherman grinned and nodded his head so hard Ben was worried he would knock himself out. The other two men stared worriedly at each other and then at their leader, before also vigorously nodding their heads.

This time Arrowbright pointed first at the fishermen's boat, and then at himself, before saying, "Will you sell us your boat?"

The three men continued to nod, and then the leader skipped forward and took hold of Ben's arm. He waited until the other two had each taken hold of one of Arrowbright's arms, before leading the way along the sandbank. As they drew level with the wooden huts, women and children began to emerge onto the verandahs. They stared at the strangers with curiosity until one of the fishermen shouted something to them, at which three of the women clambered down ladders to canoes that were tethered beneath the huts. In moments, the women had untied the canoes and were skimming across the lagoon towards them. They drew up on the sand and jumped out, then stood timidly to one side while the fishermen helped Ben and Arrowbright into the canoes. After the fishermen had climbed in behind them, the women pushed them out onto the water and – as soon as they were afloat –

sprang back onto dry sand and watched them paddle away.

The fishermen headed directly for the largest hut and tied up next to some steps. After helping their visitors out of the canoes, they indicated that they should continue up the steps and watched until Ben and Arrowbright had followed their instructions. Ben emerged onto the hut's verandah and looked across to the river mouth. The cart was still there and he thought he could detect movement, but it was impossible to make out individual figures from this distance. He wondered briefly whether Murgatroyd could see them, then his eye was drawn to the fishermen who were making their way back across the lagoon to collect the women.

"Have you noticed how careful they are not to get wet?" he murmured to Arrowbright. "Isn't that a bit unusual for people who live so near to the water?"

A voice behind them made them jump. "Not water we fear; is what lives in water."

They turned slowly to see a man dressed only in a loin cloth standing in the doorway of the hut. Arrowbright took a step forward. "We would like to buy a boat from your people."

The man had been staring at Ben, but now his eyes swivelled to Arrowbright. "We need our boats."

"I understand," said Arrowbright, "but we're willing

to pay in gold."

"Gold worthless to us; we cannot eat gold." The man's gaze returned to Ben and he addressed his next word to him. "Come."

He turned and disappeared back inside the hut. Ben looked at Arrowbright who nodded. "We need a boat; we'll have to find out what they will accept in return."

Cautiously, Ben entered the hut. It had no windows and his eyes took a few moments to become accustomed to the gloom. He heard Arrowbright enter behind him.

"Please. Sit."

Ben followed the sound of the man's voice and gradually made out a pile of cushions on the floor. As he sank down onto them, a glowing orange face loomed up in front of him. He flinched away, before realising it was the man's face illuminated by a flickering light coming from a box that he held in his hands. He watched as the man carefully transferred a glowing ember from the box onto a pile of dry tinder that ignited immediately, throwing up a flame that illuminated the rest of the hut.

Ben looked around. Apart from a sleeping platform and the pile of cushions on which they sat, the hut was largely bare. Glancing over his shoulder, he noticed a rack of fishing rods that looked as though they hadn't been used for a long time.

Arrowbright sat down next to Ben while the man busied himself in a corner of the hut. When he turned back to them, he held a small platter of dried fish which he carefully placed on the ground in front of Ben. Then he sat back on his heels. "Please. Eat."

Ben took a piece of fish and raised it to his mouth. It was as stiff as a board and had a strong smell. The man was staring at him expectantly, so Ben tentatively bit into the fish, but he immediately found that his teeth weren't strong enough to bite through it. He tried to tear off the piece in his mouth, but it was too tough. Ben glanced at the man, who now had an anxious smile on his face. Ben smiled weakly back and looked at Arrowbright who nodded encouragingly. Slowly, Ben began to chew. The fish gradually became soggy enough that he could cram more of it into his mouth, until his cheeks were bulging and his jaw was sore from the effort of chewing.

Only once the entire piece had disappeared into Ben's mouth did the man push the platter across to Arrowbright. "Please. Eat."

Soon both of them were absorbed in chewing, and for a long time it was impossible to speak. The man watched them for a while with a satisfied smile, then stood up and left the hut. Ben and Arrowbright hurriedly spat out the remains of the fish into the fire, pushing the evidence into the embers, but it had left them with a terrible thirst and they were relieved when the man returned with an earthenware jug.

He handed it first to Ben. "Please. Drink."

Ben peered into the jug, thinking of the muddy, brown water in the lagoon. The man noticed his expression and pointed to the roof of the hut. "Water from sky," he said, before pointing at his feet. "Down there not good."

Ben took a sip and found the water sweet and refreshing. He drank long and deep before lowering the jug and handing it to Arrowbright. Between them, they soon finished the water, and the man wiped the jug carefully and put it back on a high shelf before turning back to them. "You need boat." Ben and Arrowbright nodded their heads eagerly, and the man continued. "We need help to make our water good." He pointed at Ben. "He help, we give you boat."

Ben and Arrowbright looked at each other in dismay, both mindful of the head start that Lord Damien already had.

"We would like to help," began Arrowbright, "but we need a boat right away. We can offer you gold or silver —"

The man shook his head. "No gold. No silver. He help, we give you boat."

Arrowbright got to his feet with a sigh. "We're

wasting our time here," he said to Ben. "Perhaps there's another village further along the coast where we can get a boat."

The man followed them through the doorway and out onto the verandah. The sun had already begun its descent towards the horizon and the lagoon sparkled, the late afternoon rays disguising the muddy brown water.

"The canoes are gone," said Arrowbright, peering down the steps. "We'll just have to swim across – it's not far."

Ben shaded his eyes and looked across at the sandbank. "I don't think that's going to be the problem," he said. Arrowbright followed his gaze to the river mouth. The gap had widened and the water rushing through was now a raging torrent.

"High tide," explained the man, coming up behind them. "Very dangerous to cross without a boat. You stay tonight and help us; tomorrow we give you boat."

* * *

Ben and Arrowbright sat on the verandah and watched the sun set over the ocean. They could hear the man in the loin cloth moving about inside the hut. As dusk fell, they counted ten fishing boats returning to the village. They watched the fishermen expertly navigate the treacherous channel, hovering beyond the breakers until they had selected a wave that would wash them straight through the churning water and into the lagoon.

"Looks like we're stuck here for the night," said Ben glumly.

Arrowbright agreed. "There's no way we'd get across that channel without a boat."

As each fishing boat entered the lagoon it was met by women in canoes who helped the men secure the boats to the sandbank opposite before ferrying them across the water to the huts.

"Could we steal a canoe?" suggested Ben.

Arrowbright shook his head. "They're too flimsy to get us across the river mouth. No, our only chance is to wait for low tide – whenever that is – or help them in return for a boat."

Ben looked down into the lagoon. "I wonder what it is they want," he said, shivering slightly as a cool breeze blew in from the sea.

"I think we may be about to find out."

Night had fallen swiftly while they had been talking, and out of the darkness came a torch-lit procession, moving steadily across the lagoon towards them. The first canoe tied up to the steps beneath the hut and a couple appeared, the man carrying a flaming torch in his hand. They both stared at Ben with undisguised curiosity while the man placed the torch into a bracket on the side of the hut, then they disappeared inside. A second couple appeared soon after. The woman gave Ben a hopeful smile, but the man seemed almost afraid of him, and as soon as he had secured his torch in its bracket he hurried his woman into the hut without even a quick glance in Ben's direction. Two by two, the villagers climbed the steps and entered the hut. Not a word was spoken. By the time they were all inside, the verandah was ablaze with torchlight.

Eventually the man in the loin cloth came out and invited Ben and Arrowbright to join them inside. The hut was crowded and stuffy. A space had been left for them in front of the fire and the man gestured that they should sit. All eyes were on them, and Ben squirmed uncomfortably under their gaze.

"You want boat," stated the man, looking at Ben. Ben and Arrowbright both nodded. "And we need help," he continued.

A murmur rose up from the watching villagers. The man in the loin cloth held up his hand for silence, then turned back to Ben. "You help, we give you boat."

"We will help you if we can," began Arrowbright, but the man cut him off.

"Not you, *him*." He pointed at Ben. "He is special, he can help us."

"But what is it you want me to do?" asked Ben.

The man picked up a cloth bag and a stick which were placed next to the fire. Everyone in the room leaned forward as he emptied a small heap of sand from the bag onto the floor and spread it out with his hand. Using the stick, he drew a simple but recognisable diagram of the lagoon, complete with the fishermen's huts and the river winding its way along the valley floor. When he was finished, he rocked back on his heels and brandished his stick.

"Us," he declared, jabbing his stick at the huts. He glanced up to make sure that Ben was following. "Them." He stabbed the stick into the river. "They hunt our waters. All fish . . . gone!" With a sudden movement, he swept the stick across the sand and erased the lagoon. Then he raised his eyes to Ben. "You stop them, we give you boat."

The murmurings of the fishermen escalated to a loud buzz, and this time the man in the loin cloth did not silence them.

"But who are they? Who is stealing your fish?" asked Arrowbright, raising his voice to make himself heard.

The noise increased further as the fishermen and their wives all began to shout and point to the floor of the hut.

"They live within and beneath the water," said the man in the loin cloth.

"And how am I supposed to stop them?" asked Ben.

At the sound of Ben's voice, the fishermen immediately stopped talking. The man in the loin cloth stood and walked out of the hut. After a moment, he poked his head back through the doorway and motioned for Ben to join him. The fishermen and their wives filed out of the hut after Ben and Arrowbright.

The man pointed into the darkness. "Go upriver. Take canoe. Go now."

Arrowbright began to protest. "He's just a boy! You can't expect –"

"I'll do it," said Ben quickly. He looked at Arrowbright. "We'll never catch Lord Damien unless we have a boat. These people have boats; we have to try to help them. There might not be another village for miles."

Arrowbright stared at him for a long moment before turning to the man in the loin cloth. "At least let me go with him."

The man gave a quick nod, then, taking one of the torches from the verandah, he led Ben and Arrowbright down the steps to the canoes which were tied together in a long crocodile that stretched out into the lagoon.

"Wait," he instructed. Holding the torch in one hand, he ran nimbly across the canoes to the last one in the chain. They watched him fix the burning torch to its prow, then he untied it from the others and manoeuvred it back towards the steps. He held the canoe steady while Ben jumped in, but let go just as Arrowbright climbed in behind him. The canoe rocked dangerously.

"Careful! Stay in canoe," he warned, before thrusting his oar into Arrowbright's hands and pushing the boat out into the lagoon.

* * *

The light from the torches shrank to a pinprick behind them, and the murmur of voices dwindled until the only sounds were the distant crash of waves and the splash of Arrowbright's oar as he paddled the canoe upriver. The evening breeze had dropped and the air was perfectly still.

Looking ahead, Ben could see nothing beyond the bright flame of the torch fixed to the front of the canoe. In exasperation, he scrambled forward and yanked it out of its holder, intending to move it to the back of the boat; but as he turned to hand it to Arrowbright the boat gave a sudden jolt and the torch fell from his hands. It sizzled and went out as it hit the water, and they were left in total darkness.

"That wasn't my fault!" yelped Ben. "We hit something!"

"Sshh," replied Arrowbright.

Once the afterglow from the torchlight had faded from Ben's eyes, he found that the night wasn't as dark as he had first thought. Thousands of stars cast their soft light onto the glassy surface of the lagoon, covering everything in a silvery glow. It took Ben a few moments to notice that Arrowbright had stopped paddling and was staring down into the water.

"What is it?" he whispered.

Arrowbright glanced at him. "You're right, we *did* hit something. I think there's something under the boat."

Goosebumps broke out on Ben's skin. For a few long minutes, he and Arrowbright sat like statues, staring into the lagoon. Then, at the outer limit of Ben's vision, a glimmer of movement caught his eye – a stream of ripples picked out by the starlight and moving rapidly in their direction.

"Arrowbright?" breathed Ben, pointing.

As the ripples came closer, they drew together to form a single swell. The canoe began to rock, gently at first, and then more vigorously as the water seemed to be sucked from beneath them into the swell that was rapidly growing into a huge wave. It was headed straight for them.

"Hold on!" cried Arrowbright, as the wall of water towered over them. The next moment it crashed down, capsizing the canoe.

As Ben was tipped backwards into the lagoon, he remembered the last words the man in the loin cloth had said to them: "Stay in canoe." Then the stars faded into blackness as he sank beneath the surface.

15

Bella wrapped the saddle blanket tightly round her shoulders and stared at her son, who continued to look steadfastly in the other direction. Finally she sighed and looked away, trying not to dwell on how thirsty she was. The sea around them was calm now, like a mirror of black glass reflecting the dim light from thousands of tiny stars that wheeled overhead. A crescent moon near the horizon concealed itself in scraps of cloud as though to spare Bella the endlessness of the sea surrounding them.

They had lost sight of land some hours ago. At first Bella had been relieved, fearing that the rebels would find a way to pursue them across the water; but once she had taken stock of their supplies she had immediately entreated her son to turn around and head back to land. In their rush to escape, their boat had nearly been swamped by the huge waves, and the supplies that Damien had bought from the village had either been washed overboard or spoiled by salt water. They were left with a single canteen of fresh water which was already half empty. But despite their predicament, Damien had refused to turn back.

The gentle rocking of the boat eventually lulled Bella into a doze. She slid down and rested her head on the seat, allowing herself to drift off. Damien watched her out of the corner of his eye. Once he was sure she was asleep, he drew Brother William's map out of his pocket. Travelling overland had been the easy part of their journey as the landmarks marked on the map were clearly recognisable, but now they were over water he would have to navigate with the help of the stars. He glanced at the map and then up at the sky. His eye was immediately drawn to Corona Lupus: a constellation of two small, bright stars either side of the larger, reddish-tinged Wolf Star. The stars stood out in a dark patch of sky, as though the other stars were too intimidated to venture close. Looking back down at the map, he traced a line with his finger from the coastline through the centre of the Wolf Star to a cluster of islands marked at the top edge of the parchment. He didn't need starlight to read the inscription; these were the drumlins, and on one of these strange mounds he would find the heir to the throne of Quadrivium.

He felt a breath of wind against his cheek and raised his head hopefully. His sighting of Ben and the shaman had unsettled him more than he cared to admit, even to himself. Overhead, the sail flapped in the breeze and then fell limp. A moment later it stirred again and swelled beneath a stronger gust of wind that tugged insistently at the canvas until the boat started forward.

Damien took a deep breath of the fresh night air and smiled to himself. His pursuers didn't have a boat – they might not even have a map – and now he had the wind behind him. Despite a few unforeseen setbacks, his plan was still on track.

* * *

Ben woke in a cold sweat. He found himself lying on a bed of branches that were woven together to form a surprisingly comfortable mattress. All around him more branches intertwined to form a wall that arched inwards and met overhead. Fresh, green shoots sprouted from some of the branches, making it feel as though he were sealed inside a living, growing cell.

Slowly, Ben's memory came trickling back. He remembered crossing the river mouth with Arrowbright to speak with the fishermen, and being cut off from Murgatroyd and the others by the rising tide. There had been a man in a loin cloth who needed his help, then a canoe and dazzling torchlight . . . followed by sudden darkness and the sensation of being enveloped in cold water.

He looked round for Arrowbright, but the room was small and it was immediately apparent that he was alone. He sat up slowly and his head began to throb. He raised his hand and felt tentatively along his hairline until he came to a large, raised lump near his temple. Feeling suddenly anxious for Arrowbright's safety, he eased himself off the bed and stood barefoot on the floor of the hut. The anxiety deepened into panic as he realised that he couldn't see a way out. He grabbed hold of one of the branches and pulled with all his strength, but it would not break. Bracing both feet against the wall, he held onto the branch and heaved.

"Stop that!" came a voice behind him.

Startled, Ben lost his grip and fell to the floor. He lay on his back, winded, gulping helplessly at the air like a fish. Then into his line of vision appeared the most beautiful face he had ever seen. Her eyes were the clear aquamarine of tropical seas fringed with long, sweeping eyelashes, and her skin had a pearly sheen, giving the impression that her delicate features had been sculpted from the inside of a seashell. A plait of hair the colour of late afternoon sunlight hung over one shoulder, swinging inches above Ben's nose as she looked down at him. It took him a moment to realise she was scowling.

"Do you know how long it takes to cultivate a specimen like this?" she asked, gesturing angrily at the walls. "And you try to destroy it the moment you wake up!"

Ben regained his breath and attempted to sit up. He got a mouthful of hair as the vision before him spun away, her long plait whipping him across the face. "It's a good thing I got here when I did, before you did some serious damage!"

Ben opened his mouth to apologise, but the words died on his lips. He stared in astonishment at the girl, who appeared to be growing out of the floor. He blinked a few times and eventually realised that he was looking at the door to this strange room – a hole in the floor. He could only see the girl's top half through the unusual doorway, and he felt slightly sick as he watched her body sway and bob. He put it down to the bump to his head.

The girl snorted impatiently. "Well, are you coming or not? My father is anxious to speak with you, for some reason which I cannot fathom."

She rolled her beautiful eyes and Ben felt his stomach lurch. Not trusting himself to stand, he shuffled over to the hole in the floor and swung his legs over the side, then gasped in shock as they sank into something cold and wet.

"Oh, don't be such a baby!" said the girl. "Here, take this." She handed him a short reed. "It's a breathing straw – hold it tightly between your teeth and don't drop it! And whatever else you do, don't let go of my tail!"

With that final remark, she ducked under the water. A moment later a magnificent silver tail appeared above the surface, showering Ben with water. Before it could disappear, he grabbed hold of it with one hand and clamped the reed firmly between his teeth with the other. Screwing his eyes tightly shut, he allowed himself to be dragged under.

His body tensed as the water enveloped him, filling his ears and nostrils; but after a while he began to enjoy the sensation of gliding through currents that were alternately warm and icy cold, and tentatively opened his eyes. His head had stopped aching and, whenever he felt the need, he took sips of air through the breathing straw. It was sweeter and thicker than the air he was used to, and he rolled it around his mouth before drawing it down into his lungs.

He was enjoying himself so much that he didn't pay attention to where they were going and almost dropped his breathing straw as he bumped into the mermaid when she slowed unexpectedly. He looked over her shoulder and saw a wall of pale limestone in front of them, stretching in both directions as far as he could see. Before he realised what she was doing, the mermaid had turned and was pushing him upwards. He sensed a ceiling above him and instinctively thrust his hands upwards to cushion the blow, but instead of rock he felt the caress of dry air as he broke the surface.

Another pair of hands grasped his and pulled him up through the invisible barrier between air and water, and soon he was standing on a limestone slab, dripping and shivering like a puppy. Someone placed a blanket around his shoulders and he looked up into Arrowbright's face.

"Welcome, Deliverer."

Ben turned towards the familiar voice, a smile spreading across his face even before he laid eyes on his old friend. "Prince Trestan!"

The leader of the mermen lounged in the water before him.

"What are *you* doing here?" exclaimed Ben. "Where are we, anyway?" He looked around. He and Arrowbright were standing on a narrow strip of rock that jutted out into an underwater pool. Overhead, a low limestone roof emitted a pale glow that appeared to come from the rock. Taking a second look, Ben realised that the roof and walls of the cave were undulating under a blanket of tiny glow worms.

"This is our meeting chamber," said Prince Trestan

in his booming voice. "I apologise for disturbing your rest, but after your friend explained why you were here, I thought it best we act swiftly."

"Prince Trestan knows about our mission to find the heir," added Arrowbright, "and our urgent need for a boat."

"You wish to journey to the drumlins," stated Prince Trestan. A rumble echoed around the cavern and Ben noticed that the pool behind the prince was full of mermen, a few of whom he recognised from his previous encounter with Prince Trestan's clan. "Your proposed voyage is exceptionally dangerous," continued Prince Trestan. "Are you sure this is where you will find Prince Alexander?"

"Almost certainly," said Ben. "And we're not the only ones who think so." He quickly explained that they had seen Lord Damien set out in a sailboat in the direction of the drumlins. "If he reaches the prince first, he'll use him to take control of the kingdom!"

Prince Trestan's expression grew more serious at the mention of Lord Damien who had imprisoned him and his people in an underground lake beneath the palace in Quadrivium. It had been Ben who had freed them.

He nodded as Ben finished speaking. "The drumlins lie thirty leagues or so off this coastline, in the middle of the open sea. With a good wind, the journey might be expected to take no more than three days; but there are dangerous currents, hidden reefs, and storms that strike without warning – and it gets worse once you enter the drumlins."

"You've been there?" asked Ben.

"No, only one of our kind has ever ventured near, and that was many moons ago. But we hear things from the whales and dolphins: stories of shipwrecks and sea monsters, sudden mists and churning seas. I can't let you go alone."

"You'll come with us?" asked Arrowbright hopefully.

"Alas, I cannot, but I will send an escort; it's the very least I can do for the Deliverer." He turned then and addressed the gathered mermen. "Who will volunteer to accompany the Deliverer and his companions to the drumlins?"

There was a long silence unbroken even by the drip of water. Then, from the very back of the cavern came a faint and wavering voice, "I will go!"

The mermen drew back to allow the volunteer through. He approached slowly, dragging himself sideways through the water in a crab-like fashion. Prince Trestan appeared taken aback. "Tribold," he began, "I don't think . . ."

The merman finally reached the front and steadied himself against the slab of limestone where Ben and Arrowbright stood. He looked very frail besides Prince

Trestan. "What's the matter, Trestan, too scared to go yourself?" he growled.

Looking down at the old merman, Ben could see the shape of his skull through the wisps of green hair plastered to his scalp like seaweed. Then the ancient merman raised his head and looked up at him, and Ben took a step back in shock. One side of the merman's face was completely covered in hideous scars. The eye socket was an empty hollow and only a small flap of skin remained of his ear.

The merman stared back at him through his remaining sea-green eye and cackled. "You've never seen scars like these before, have you, Deliverer? I earned these battle wounds, I did, which is why you'll be glad to have me along when you set out for the drumlins!"

"This is out of the question, Tribold," said Prince Trestan, finally finding his voice. "You'll never make it."

"I'm the only one who has ever been near the drumlins – the only one who lived to tell the tale, that is," wheezed Tribold. His one good eye swivelled towards Ben. "Oh, the drumlins are a fearful place where myths take form and your worst nightmare becomes reality! If you want to have any hope of reaching your destination, you'll take me as your guide."

Prince Trestan ran a huge hand through his mane of greenish hair. "Someone else will have to go with you." He looked expectantly at the sea of faces staring back at him. There was another long, awkward silence.

"I will go, Father."

It was the mermaid who had brought Ben to the council chamber, the beautiful mermaid with the porcelain skin and piercing gaze. Prince Trestan opened his mouth, but before he could respond there came another voice, "So will I!"

A merman only slightly older than Ben swam to the front of the cavern. His skin was a sallow grey and his face was thin and pinched.

"Trenorsen, are you sure?" asked Prince Trestan.

The young merman's adam's apple bobbed up and down in his throat as he nodded.

Prince Trestan turned back to his daughter. "Tremelia," he began, "this journey will be very dangerous –"

"Too dangerous for your precious daughter, but not for my son?"

Ben tore his gaze from Tremelia's face to see an older merman who bore a striking resemblance to Trenorsen approach the limestone slab.

"She's just a maid, Trenor!" said Prince Trestan sharply.

"Father!" cried Princess Tremelia indignantly. "I

can swim just as fast as any merman! You have to let me go!"

"She's right, Trenor," said Tribold with a sly, toothless grin. "If you can't make the journey yourself, the least you can do is send your daughter."

Prince Trestan glared at Tribold and then turned the glare on his daughter. "We'll talk about this later, young lady. Right now the fish are biting and we have to get Ben a boat."

He handed Arrowbright a breathing straw identical to the one which Ben still clutched in his hand, and said, "Stay close to me, and don't drop the straw, whatever you do." Then he turned back to the mermen. "You know the plan. Stay hidden until I give the signal."

Ben and Arrowbright slipped back into the water and took hold of Prince Trestan's huge tail. After making sure their breathing straws were in place, the great merman eased himself round and, with a single flick of his powerful tail, dived below the surface.

As they sank, Ben allowed himself a brief glimpse over his shoulder. Tremelia was directly behind them, and beyond her he could see rank after rank of mermen following them down into the depths.

* * *

Ben's head broke the surface. He looked around

and spotted the shadowy shape of the canoe drifting close by. A moment later, Arrowbright appeared beside him and together they swam towards the canoe. They hauled themselves in and sat for a moment, watching and waiting. The surface of the lagoon was undisturbed and the only sound was the waves crashing onto the shore. Dawn had not yet broken, but there was a brightening in the sky to the east. Arrowbright began to paddle towards the fishermen's huts, dipping the oars carefully into the water so as not to disturb its surface.

The line of canoes appeared out of the darkness as they approached the main hut. Arrowbright manoeuvred the canoe up to the edge of the steps and they clambered onto the small wooden platform. The canoe bumped gently against the hut's wooden stilts and they heard someone stir above. A moment later, the man in the loin cloth appeared at the top of the steps. He stared at them for a long moment, and then leapt down the steps and threw his skinny arms around Ben. Finally he released him and looked eagerly from him to Arrowbright.

"You make water good?" he said, nodding vigorously as though answering his own question.

"Come and see," said Ben.

Together, he and Arrowbright led the man up the steps and onto the verandah. The other fishermen and their wives staggered out of the hut, roused by the sound of voices. Ben and Arrowbright looked out across the lagoon and motioned for the others to watch. The stars were fading fast, and the mirror-smooth water glimmered in the growing dawn light. Suddenly the reflection was shattered as a shoal of fish skimmed across the surface towards the hut. It stopped directly in front of the watching fishermen as though it had hit an underwater wall, then turned and headed back across the lagoon. Once more the shoal stopped, and then darted back towards the hut, hundreds of fish flinging their silvery bodies into the air over and over again. The fishermen watched intently, their heads turning back and forth as the fish were herded slowly towards them.

The patch of water below the verandah began to churn and boil as the numbers of fish grew. The fishermen stood in silence, their mouths agape at the sight – and then slowly, majestically, Prince Trestan rose up out of the water, joined on each side of the shoal by the other mermen. The fishermen gasped, and a few stepped back in fear, but Prince Trestan held up his hands and began to speak.

"Fishermen of the lagoon, please accept our gift to you," he said with a small bow. "It was never our intention to take your fish. There are plenty for both of us if we work together. I hope you will accept my humble apology."

Ben looked at the man in the loin cloth. The man was staring in astonishment first at Prince Trestan and then at the shoal of fish. Suddenly a grin flooded onto his face and he clapped his hands and turned to Ben.

"You shall have your boat."

16

Ben clung to the rail of the fishing boat and shouted in delight. He was drenched from the spray that flew high into the air each time the boat crested a wave, but this only added to his sense of exhilaration. Tobias sat beside him, his snout in the air and his long ears flying in the brisk wind. Ben glanced down at the dog, giddy with pleasure at having him by his side once more, then he tightened his grip as the prow of the boat tilted skyward, and whooped happily as they reached the peak and crashed down into the trough below.

Arrowbright stood at the wheel, grinning at Ben's excitement. He manoeuvred the boat expertly through the breakers until they reached the gentle, rolling swells, then he relaxed and enjoyed the warm sun on his back as he surveyed their vessel. The grateful fishermen had insisted on giving them their largest boat, and the man in the loin cloth had steadfastly refused their offer of gold and silver coins, saying over and over again, "You helped, we give you boat." And it was a fine boat, thought Arrowbright as he admired its clean lines. There was plenty of space on deck and a small galley below with a seating area, which was where they had put the abbot. Glancing down through the hatch, Arrowbright could see the old man rocking from side to side with the motion of the swell and smiling dreamily to himself. The Book of Prophecies was safely stowed in the storage space beneath the abbot's seat, away from the salty sea spray.

Arrowbright's attention was brought back to the boat as it suddenly listed heavily to one side. He spun the wheel to bring the prow back round to face into the swell, and then glanced up to check the sails. His breath caught in his throat as saw Gretilda. She stood like a dancer, beautiful and carefree, with her bare feet braced against the motion of the waves and one hand resting lightly on the mast.

"She's like a different person, isn't she?"

Arrowbright jumped as Murgatroyd's words echoed his own thoughts. The eagle was perched behind him on the captain's chair, which already bore deep scratch marks from his talons. "The longer she's separated from her Stone, the more normal she becomes," observed Murgatroyd. "Don't you agree?"

"Perhaps," said Arrowbright noncommittally.

"She was frantic when you didn't return before nightfall," continued the eagle. "It took all my powers of persuasion and common sense to stop her swimming the channel to go and look for you. Even Samswift had to have a word with her."

"I hope he makes it home safely," said Arrowbright, quickly changing the subject. To his relief, Murgatroyd took the bait.

"It's a well kept secret that centaurs cannot abide water," replied the eagle. "His feelings of revenge must have been exceptionally deep for him to even attempt to board the boat."

Arrowbright thought back to their departure from the fishermen's village, where Samswift's burning desire to avenge his cousin's death had not been enough to overcome his fear of water. The centaur had got halfway up the gangplank, his flanks drenched with nervous sweat and his eyes rolling in terror at the wavelets which gently rocked the boat at its mooring, but ultimately his fear had beaten him back to dry land. Reluctantly, he had agreed to return to Quadrivium with the sun leopards to take news of their progress to the queen.

A volley of barks brought Arrowbright back to the present. He looked round, all thoughts of the centaur forgotten. Ben was leaning out over the rail, staring down into the water. Tobias was beside him with his paws on the rail and his hackles bristling.

"Look!" cried Ben, pointing towards the prow.

Arrowbright called Gretilda over. "Keep the wheel steady," he instructed, before moving swiftly across the deck to Ben's side. Murgatroyd was already there and they all peered down into the water where the shadows shifted in the depths. Arrowbright was about to dismiss the movement as the interplay of sunshine and clouds, when a sleek, silver shape suddenly erupted out of the sea. It was visible for less than a second before it disappeared back into the water with barely a splash. A moment later it reappeared along with three or four similar creatures. They launched themselves out of the water again and again like stones skipping along the surface.

"What are they?" breathed Ben.

Princess Tremelia appeared and swam alongside the boat, a glorious smile on her face. "Trenorsen and I found this pod of dolphins a little way offshore and persuaded them to join us. They make excellent guides –" She was interrupted by a shrill squeak followed by a series of loud whirring clicks from one of the larger dolphins. With her head on one side, she waited until the dolphin had finished, then looked up at Arrowbright. "You may want to check your bearings," she suggested. "Chik-ak-ak thinks you're veering off course."

Amused but indignant at receiving navigation tips from a dolphin, Arrowbright strode back to the wheelhouse and consulted the ship's large brass compass, glancing back at the shoreline to get a better idea of their position. Already the fishermen's huts were no more than tiny bumps on the horizon, but he could tell immediately that the boat had indeed veered off course. Taking the wheel from Gretilda, he spun it until the compass showed they were back on track, and watched the thin strip of land recede until finally it disappeared altogether.

He glanced at Gretilda who was staring out at the ocean with a look of intense concentration on her face. She jumped slightly as he laid a hand on her arm and then looked up at him questioningly with her large, grey eyes.

"Is he close – Lord Damien?"

She looked away and Arrowbright immediately wished he hadn't asked. "I'm beginning to sense his presence," she began, "but I can't pinpoint his whereabouts. The water gives a totally different perspective to land." Ending the conversation abruptly, she ducked her head through the hatch and disappeared below deck.

Murgatroyd, Ben and Tobias were still at the prow of the boat watching Tremelia and Trenorsen cavorting with the dolphins. Chik-ak-ak was competing with the young merman to see who could perform the best somersault whilst staying ahead of the boat.

"Where's Tribold?" called Arrowbright as he watched Trenorsen flip himself higher than the wheelhouse before disappearing smoothly back into the water. Without looking up, Ben pointed back towards the stern. Arrowbright glanced over the side and chuckled. The old merman had managed to fashion himself a hammock from some fishing nets hung from the side of the boat. He looked extremely comfortable with his lower half submerged just below the waterline and his face bathed in sunlight.

The fishing boat's sails billowed outwards, filled by a brisk wind, and the boat picked up speed. It plunged through the rolling swells, preceded by the dolphins that leaped and dived ahead of the boat like galloping horses pulling a chariot. Trenorsen and Tremelia couldn't match their stamina and had fallen back to swim alongside Tribold's hammock, but Ben continued to watch the dolphins. He was fascinated by the way their slim bodies seemed to fly beneath the surface, shrouded in a flurry of bubbles as they gathered speed until they shot out of the water for a few glorious seconds, the sun flashing on their silver bodies. For a while he forgot where they were headed and revelled in the dolphins' sense of freedom and joy of living.

Gradually he became aware of a low rumbling voice. He half-turned his head to catch the words.

" . . . so I lassoed the beast with a rusty, old anchor chain and left him circling the treasure. As far as I know, he's still there."

"You've never been back?" Ben recognised Tremelia's voice. With one last glance at the dolphins, he turned and ambled to where Tribold was lounging in the fishing net, Tremelia and Trenorsen swimming alongside.

"That treasure is my pension," said Tribold, winking up at Ben with his one good eye. "I'll go back there one day – the location is memorised in this old head of mine."

"Why don't you tell *me* where it is and I can get it for you?" suggested Trenorsen, ignoring Ben who sat down on the sun-warmed deck, letting his legs dangle through the rails.

"You'd like that, wouldn't you?" chortled Tribold. "But you wouldn't last a minute with that crafty old shark. He's guarding the treasure like it's his own!"

"I'm not afraid of sharks," said Trenorsen. He glanced up at Ben. "I bet *you'd* be terrified – I saw the look on your face when you first saw the dolphins!"

"Ben's faced worse things than sharks," said Tribold. "He's famous for his courage, that boy is."

Ben felt a flush creep up his face as Tremelia stared

at him, while Trenorsen looked away moodily. "Tell us what happened in the Mountains of the Outer Boundaries, Ben," she asked shyly. "I know the story, but I'd like to hear it from you."

Ben's mind went blank as he searched frantically for a suitable point at which to start. His thoughts took a different direction as a cloud passed over the sun. In an instant the colour of the sea changed from shifting greens and blues to an almost impenetrable black. He looked up at the sky. Where a moment before it had been perfectly clear, it was now liberally scattered with thick, fluffy clouds which gathered on the horizon in a huge mass edged in ominous shades of grey. The wind was getting stronger. It whipped spray from the top of the swell, and as the sea grew rougher the boat bucked and reared.

Standing abruptly, Ben turned his back on the mermen and made his way to the wheelhouse. He found Gretilda standing beside Arrowbright who was struggling to hold the wheel steady. The shaman's face was almost as grey as her dress.

"I don't like the look of this," observed Murgatroyd from the back of the captain's chair. "Those clouds are coming in fast. We could be in for an interesting ride."

They all staggered forward as the boat plunged into a deep trough. A wave broke over the prow and Ben felt the stinging blast of spray on his face. He shivered as the sky began to grow darker. There was suddenly no sign of the dolphins, or the mermen.

"Gretilda, take the wheel," instructed Arrowbright. "Ben, come with me."

The canvas sails overhead whipped from side to side as the wind seemed to blow from three directions at once. Arrowbright made his way to the main mast and took hold of the rope. "We have to take the sails down," he shouted against the howl of the wind.

Ben reached for the boom, but a gust of wind snapped the sail away from him. He stumbled and fell against the canvas just as the boom swung back the other way, knocking him onto his back. Arrowbright leaned down and hauled him to his feet, and together they struggled with the sail until eventually they had it lashed securely to the mast.

As Ben turned back towards the wheelhouse, he caught a glimpse of something on the horizon. He stopped and stared, but the towering waves obscured his view and at that moment the first fat raindrops began to fall. The individual drops soon became a downpour, and Ben raced after Arrowbright for the cover of the wheelhouse. Before long the fishing boat was surrounded by a grey curtain of driving rain, making it impossible to see anything beyond a stone's throw away.

"You're sure you saw a boat?" Arrowbright was asking Murgatroyd as Ben joined them in the wheelhouse.

"I saw it too," said Ben, shaking the rain from his hair.

"Lord Damien?"

"Who else?" said Murgatroyd. "If my wing was strong enough I'd brave the storm just to be sure, but nevertheless I would wager it is he."

They all looked to Gretilda for confirmation. The shaman was clinging to the wheel which was trying to wrench itself out of her hands with each buffeting the boat took. Her pale skin had turned a peculiar shade of green.

"I don't know," she said miserably. "I can't seem to get a feel for how near or far he is."

The conditions were growing worse every minute. The covered wheelhouse provided scant shelter from the wind and the rain, and they were all soaked to the skin. Arrowbright took the wheel from Gretilda and waved the others down into the galley, to where Tobias had already retreated. Using a thick rope, he secured the wheel to the post of the captain's chair in the hope that it would keep the boat on an even keel, then joined the others down below. Gretilda was curled up in a corner, hugging her knees to her chest, while Tobias cowered beneath the table with his head hidden in the abbot's long robes. The abbot, however, appeared to be enjoying himself and grinned wordlessly at Arrowbright as the soldier squeezed in next to him. For a while they listened in silence to the storm.

"If it is Damien, he'll be lucky to come through this unscathed," said Arrowbright finally. "His boat is much smaller than ours."

"I hope Bella's alright," said Ben glumly, glancing at Murgatroyd.

But Murgatroyd seemed distracted. "Something doesn't feel right. Damien had almost a day's head start on us; how have we managed to catch him up so quickly?"

"Maybe Bella's slowing him down," suggested Ben hopefully. "She might have realised what he's up to."

"I doubt it, she was totally taken in by him when I last spoke to her," said Murgatroyd bitterly. "It's more likely his map is wrong. They must have gone off course or –"

He was interrupted by a sudden knocking on the hull of the boat. They all looked at one another, and then Arrowbright stood up abruptly and went outside. Ben followed him. "What is it?" he asked, raising his voice against the storm.

Arrowbright ran from one side of the boat to the other, peering over the side. "We must have gone aground," he shouted. "I should have kept a lookout, but I just didn't think there were any reefs this far out to sea."

"I can't see the bottom," said Ben, peering down into the waves. Then he caught sight of something pale floating to the surface.

"Tremelia!" he cried as the mermaid's golden hair broke the surface. He was less pleased to see Trenorsen appear beside her.

"Sorry if we gave you a fright," called the merman breezily, not sounding sorry at all. "There was no one up top and we had to get your attention."

Tremelia interrupted him. "This storm is going to get worse before it gets better, so we're going to take you somewhere safe to sit it out. Throw me a rope."

A large swell lifted the two mermen almost level with Ben and Arrowbright before dropping them back down again. Arrowbright tied one end of a large coil of rope to the captain's chair and waited until the swell rose again, then threw the rope to Tremelia. She caught it and darted away, followed by Trenorsen, and they were soon lost amongst the towering waves. Ben swung himself onto the roof of the wheelhouse and shielded his eyes from the horizontal rain. The boat lurched drunkenly to one side as it turned sharply, almost throwing him from his perch, then it drew itself upright as the two mermen pulled it through the rough seas. Ben clung to the roof, every now and again catching sight of Tremelia.

After what seemed like hours, she swam back to the boat. "Weigh anchor here," she called. "Everyone into the rowing boat and I'll ferry you across while Trenorsen makes sure the boat is secure."

Ben peered through the pouring rain. If anything, the sea ahead looked even rougher than before, a mass of waves churning the ocean into white froth. Then he noticed that beyond the restless waves was a small patch of calm. He squinted against the driving rain, hardly daring to believe that what he saw was land.

"Give me a hand with this, Ben," called Arrowbright. A small rowing boat was lashed to the rear of the fishing boat, suspended over the water. Together they released the ropes holding it and watched it crash down into the waves below.

"We'll never get Gretilda in that," observed Ben, as the waves picked it up and hurled it against the side of the fishing boat. His words were drowned out by the rattle of the anchor chain. The noise brought Murgatroyd on deck and Arrowbright quickly explained the situation.

The giant eagle eyed the small rowing boat dubiously. "Are you sure about this?"

Gretilda's pale face appeared in the hatchway behind the eagle. Arrowbright leant down and took her arm. "You'll have to be brave, Gretilda. We'll soon be on dry land."

As he spoke, the fishing boat lurched to one side, battered by the waves that rushed towards the island. Taking a few deep breaths, Ben clambered over the side and let himself drop down into the rowing boat. The shaman appeared almost in a trance as she allowed Arrowbright to hand her down into the tiny bucking boat. The abbot went next, but Tobias refused to follow. Whining loudly, he trotted backwards and forwards across the yawing deck, continuously drawn towards the rowing boat where the abbot sat patiently waiting for him. He jumped up and stood with his front paws on the rail, looking down at them. Suddenly a large wave rammed the boat and the large dog was catapulted head over heels over the side. He landed with a splash in the water and went under, before reappearing in the arms of Tremelia who deposited him safely into the rowing boat.

Arrowbright turned to hoist Murgatroyd onto his shoulder but the eagle was busily tugging at the bandage on his injured wing. As it finally came free, the wind caught it and flung it up into the air like a streamer. Murgatroyd tentatively stretched out his wing, then fluttered up to the boat's rail and hopped over the side. Arrowbright watched to see that the bird landed safely in the boat, then followed him.

The conditions were even worse this close to the

water. The waves washed over the boat, threatening to capsize them at any second. They caught brief glimpses of the island as they were tossed about on the swell, before it disappeared again behind the towering seas. But Tremelia appeared unconcerned. Steadying the boat with her arms, she rode the waves, propelling them forward with her powerful tail. Eventually they crested a huge breaker and the little rowing boat rushed down the other side and came to a sudden stop on a wet and sandy beach. Gretilda immediately fell out of the boat and scrambled out of reach of the water which rushed up behind her as though to pull her back in. Tobias wasn't far behind, his spirits remarkably recovered as soon as he found his paws on solid ground.

Ben climbed out of the boat and got his first proper look at the rain-drenched island. It was little more than a mound of sand, adorned at its highest point by a few pitifully twisted trees that grew almost horizontal to the ground. A wave smacked against the back of his legs and carried on up the beach almost as far as the trees before hissing angrily back into the sea. Arrowbright carried the abbot up the beach and deposited him beside Gretilda who was huddled beneath the stunted trees, trying to find some shelter from the rain. Then he returned to help Ben drag the boat up above the water line while Murgatroyd half flew, half hopped up the beach, too proud to accept Arrowbright's offer of help.

They finally collapsed exhausted beside the others and stared out at the raging storm. The fishing boat was barely visible through the sheets of rain. The sky had grown darker, but it was impossible to tell whether the storm was getting worse or whether night was drawing in. Sure that it would be impossible to get any rest, they huddled together and waited for the storm to pass.

* * *

Ben was woken by sunlight shining pinkly through his eyelids. He opened his eyes and tried to remember where he was. The first thing he saw was a beach of fine white sand sloping gently down to an aquamarine sea. Beyond the curling waves lapping against the shore was their fishing boat, bobbing peacefully at anchor. He sat up slowly, shaking sand out of his hair. The others were lying in a heap around him, still sound asleep. The abbot gave a juddering snore and Tobias, who was curled up beside him, opened one eye and watched Ben get to his feet.

Ben stretched his arms over his head and gazed out over the ocean, which was now as flat and calm as a pond. He walked slowly down to the water's edge, looking out for the mermen. Suddenly he stopped dead. Half-hidden behind their fishing boat was another craft floating a little further out to sea – although floating may be too generous a term for it, thought Ben. He walked a few paces along the beach to get a better view and could see that the boat was wallowing low in the water. Its mast had snapped and was trailing its sail over the side. As he watched, a figure appeared on deck. It staggered to the side and hung there for a long moment. Ben narrowed his eyes, but the boat was too far away for him to identify the figure. He turned and raced back up the beach.

"Arrowbright, Murgatroyd, wake up! I think Lord Damien's been shipwrecked! I can see his boat – look, it's just behind ours!"

At the mention of Lord Damien, Arrowbright, Murgatroyd and Gretilda quickly opened their eyes. Tobias stood up and stretched, then nosed at the abbot until he too opened his eyes.

Ben tugged at Arrowbright's arm, pointing towards the sea. "He must have been blown here by the storm. His boat is ruined!"

Arrowbright got to his feet and gazed in the direction indicated by Ben. His eyes widened in shock, and then he began to ask questions. "Did you see anyone on board? How many? And Tremelia and the others – have you seen them?"

Ben nodded and then shook his head. "I only saw one person on board, and there's no sign of the mermen."

Gretilda still hadn't said a word. She was staring at the shipwrecked boat.

"Gretilda, you stay here with the abbot," ordered Arrowbright. "Murgatroyd and Ben, you come with me. Hopefully he won't put up a fight – it looks like he's had a bad night."

Ben and Arrowbright waded into the warm, clear ocean and pushed the rowing boat out. Murgatroyd tested out his wing by flying close to the boat before landing on the prow. Arrowbright handled the oars easily in the gentle surf and kept the fishing boat between them and the wreck. None of them said a word. The only sound was the creak of the boat and the gentle splash of the paddles. Finally they rounded the fishing boat and made their way slowly towards the wreck.

As they approached, Ben observed that the other boat was larger than he remembered. It was just over half the length of their own boat, with a small cabin built on the deck. There was no one in sight. Bringing the rowing boat alongside, Arrowbright motioned for Murgatroyd to board first. Murgatroyd hopped onto Arrowbright's forearm and from there up onto the side of the boat, his claws making a faint scrabbling sound against the wood. Ben found the tension almost unbearable as he watched Murgatroyd make his way along the rail towards the cabin. Finally the giant eagle reached the doorway and peered in.

The bird's head turned swiftly and he looked back at Ben and Arrowbright with an expression of such shock that Ben almost laughed out loud. Murgatroyd made a quick beckoning motion with his wing and Arrowbright climbed on board, followed by Ben. As the stricken boat shifted under their combined weight, Ben heard a groan from the cabin. In a few steps, he was standing in the doorway, his face pressed up against Arrowbright's as they peered in.

The interior of the cabin was a mess. Smashed plates and broken navigational instruments lay strewn across the floor. In the middle was a tangled heap of sodden material. Ben gave a start as it moved and a face appeared from amongst the folds of fabric.

"Cardinal Bolt!" said Arrowbright. "What in Tritan's name are you doing here?"

17

A quick search of the boat revealed another man on board besides the cardinal. Arrowbright found him barricaded inside a small, airless berth off the main cabin. Like the cardinal, he was badly dehydrated, but his face lit up at the sight of his rescuers.

Arrowbright beckoned for Ben and Murgatroyd to join him on deck. "We'll have to take them with us," he said.

"What?" cried Ben loudly, before lowering his voice to a whisper. "But that's the man who tried to kidnap me – on the orders of Cardinal Bolt! Can't we just leave them both here?"

But Murgatroyd agreed with Arrowbright. "The first rule of combat, Ben: keep your friends close and your enemies closer. We need to find out what they're doing here."

The rowing boat was too small for all five of them,

so Arrowbright rowed the cardinal across to the fishing boat while Murgatroyd and Ben kept an eye on the other man, whose name, Ben recalled, was Glarebourne. The man's distinctive scar was white in his sunburned face. Despite his cracked and blistered lips, he managed a grin. "Not exactly how I planned it," he croaked, "but it couldn't have worked out better."

"What do you mean?" asked Ben, suspiciously. But Arrowbright returned just then with the rowing boat, and it was a few minutes before they were safely back on board their own boat, and a few minutes more while Glarebourne gulped down several mugs of fresh water.

Finally, Arrowbright took the mug off him. "Right, do you want to tell us what is going on?"

Cardinal Bolt had shed his sodden robes and looked thin and vulnerable in his white underclothes, but despite his undignified appearance he appeared cheerful.

"We're after the same thing as you: Prince Alexander – or should one say *King* Alexander? The council was wasting too much time talking about what should be done to find him, so Glarebourne and I decided to take the bull by the horns and mount an expedition by ourselves." He caught Ben staring at him and gave him a broad smile. "And what a happy coincidence we ran into you. Neither of us are accomplished sailors – when the storm blew up unexpectedly, we thought it was the end for us!"

"You're lying," said Ben flatly.

The cardinal put on a hurt expression.

"You tried to have me kidnapped," continued Ben, "and when that didn't work, you followed me from Quadrivium. You're working for Lord Damien, aren't you?"

"Damien?" The cardinal looked shocked and shook his head from side to side. "I barely know the man."

Glarebourne hid a smile, which didn't go unnoticed by Murgatroyd. "What did your man here mean when he said it couldn't have worked out better?" he asked, directing the question at the cardinal, but keeping a close eye on Glarebourne.

Cardinal Bolt glanced scornfully at his henchman. "I wouldn't listen to anything he says; he told me he could handle a boat, but the moment the wind got up he locked himself in the cabin! Perhaps I was foolhardy in setting out so ill-prepared, but the young prince's wellbeing took precedence over everything else."

As he finished speaking, a gentle swell lifted the fishing boat. The cardinal instantly turned green and staggered to the side of the boat, then reeled backwards, pointing wildly at the water. "There's something down there!"

Ben looked over the rail into Tribold's ravaged face. The ancient merman leered back at him. "Got company, have you?" he cackled. "I knew those landlubbers wouldn't last long in the storm, so during the night Trenorsen and I pulled their boat into the lee of the island." He noticed Ben look searchingly at the ocean and laughed. "I've sent Tremelia to collect the others from the island. It's high time we were off; the weather's cleared and we should take advantage of this wind."

Ben wondered how the cardinal would react when he saw the abbot. He didn't have to wait long to find out. Tremelia soon returned with the rowing boat and the moment the abbot clambered back on board, the cardinal's face froze with shock. "Father Abbot," he stuttered, "I didn't expect . . . I mean, I thought that . . ."

The abbot waited politely for the cardinal to finish his sentence, but when it became obvious he had nothing further to say the old man turned his back on him and allowed Arrowbright to help him to his spot in the galley.

Murgatroyd herded the cardinal and his henchman towards the back of the boat where he could keep an eye on them. They both looked increasingly miserable as the wind picked up and the fishing boat began to roll from side to side with the growing swell. As soon as the anchor was hoisted, the boat sprang forward as though eager to be off. The wind filled their sails and propelled the craft swiftly through the waves.

As the island disappeared into the distance and they entered deeper waters, the dolphins returned. Their slender bodies streaked ahead of the boat, trailing streams of bubbles through the water. Tremelia and Trenorsen vied with them to see who could leap the highest, while Ben watched enviously from the prow. With her long plait streaming behind her, Tremelia launched herself into a neat triple somersault before re-entering the water with barely a splash. Trenorsen immediately went one better, executing a fast, spinning quadruple twist with a look of sheer delight on his normally sulky face. Despite his skinny frame, he was a fast swimmer and managed a number of manoeuvres that Ben found himself spontaneously applauding.

Eventually Tremelia tired of competing with Trenorsen and the dolphins, and fell back to swim alongside the boat near Ben. After a while, she glanced up at him.

"I owe you an apology," she began. "I was a little jealous that my father had given you one of his precious silver strands of hair, but I realise now that he wouldn't have done this lightly. Can you tell me how it came to be?"

Ben touched the chain around his neck. His most

treasured possession – the silver locket containing the portrait of his mother – hung from the chain, along with the skeleton key which Bella had given him. Prince Trestan had created the chain from a strand of his hair, which Ben discovered later was not only exceptionally strong, but also had magical properties.

Tremelia was looking up at him, waiting for an answer. Ben cleared his throat. "Erm, it happened in the underground lake beneath the palace," he began. "I was searching for the Book of Prophecies. Your father gave me this before taking me to where he thought the Book was –"

"But it wasn't there!" finished Tremelia. "And that's when you released my father and all the other grown-ups from the lake's enchantment!"

Ben looked away modestly. "Yes, but I didn't know at the time . . ."

At that moment Trenorsen erupted out of the sea in front of them, saving Ben from further explanation. The merman executed a complicated somersault, but instead of entering the water smoothly he let the full length of his body crash down, throwing up a huge geyser of water that soaked Ben.

"Trenorsen!" cried Tremelia crossly.

The young merman reappeared with a large grin plastered across his face. "What are you two jabbering on about? Why don't you come for a swim, Ben? The water's lovely, and I can teach you a few tricks if you like."

A look of terror passed over Ben's face that didn't go unnoticed by Trenorsen. "Awww, you can't swim, can you?" he laughed. Tremelia shot Trenorsen a warning look. "What?" he protested. "I'm offering to teach him! The wind's dropped so we're not going anywhere in a hurry, and I'll be right here if he gets into difficulties."

Ben looked nervously down into the depths. He vividly remembered the terrible feeling of sinking through the icy waters of the underground lake – the weight of the key around his neck; the feeling of not being able to breathe; the water flooding into his nose and ears and mouth. But now Tremelia was looking at him expectantly, and the sea *was* calm.

"Give me a moment," he said, and rushed towards the galley. Under the bright, watchful eyes of the abbot he stripped down to his shorts and took Prince Trestan's chain with his locket and key from around his neck. The abbot shifted along so that Ben could place his things with the Book of Prophecies in the space beneath his seat. They had been careful to keep the Book hidden from the cardinal and Glarebourne, who were still on deck under the watchful gaze of Murgatroyd and Tobias. As Ben padded back on deck, the two men were leaning over the side and didn't even raise their heads. Ben looked around, but Arrowbright was trimming the sails with Gretilda's help. She, at least, appeared to have recovered from her seasickness.

Ben bounded to the front of the boat. "Where's Tremelia?" he asked as he looked over the side to find Trenorsen by himself.

"Tribold wanted her for something. Don't worry – she'll be back soon. Now, if you're ready, just jump straight in."

Ben hesitated, but the sun was warm on his back and the water sparkled invitingly. He climbed onto the rail and stood for a moment, perfectly balanced. Then a slight swell lifted the boat, and he let himself fall forward and drop into the ocean.

He plunged down for what seemed an eternity. The shock of the cold water knocked the breath out of him and his lungs began to scream for air. He lashed out with his arms and legs, trying to kick his way to the shimmering ceiling of light above him; but the ocean was alive with currents which tugged his body first one way and then another – any way, it seemed, but up. Just when he thought his lungs would explode, someone grabbed hold of his upper arm and hauled him upwards. In a sudden rush he broke the surface and was into the open air.

Once he had taken a few gasping breaths, he looked around and was startled to find himself some distance from the fishing boat. He turned to see Trenorsen's grinning face inches from his own.

"Good first jump," said the merman. "I can now safely assume that you know how to go *down*, now it's time to see you go *up*!"

Before Ben could protest, Trenorsen had disappeared beneath the surface. The next thing Ben knew, his legs were clasped in an iron grip and he was yanked downwards. His eardrums squeaked in protest as Trenorsen dragged him deeper. Then abruptly the merman changed direction and pushed Ben upwards, faster and faster until suddenly, like a cork out of a bottle, he broke the surface and flew through the air. He felt a brief moment of exhilaration as the air rushed past his body before he found himself plummeting downwards. His bare chest slapped the water with a sound like a pistol shot, and a burning sensation spread through his entire body. Sea water flooded into his lungs as he gasped in pain. His eyes stung with a mixture of tears and salt water and he didn't know which way was up. All he felt was burning: on his skin, in his lungs, his throat, his nostrils. Panic took hold and he thrashed from side to side.

Then suddenly a pair of arms went round his body, gently pinning his arms to his sides, and he felt his body glide through the water. When his hair plastered itself across his eyes, some part of him registered that they had broken the surface; but when he attempted to draw breath a fit of coughing shot needles of pain into his throat and he felt himself sink beneath the water again. He was powerless to do anything about it. All the strength had seeped from his limbs and he felt as weak as a baby. The bright light behind his closed eyelids began to fade until everything went black.

* * *

The voices were the first thing to penetrate Ben's consciousness. At first he couldn't make out the words, but he recognised the shrill tones of Murgatroyd at his most furious, and in the background a deeper rumbling that echoed the eagle's angry sentiments. Then he felt a cool hand on his forehead and a voice near his ear said, "Hush, I think he's waking up."

Ben's eyelids fluttered open and he stared up into Gretilda's anxious face. The sun shone brightly behind her and she seemed to sway from side to side without actually moving. Dark blotches swam across Ben's vision and his stomach heaved in sympathy; without any warning a flood of seawater came pouring from his mouth. Strong hands lifted his shoulders and turned him onto his side, and he heard Arrowbright's voice say, "That should be the last of it. I can't believe there's any more left inside him."

A flask was held to Ben's lips and he took a tentative sip. The water felt fresh and cool as it slid down his throat and he raised his head to gulp more deeply.

"Not too much at once," said Arrowbright, taking the flask away and laying Ben's head gently back down on the sun-warmed deck.

"Is the young buck alright?"

Ben opened his eyes again to see Cardinal Bolt, dressed once more in his crimson robes, peering over Gretilda's shoulder. He was surprised to see an expression of genuine concern on the man's face.

"He seems to be," said Gretilda, shifting slightly to block the cardinal's view. "Move back – give him some air."

"Of all the idiotic, irresponsible, ill-conceived ideas!" Ben now identified the rumbling voice as that of Tribold. "What were you thinking, Trenorsen?"

"I was teaching him to swim, that's all," came Trenorsen's plaintive whine. "I didn't know –"

"He almost drowned," snapped Murgatroyd. Ben's eyes moved up to the rigging where Murgatroyd was perched, looking angrily down into the water. "How could you be so careless?"

Ben heard Trenorsen mutter something in reply, but he didn't catch the words. His attention had been caught by something out of place in the rigging behind Murgatroyd's head. It looked like a long, dark green finger and it was waving about in the air. He watched it absently while only half listening to the scolding being meted out to the hapless young merman.

"I leave you alone for five minutes," said a high, clear voice from the water. Tremelia. Ben smiled dreamily to himself as he pictured her blue eyes and perfectly formed nose. "Five minutes, Trenorsen, and I come back to find you flipping Ben in the air like a performing seal!"

Ben watched the giant green finger wave to and fro as though conducting the conversation. He almost giggled out loud as it pointed to Murgatroyd who opened his beak as if on cue. "If it wasn't for Ben, your father would still be trapped in the underground lake – and this is how you repay him!"

"I didn't mean any harm –"

"You were showing off!"

Ben winced at Tremelia's scornful tone. Trenorsen *had* been showing off, but Ben understood why: acrobatics were the only thing the skinny merman was good at. He almost felt sorry for Trenorsen, but he was slowly beginning to realise how close he must have come to dying as his hallucination grew more real by the second. The solitary green finger had been joined by three or four more fingers, each turning and swaying independently of each other. He noticed idly that the tips were covered in tiny purple suckers.

One had wrapped itself around the mast and, as he watched, he felt the boat tilt suddenly to one side.

Gretilda stumbled into Arrowbright, knocking him off his feet. The soldier landed on the deck next to Ben, and as Ben watched his friend's expression change, he realised that he hadn't been hallucinating after all.

"Squid!" shouted Arrowbright, pointing at the tentacles that were now entwined in the rigging and slowly pulling the boat over.

Murgatroyd flew at the nearest tentacle, attacking with his beak and claws. He slashed off the tip and sticky green fluid began to spurt from the wound. The tentacle reared back, flicking the green goo across the deck and narrowly missing Ben who scrambled for the cover of the wheelhouse, suddenly wide awake. He rolled down into the cabin and found Glarebourne and Cardinal Bolt there, cowering one on either side of the abbot.

"You have to come and help us!" Ben cried, before snatching a kitchen knife from one of the drawers.

He staggered back on deck and skidded in a patch of the slippery green mess, almost going overboard. The boat was leaning to one side and he had to use the ship's rail to pull himself along the deck. Two tentacles were now wrapped around the mast and another three swayed back and forth above the boat, as though blindly searching for something to grab hold of. Arrowbright had scaled the rigging and was hacking desperately at the waving tentacles with his hunting knife, ducking each time they came too near. Ben looked round and saw Gretilda standing on the roof of the wheelhouse, using her bare hands to prise the suckers from the mast. He clambered up next to her and began sawing at a tentacle with his knife.

By now, the sail was almost parallel to the water as the boat listed heavily. The suckers seemed to have welded themselves to the mast and were not budging. Gretilda began to beat at them with her fists as tears of frustration streamed down her face. Arrowbright was still valiantly fighting off the thrashing tentacles with quick thrusts of his dagger, but this only served to give away his position to the creature, and, as Ben watched, one of the tentacles wrapped itself around the soldier's arm. Without stopping to think, Ben grabbed hold of a rope and swung himself onto the rigging near Arrowbright. But Murgatroyd had got there first. Swooping down from above, he lashed out at the tentacle, severing it a hair's breadth from Arrowbright's arm. It fell back into the water with an almighty splash, leaving Arrowbright to peel away the lifeless suckers and drop them into the water after it.

Ben watched the tentacle sink as he clung to the rigging, suspended over the ocean. He saw flashes of movement below, followed by tiny spurts of green that clouded the water. Then a head broke the surface and he looked down into Tribold's single eye. The old merman gave him a quick nod and dived back down again.

A loud crack made him look round. The pressure on the mast was too much; it had snapped in two, dropping the sail into the ocean. Arrowbright had become entangled in the rigging and was struggling to keep his head above the water. Ben tried to free him, but he was on the wrong side of the rigging and the boat was still tipping sideways. The tentacles had released the broken mast and instead taken hold of the rails, and were still pulling the boat, slowly and surely, into the sea. Murgatroyd darted to and fro, jabbing at the tentacles with his sharp beak and claws; but although he was opening up more gashes, it didn't seem to be weakening the creature at all.

Ben felt anger well up inside him; he hadn't come all this way to be beaten by a giant squid. Ducking the tentacles, he scrambled back along the rigging and into the cabin. Cardinal Bolt and Glarebourne were sprawled over each other in a corner, but the abbot was still clinging to his seat. When he saw Ben, he moved to one side and lifted his seat. The cardinal's eyes widened as he spied the Book of Prophecies. He watched, open-mouthed, as Ben lifted the Book out and opened it.

As soon as he came to the right page, Ben knew what he had to do. Leaving the Book where it lay, he grabbed the kitchen knife and climbed back onto the listing deck. Pausing only to thrust the knife between his teeth, he slid down the deck, hit the boat's rail and then he was over the side and into the churning water. His eyes began to sting again, but he kept them open. The creature's tentacles were close enough to touch as they stretched past him to enclose the boat in a tight embrace. Ben grabbed hold of one of the tentacles and began to haul himself, arm over arm, through the water.

He soon found what he was looking for. Directly beneath the boat was the body of the squid, a giant, torpedo-shaped head that ran the entire length of the boat. Staring straight at him was a huge eye. Ben drew the knife from between his teeth. He just needed to get a little closer.

Hurrying now, feeling his lungs already crying out for air, he moved towards the eye. But as he drew back his arm to plunge the knife into it, the tentacle he was holding loosed itself from the side of the boat and lashed out. Ben felt the tentacle slide from his grasp, and then he was spiralling downwards into the depths. His flailing hand touched something in the water and instinctively closed around it. Immediately he felt the pressure on his chest ease as he was pulled upwards.

As soon as his head broke the surface, he realised it was Tremelia's long plait which was grasped in his fist.

"Take me back down," he gasped, brushing the streaming water from his eyes.

"What?"

"Take me back down – as close as you can get to the eye!"

Tribold appeared beside them and immediately understood Ben's intention. "Grab this, lad," he said, offering his scarred tail.

Ben put the knife back between his teeth and grabbed hold of the old merman's tail. The water was filled with bubbles from the thrashing tentacles and he could barely see a thing as they sank. Tribold shuddered as one of the tentacles lashed his chest, but he kept going. Another tentacle appeared from behind the curtain of bubbles and almost knocked Ben off the merman's tail. As he tightened his grip, a familiar dark shape flashed past, darting in and out of the tentacles. Ben stared after it as it disappeared into the gloom.

Suddenly the eye appeared, its shimmering blackness looming large in front of him, and he instantly forgot about the darting shadow. With one hand he let go of Tribold's tail and took the knife from between his teeth. He held it straight out in front of him like a lance as the merman bore down on the giant squid.

The collision when it came was gentler than Ben had expected. The knife went into the eye as though through butter, and his arm sank in up to the elbow. The shock of it made him release his hold on Tribold's tail and he was left dangling from the creature's eye. Ben looked round for the old merman and flinched as a tentacle plummeted past with Tribold in its grasp. The squid's other tentacles crashed into the water around him. He felt the creature's body shift as the hull of the boat began to swing upright, then there was a tug on his leg and he turned to see Tremelia. Leaving the knife embedded in the creature's eye, he grabbed hold of her tail with both hands.

They surfaced next to the boat and Ben dragged himself onto the sail which now trailed in the water. "It took Tribold!" he gasped to Tremelia.

The last of the tentacles fell limply from the side of the fishing boat and splashed down into the sea behind Ben. He heard a groan and turned to see Tribold appear out of the water, clinging to a large dolphin. Tremelia darted over and gently helped the old merman off the dolphin's back as it clicked and cheeped at her. She listened patiently, then gave a complicated response of clicks and whirrs.

Then she repeated what she had said so that Ben could understand. "I thank you for your warning, Chik-ak-ak, but we *must* go forward. It is where our destination lies."

She rested her hand gently on Chik-ak-ak's glistening dorsal fin before the dolphin flipped onto its side and disappeared into the depths.

Tribold raised his head and squinted at them. "It's gone," he said. "Back down into the depths where it belongs."

They pondered his words. After the onslaught, everything suddenly seemed very quiet, yet no one felt inclined to break the silence. Ben dragged himself up the side of the boat and collapsed on deck. He began to shiver. The weather had changed while they had been battling the squid, and a thick white cloud now covered the sun.

Suddenly Tremelia spoke up. "Where's Trenorsen?"

It didn't take them long to realise that no one had seen the young merman since the giant squid had made its appearance. Tribold did a quick sweep of the area, but returned alone.

"He's gone," he said grimly, "and even if he wanted to return he couldn't; there's a thick fog moving in fast. It will be upon us at any moment."

18

Trenorsen skittered backwards as the creature brushed against his body. His survival instincts kicked in and he quickly propelled himself out of range of the flailing tentacles, surfacing a safe distance from the boat. He watched with horrified fascination as the giant squid wrapped its tentacles around the mast and began to pull the boat over. He'd heard Tribold tell of such creatures, but he hadn't really believed the stories. The thought of the old merman brought back the anger he'd felt at being humiliated in front of the boy. It wasn't *his* fault Ben had forgotten to hold his breath underwater. He hadn't been trying to hurt the boy, he'd been trying to do him a favour by teaching him how to swim.

Before he realised it, he'd drifted so far from the fishing boat that he could no longer distinguish the figures on deck. He felt a sudden rush of shame and knew that he should return to help fight the giant squid – but his tail was unresponsive, and his good intentions were soon swamped by the resentment in his chest which grew heavier as he recalled all the hurtful words that had been used against him. Why should he help them? he thought. He'd probably just end up doing something wrong, or they'd find a way of blaming him for the squid's attack. Without him realising it, his face had rearranged itself into an ugly scowl, and he turned his back on the floundering boat and swam in the opposite direction.

Trenorsen was so preoccupied with justifying his decision to himself that he didn't notice the fog until he was completely enveloped by it. Startled, he looked around and immediately regretted his impetuous retreat. It was impossible to see more than a few yards in any direction. The fishing boat had vanished. He strained his ears, but all was still. Even the sea was motionless, its surface as smooth as glass and reflecting nothing more than the swirling white cloud which surrounded him.

Trenorsen sank beneath the surface, but that was no better. The visibility underwater was limited by the lack of light from above, and there was no sign of the boat's hull or the giant squid. The ocean was deserted as far as he could see; there weren't even the usual specks of plankton hanging suspended in the water. He felt completely and utterly alone.

Not knowing what else to do, Trenorsen resurfaced. The fog drifted slowly across the water like a living thing, even though there was no wind. Shapes appeared, and then dissolved before he could make sense of them. He heard a voice and started to swim towards it, ignoring his instincts that told him he was moving in the wrong direction. He tried to overcome his fear by recalling the humiliation that Tribold and Murgatroyd had made him endure. Tremelia was no better, he thought to himself. She looked down on him just because she was Prince Trestan's daughter; she thought she was too good for him. A shard of jealousy pierced his heart as he thought of the growing friendship between her and Ben.

Suddenly, out of the fog, the prow of a boat appeared. Trenorsen stared in surprise and blinked a few times, half expecting it to disappear; but instead it drifted closer, heading directly towards him. Then he heard a frail and weary voice, "The drinking water's all gone. We need to find land soon, or –"

"Don't worry, Mother, I know what I'm doing," interrupted a second voice, loud and confident.

Open-mouthed, Trenorsen watched the boat drift past. It had almost disappeared back into the mist before he came to his senses and swam after it.

"Lord Damien," he called out, but his voice was

hoarse and didn't carry through the fog. He cleared his throat and tried again. "Lord Damien!"

In the boat a tall figure half-rose and turned. Trenorsen nervously watched the man's eyes sweep over the ocean until finally they came to rest on him. "Who are you?" asked the man.

Trenorsen approached the boat. "My name is Trenorsen."

The man stared at him with narrowed eyes. "What are you doing here? Have you been following us?"

Trenorsen swallowed nervously. His adam's apple felt even larger than normal and he swallowed a few more times while he thought about what he was going to say.

"I was with the one they call the Deliverer: Ben," he began, and was immediately gratified by the spark of interest in Lord Damien's eyes. He was about to continue when a woman's face appeared over the side of the boat. Her snowy white hair was dishevelled and her face was pale and drawn.

"Did I just hear someone say *Ben?*" She stared down at Trenorsen. Lord Damien appeared irritated by her interruption, but let her continue. "Where is Ben now?" she asked the merman.

Trenorsen looked over his shoulder into the fog that was, if anything, thicker than before. "Close by," he said vaguely, reluctant to admit that he was lost.

Lord Damien scanned the mist before turning back to the young merman. "Why aren't you with him?"

Trenorsen hesitated for only a second. "I wanted to warn you," he said, thinking quickly.

Damien cast a glance towards his mother. "Warn me? About what, exactly?"

"About the shaman – she's on the boat with Ben and the others. She can sense your presence."

"What is he talking about, Damien?" asked Bella, sharply. "Why is he warning you about this shaman? What does she want with you? If she's a friend of Ben's we should find them and see if they have any fresh water."

Damien fixed his mother with a piercing gaze. "Mother, let me deal with this. Why don't you try to get some rest?"

Reluctantly, and with a suspicious glance at the merman, Bella allowed her son to settle her in the prow of the boat. Lord Damien returned to Trenorsen. "Tell me, how many of them are there?"

"Well, there's two of my kind, but one's an old man and the other's just a girl. Then there's the soldier from Quadrivium who looks quite tough, and a vicious eagle, and the abbot and his dog –"

"The abbot?" Lord Damien was unable to hide his surprise. He thought hard for a few moments, and then his brow lifted. "Ah, but of course – that's how they've managed to get this far! Anyone else?"

"Just the men we rescued after the storm – their boat was badly damaged. One of them is a cardinal, I think. His name is Bolt and the other is called Glarebourne."

"Bolt and Glarebourne?" Lord Damien sat up straighter. "And tell me: does Ben have the Book of Prophecies with him?"

Trenorsen swelled with importance. "Yes," he said. "I saw him take it on board."

At this, Lord Damien's face broke into a sinister smile. "Then perhaps mother is right," he said. "We *should* find Ben and his companions . . ."

* * *

The fishing boat lay motionless on a tranquil sea, surrounded by thick fog. There wasn't a breath of wind, but even had there been they could not have benefitted from it as the mast was now gone, broken in two by the giant squid. Arrowbright had cut away the torn remnants of sail which was the only thing holding it together, and they had watched the huge sheet of canvas sink into the depths, dragged down by the heavy oak beam.

Everyone apart from Tobias and the abbot were on deck. For once, Glarebourne and the cardinal didn't look ill; the sea was so calm that their seasickness had vanished. Murgatroyd kept a close eye on them, in between casting glances into the fog for signs of a break. Gretilda sat atop the wheelhouse gazing forward. Arrowbright tried to speak to her, but she seemed to be in some kind of trance and couldn't be roused.

With a blanket wrapped around his shoulders, Ben made his way to the prow of the boat where he found Tribold and Tremelia lolling silently in the water. The old merman looked exhausted after his battle with the giant squid and he had an ugly laceration across his chest where the suckers had torn away the skin. Tremelia offered Ben a small smile as she looked up and saw him peering over the side of the boat.

"You saved us all back there, Ben," she said. "My father would have been proud."

Ben did his best to look modest and was about to reply when he heard a sound in the fog. "Did you hear something?"

Tremelia put her head on one side and listened carefully. The fog had created a cocoon of silence, but when the sound came again it was unmistakably the flap of a canvas sail.

Arrowbright appeared by Ben's side. "Did I imagine that, or did you hear it too?"

Ben nodded, and together they peered into the fog,

listening hard, but this time there was only the familiar creaking sounds of their boat and the soft splash of water as the mermen looked around.

"Perhaps we did imagine it," said Arrowbright, softly. "There's no wind, after all."

"Certainly not," called Murgatroyd, whose sharp ears were listening to their conversation while he kept an eye on Glarebourne and the cardinal at the other end of the boat. "I heard it too, and the only other boat that we know of in this area is that of Lord Damien, so I suggest we all keep our eyes and ears open."

They all fell silent and strained their ears for any further sound, but the fog not only muffled all sounds, it also prevented them from seeing much beyond the edge of the boat itself. It was like being suspended inside a big ball of cotton wool, thought Ben.

When the silence was finally broken, the sound was not what they had been expecting to hear. It was the long, shrill cry of a bird, almost immediately answered by another cry from a different direction.

Ben and Arrowbright looked at each other in surprise, and then Arrowbright broke into a grin. "This must mean we're close to land," he said, gazing upwards to catch sight of the bird.

The call came again, closer this time. Overhead, Ben caught a glimpse of sky through a break in the fog. It was quickly covered again by white cloud, but the fog appeared to be thinning and through the wisps of cloud Ben caught sight of a dark shadow. He looked away as Tobias appeared on deck and bounded towards him. The dog barked once to get his attention and then raced back towards the cabin, where he stopped and barked again.

Ben glanced back at the sky. The shadow was still hidden from view by the swirling fog, but it was getting closer. "Arrowbright," he began, "I think we should get inside . . ."

The words were barely out of his mouth when a huge bird broke through the fog and dived towards the boat. Ben and Arrowbright ducked as it swept past, feeling the hair on their heads shiver in the chill breeze caused by its outstretched wings. The creature was enormous, with a wingspan wider than the boat. Its wings had no feathers, instead, dark leathery skin was stretched taut across a latticework of fine bones.

Glarebourne dived for the cover of the wheelhouse, with the cardinal close behind him. The bird wheeled round for another pass over the boat, and Ben caught the look of horror on the cardinal's face before he stumbled on his robes and half fell through the cabin hatch. Murgatroyd, instead of following his prisoners to safety, spread his wings and flung himself upwards into the bird's path. He looked like a sparrow next to the monstrous creature, which simply swatted him aside with one of its huge, black wings. The mighty eagle fell to the deck while the bird kept on coming, headed straight for Ben.

Ben stared at Murgatroyd's motionless body in dismay, then raised his eyes and looked up into the pale underbelly of the creature with its human arms hanging limply by its sides. He didn't realise how fast it was approaching, or notice the talons reaching out for him. The bird let out a victorious scream as it descended, bringing him suddenly to his senses. But it was too late to run. The sight of the bird filled his vision.

Then a streak of gold flashed before his eyes and knocked the creature sideways. A cacophony of growls, shrieks, yelps and whines filled the air, before the creature managed to drag itself to the rail and plummeted over the side, leaving a trail of blood on the deck. Tobias stood panting heavily, pink saliva dripping from his open mouth. Ben had only a moment to comprehend what he had witnessed before Arrowbright hauled him to his feet and began to drag him towards the wheelhouse.

"Wait!" cried Ben, yanking his arm free and running back to Tobias. He fell to his knees and threw his arms around him. "I knew you hadn't forgotten me completely," he mumbled into the dog's neck. "You saved my life *again*, Tobias!"

"Come on, Ben!" cried Arrowbright from the safety of the wheelhouse.

Tobias shook himself free of Ben's embrace and padded across the deck to where Murgatroyd lay. He nosed the fallen eagle, then opened his mouth and took him in his jaws. With his head bent low, the dog half-dragged, half-carried the eagle across the deck towards the cabin.

Suddenly realising how exposed he was, Ben jumped up to follow him. He had almost made it when a second bird appeared through the clouds and dived across his path. Ben skidded to a halt and stumbled backwards. The bird's momentum carried it over the side of the boat, where it banked sharply and returned for another pass, reaching forward with its talons as it swooped directly towards him.

Ben froze, unsure of which way to run. Just as it seemed he would be caught in the bird's grasp, there came a rasping shout from the water. "Hey, birdman, over here!"

The bird veered towards Tribold's voice, and Ben darted to the rail just in time to see it disappear into the water with a great splash. "No!" he cried, as he watched Tribold sink under the weight of the bird.

Tremelia's face appeared above the surface. "Go!" she screamed at Ben.

Arrowbright appeared and dragged Ben through

the wheelhouse and into the cabin, slamming the hatch shut behind them just as a third bird appeared. It passed close overhead, shredding the canvas roof of the wheelhouse with its talons.

Inside the cabin, Tobias had deposited the limp figure of Murgatroyd at the abbot's feet and was busily licking him, smoothing down the eagle's ruffled feathers with his long, pink tongue.

Ben hesitated in the doorway. "Is he . . .?"

At that moment, Murgatroyd let out a groan and raised his head. "Will someone get that dog off me before I have no feathers left?" he grumbled.

Ben collapsed onto the seat next to the abbot with a sigh of relief. A second later, he jumped to his feet as something heavy slammed into the cabin hatch. The hatch shuddered but held firm.

Cardinal Bolt began to wail. "We're all doomed! The gatekeepers have seen us! We're all doomed!"

"Snap out of it!" cried Arrowbright, grasping the cardinal's shoulders. "They can't get to us in here."

At that moment, the glass in one of the small porthole windows exploded inwards, and the bird's head appeared. Its long, sharp beak slashed back and forth, but its head was too big for it to reach very far into the cabin and it quickly retreated, uttering its shrill cry as it went.

An eerie silence filled the cabin. Even the abbot

looked anxious as they waited for the next attack. After a while, Arrowbright stood up and covered the broken window with a length of canvas that was intended to repair storm-damaged sails. They had no further need for it.

The cries of the birds sounded overhead. In the cabin, everyone's eyes went to the ceiling, expecting it to collapse at any moment under the force of a renewed attack. The abbot moved from his seat to allow Arrowbright to secure a piece of canvas to the window behind him. As he stood, Ben noticed that part of the oilcloth in which the Book of Prophecies had been wrapped was sticking out from the seat. He stepped forward and lifted up the seat and stared into the empty space, unable to believe his eyes. The Book was gone.

He spun round. The cardinal had retreated to the far corner of the cabin where he was huddled on the floor, wrapped in his crimson robes. "Where is it?" said Ben in a low voice, advancing on the cowering man. He glanced around the cabin and noticed Glarebourne's absence for the first time. "And where is your sidekick?"

There was a renewed burst of shrill bird screams, fainter than before, and – almost lost beneath it – a human cry. Ben tore the canvas from the porthole and stared out. It was impossible to get a good view from the tiny window, but there was no sign of the birds. Arrowbright picked up his hunting knife – still sticky from the blood of the giant squid – and cautiously opened the cabin door. With a backward glance at the cardinal, Ben followed Arrowbright out onto the deck.

The first thing they noticed was the absence of the rowing boat. It was missing from its mooring at the back of the boat; the ropes which secured it had been cleanly severed. Ben looked round and spotted the birds. All three were circling in a tight formation a little way from the fishing boat. Below the birds, crouched in the tiny rowing boat and holding aloft the leather and bronze-bound Book of Prophecies, was Glarebourne. One by one the birds darted forward, almost skimming the Book with their claws, but at the last second each veered away.

Ben watched in amazement as Glarebourne reached down and picked up an oar in one hand while still holding the Book above his head with the other. The birds chattered loudly to each other as they continued to swoop and dive around the boat, but it seemed there was nothing they could do to get to the man. Dipping the oar into the still water, Glarebourne began to draw away.

"Stop!" cried Ben, banging his fists against the rail with helpless fury. "Come back."

Glarebourne glanced over his shoulder and grinned.

"Come and get me," he sneered. "I suppose you want your precious Book of Prophecies back, but I know someone else who wants it."

Ben glanced back towards the hatch where he could see the cardinal's pale face peering out. Glarebourne followed his gaze and snorted. "Bolt is a mere collector; he wanted to lock the Book away in a glass case to gather dust. I was merely using him to help me get close to the Book, and now it's in my possession I'm taking it to someone who knows its true value."

"Lord Damien," said Arrowbright in a disgusted voice.

"Right first time," said Glarebourne. "And he's going to make me rich beyond my wildest dre–" He stopped abruptly and looked down at his oar, then pulled hard on it. The oar would not budge. Giving the onlookers an evil look, Glarebourne gave the oar a sharp tug. The rowing boat rocked dangerously and the birds swooped down from above, coming even closer to the Book that Glarebourne still managed to hold one-handed above his head. But still the oar wouldn't give. Putting all his weight against it, Glarebourne heaved backwards.

Suddenly the oar came free and a number of things happened all at once. Glarebourne stumbled backwards and fell over the side, while the Book flew out of his hand and into the air, spinning end over end.

Ben instinctively stretched out his arms towards it, but he was much too far away and he could only follow its upward arc with his eyes, his mouth falling open in a horrified, silent "Nooo!" The birds darted around the Book and dived into the water after Glarebourne. As they disappeared beneath the surface, Tremelia appeared. She threw her body upwards in a spiralling twist – leaping higher than she had ever done before – and snatched the Book out of the air. As gravity pulled her back down, she turned in mid-air and dropped the Book into the rowing boat before re-entering the water with barely a splash.

Ben let out a triumphant "Yes!" as he heard the Book hit the bottom of the boat with a thud. A moment later, the three birds emerged from the water holding Glarebourne, kicking and screaming, between them. Without a backward glance they disappeared into the swirling fog.

Ben gripped the rails and stared after the creatures, listening to Glarebourne's cries becoming fainter until they faded altogether. As he gazed into the fog, it began to break up, drifting into shreds of tattered cloud and leaving gaps through which he caught a glimpse of land. At first he wasn't sure whether he had imagined it, but gradually the islands took shape: low mounds, some of which barely broke the surface of the sea.

Ben turned to find the abbot standing beside him.

The old man was staring eagerly at the islands.

"The drumlins," said the old man softly. "We're almost there."

19

Trenorsen found Lord Damien's boat easier to pull than the cumbersome fishing boat with its larger crew, but nevertheless he made a great show of effort as he dragged it through the water. The truth was he wasn't at all sure in which direction the larger boat lay; he was as disorientated by the fog as the boat's occupants.

Overhead, the large sail hung limply from the mast, ragged and torn from the battering it had received in the storm. It swung from the boom, making a lonely flapping noise that was unexpectedly loud in the silence. Irritably, Lord Damien stood and lashed it to the mast.

Bella lay in the bottom of the boat. She opened her eyes to watch her son secure the sail, and then closed them again. Her eyelids shot open again as she heard a shriek. Damien, who had been about to sit down, lurched to his feet, his hand going straight to his pocket. "What was that?" he asked Trenorsen sharply.

Trenorsen peered wide-eyed into the mist. Tribold's tales of sea monsters came unbidden into his head, but when the shrill cry came again and he recognised it as that of a bird, relief flooded through him. He was about to answer Lord Damien when a shape broke through the low clouds. Trenorsen's mouth dropped open as the huge creature swooped towards them, throwing the boat into shadow.

The young merman was seized with panic. Instinctively, he immediately retreated to safety under the water. He cowered beneath the hull of the boat, expecting at any moment for his cover to be torn away and to be snatched from the water like a common fish. Instead, he was suddenly blinded by a brilliant white light – like a huge bolt of lightning illuminating the entire ocean. The light didn't fade, instead it seemed to grow brighter and stronger. Trenorsen flinched and his head thudded against the bottom of the boat. He was comforted to know that it was still above him, but confused and shaken by the strange light shining through his closed eyelids.

Cautiously, he opened his eyes and realised immediately that he could see for miles. He rotated slowly, but there was no sign of Tribold or Tremelia, or the fishing boat. Far below him, the ocean floor was covered with huge, cone-shaped mounds, some of which soared upwards and broke the surface. The bright light threw deep shadows behind them and Trenorsen remembered the giant squid with a shudder. The thought was driven from his mind as something crashed into the water next to him and began to sink. He caught a glimpse of a shrivelled, blackened wing before it descended out of sight into the gloomy depths as the brilliant light faded and finally went out.

His heart beating loudly, Trenorsen poked his head above the surface and spotted Lord Damien in the boat. The pale man was leaning over the side and staring down into the water. In one hand he held a rock that shimmered with a restless light. Trenorsen stared in fascination as a final glimmer of light shot around the rock's circumference and then vanished.

As soon as he saw Trenorsen, Lord Damien lowered the rock and slipped it into his pocket. "Ah, there you are," he said. "Change of plan. The fog appears to be lifting so we're going to make for that island over there."

Trenorsen raised his eyes and caught sight of a tower rising up out of the fog. As he stared at it, a bell began to toll.

* * *

Ben stood at the prow of the boat, staring at the

solid shapes emerging from the fog. Beside him, the abbot had lapsed back into his customary silence, but his eyes were wide and bright and he had an expression of anticipation on his wrinkled face. Tobias sat at the abbot's feet with a similar eager expression on his canine features. Ben experienced a pang as he realised that the dog was unlikely to return to Quadrivium with him when this was all over. He drove the thought from his mind and concentrated on trying to make sense of the shapes in the swirling cloud. Once or twice he caught a glimpse of a tower or a section of wall, but the light was poor and his eyes were growing tired, and he was never quite sure whether he had imagined it.

He heard footsteps on the wooden deck behind him and turned to see Gretilda approaching. The shaman's face was pale, but her eyes burned as brightly as the abbot's. Without a word, she joined them at the rail.

Ben turned back just as the mist parted, and through the ragged gap he caught sight of a wall and part of an archway. At that moment, a brilliant white light lit up the sky and the building in front of them was silhouetted in stark relief. He heard Gretilda cry out, but his attention was caught by the sight before him. He saw a square tower beyond grey stone walls which stretched in both directions, punctuated by an archway here and there through which the strange light streamed.

"Ben, help me!"

Ben dragged his gaze from the sight to find Arrowbright grappling with Gretilda. The agitated shaman seemed determined to throw herself overboard. She repeated something over and over, and it didn't take Ben long to make out the words: "Sacred Stone . . . Lord Damien . . . He's using it again . . ."

Hearing the commotion, Murgatroyd appeared in the entrance to the cabin. He leant heavily against the side of the door and stared at Arrowbright and Ben. "Lord Damien? If he's already reached the abbey . . ." He didn't need to finish his sentence; they all knew the future of Ballitor would be in jeopardy if Lord Damien got to the prince before they did.

Between them, Ben and Arrowbright dragged Gretilda away from the rail. They had almost reached the wheelhouse when the light faded and then went out altogether. Gretilda slumped heavily in their arms, still mumbling Lord Damien's name. A moment later her moans were drowned out by a bell that began to peal, over and over again.

Ben dropped Gretilda's arm and ran to the side of the boat. "Tremelia!" he called.

The mermaid's golden locks broke the surface and she looked up at him. "Did you see that flash of light?" she said wonderingly. "It lit up the under-sea for miles, but there's not a living thing to be seen –

it's quite eerie." She paused. "What is that dreadful noise?"

"Tremelia, we need your help," shouted Ben above the sound of the bell. "We can see the abbey straight ahead, but we can't reach it without your help; there's no wind. Can you manage to pull the boat by yourself?"

Tremelia looked in the direction he was pointing, then sank down under the water. She resurfaced moments later. "You won't be able to reach the island in this boat; the rocks are too close to the surface. You'll have to use the rowing boat."

She had barely finished speaking when Arrowbright began untying the small rowing boat from where they had secured it after Glarebourne's ill-fated attempt to escape with the Book of Prophecies, which was now wrapped safely in its oilskin in the cabin.

"Ben, you go first," he said as he worked on the knots. "Take the abbot; you might need him with you to convince the monks we're friends. If Lord Damien has beaten us there, they may need some persuading."

Ben turned and collided with the abbot who was standing right behind him, ready to go. Arrowbright released the ropes and the rowing boat dropped down onto the water with a great splash. Ben helped the abbot climb over the side and into the boat.

Murgatroyd fluttered weakly to the rail and paced

anxiously up and down. "Arrowbright can't handle both Gretilda and the cardinal by himself," he twittered. "I'll have to go with him in the second boat."

Ben nodded once, then followed the abbot down into the rowing boat. After a moment's hesitation, Tobias jumped in after them, almost causing the small boat to capsize. Tremelia steadied it with her arms, then took hold of the rope and disappeared beneath the surface.

"Wait for us!" called Murgatroyd. "We'll be right behind you!"

Ben nodded distractedly and turned away. He looked over the side of the rowing boat and caught a glimpse of Tremelia's tail as she pulled them along. The boat made little impression on the smooth water as it surged forward. Peering ahead, he gradually began to make out the walls of the abbey emerging from the tattered remnants of the fog. It did not appear a welcoming place. The stone walls seemed to plunge straight down into the sea as though the abbey was built on water. The grey stone from which it was built was almost exactly the same shade as the sea and the overcast sky; if it hadn't had been for the mysterious light they might never have seen the abbey at all.

The boat began to snake from side to side as Tremelia made her way carefully around the submerged rocks. Tobias placed his paws on the front of the boat and stared towards the abbey, his tail swaying gently to and fro. He began to wag faster as a procession of robed figures appeared through an archway in the wall and made their way along the narrow, rocky shore. They came to a stop and arranged themselves in a line to watch the boat approach. When it finally bumped against the low jetty, which was barely visible above the water, one of the monks stepped forward and pulled the boat in. Tobias leaped out first and stood patiently while a second monk took the abbot's arm. As soon as he was safely on dry land, the first monk let go of the boat which immediately began to drift away. Ben, who had one foot on the jetty and the other still in the boat, almost fell into the water; but Tremelia caught the boat just in time and pushed it back, and he managed to scramble safely ashore. He looked up to see the monks surround the abbot and begin to move away.

Ben felt something brush against his legs and looked down in surprise. Tobias had settled himself at his feet and was calmly watching the abbot being escorted away by the monks, who left the way they had come. As the last monk disappeared, Ben caught sight of a large dog, golden-haired like Tobias, sitting in the archway through which the monks had just passed. The dog stood up and began to make its way towards them. It walked stiffly and as it came closer

Ben noticed that its muzzle was completely grey. Tobias got to his feet and stood absolutely still as the older dog came up and touched his muzzle gently with its own. Then it looked up at Ben and began to speak in a low, husky voice.

"From this moment on, I release Tobias from his obligations. He has done an excellent job of bringing my master safely home, and now I, Arturius, return him to you, Deliverer – his rightful master."

Ben felt a wet tongue on his hand and looked down into Tobias's warm brown eyes, which were the mirror image of the older dog's. He suddenly understood how the elderly abbot had mistaken Tobias for his own dog, Arturius, and why Tobias had accepted this role. Now that he had returned the abbot safely to Arturius, he was Tobias once more.

Ben patted Tobias on the head and suddenly felt more cheerful than he had for a long time. When he finally looked up, Arturius had turned and was picking his way, slowly and with great care, across the rocks towards the abbey.

"Wait!" said Ben. "We need your help." Arturius kept on walking. Ben raised his voice, "Is Lord Damien here, on the island?"

The dog paused and raised one ear. "Lord Damien?"
"Is he here?"

Slowly, Arturius turned to face Ben. "What possible

business could Lord Damien have in the Abbey of the Ancients?"

"He's here for the baby: Prince Alexander."

"Why?"

"The king is dead! Alexander is his heir and whoever becomes his guardian will hold the power to the throne!"

Arturius appeared to consider this news carefully before fixing Ben with his milky eyes. "You'd better come with me," he said.

Ben glanced over his shoulder. Tremelia had disappeared with the rowing boat and the fog was starting to close in again. He could only just make out the shadowy outline of the fishing boat in the distance. He hesitated for a brief moment, then scrambled over the rocks after Arturius with Tobias close behind him.

The old dog led them through the archway and up a flight of stone steps into an enclosed passageway. The bell seemed louder in the confined space and the sound echoed off the stone walls until Ben's ears rang with it. It wasn't long before he spied daylight up ahead and the passageway opened up into a cloister with a large, grassy quadrangle surrounded by stone arches. In the centre of the quadrangle stood the abbot, in the middle of a crowd of monks.

"Stay here," said Arturius, stepping through the arches and onto the grass. The crowd around the abbot grew as more monks entered the cloister. They milled silently round the old man, jostling each other in their efforts to get closer to him. Ben watched from the shadows as Arturius disappeared between their legs. Still more monks continued to emerge from hidden doorways and passages to join the throng, completely ignoring Ben and Tobias.

After a while, Ben's attention was drawn to one particular monk standing on the far side of the quadrangle. He seemed to be holding back as the other monks rushed forward to greet the abbot. Without thinking, Ben moved out of the shadows to get a better look, and at that moment the monk turned his head and looked straight at him.

Ben gasped as he recognised Brother Bernard, the monk who had unwittingly led him to the underground lake beneath the palace in Quadrivium, where Ben had found the page that had ultimately led him to the Book of Prophecies. The colour drained from the monk's face and he began to back away, then suddenly he turned and fled. Ben raced across the grass to the spot where he had been, but Brother Bernard had vanished. Quickly, Ben shinned up a nearby pillar and looked out over the heads of the monks. He immediately caught sight of Brother Bernard pushing against the tide of bodies. The fleeing monk glanced over his shoulder and picked up his pace as he spotted

Ben staring down at him.

Ben jumped to the ground and raced after him, pushing through the crowd until he was through the last of the monks and into a narrow passageway. He stopped for a moment to allow his eyes to adjust to the gloom and Tobias trotted on ahead, giving an encouraging bark that echoed against the walls. Ben hurried after him and soon came to a flight of shallow stone steps. Bounding up the steps, he emerged into daylight and found himself in a paved courtyard. There was no sign of Brother Bernard, but on the far side he recognised the tower he had seen from the boat, rising up above the walls surrounding the courtyard. As Ben stared up at it, he saw a flicker of movement as though someone had hurriedly stepped away from one of the windows.

Tobias put his nose to the ground and made a beeline for the tower. Ben followed the dog into the shadows beneath the arches where he found a door standing ajar. Tobias pushed it open with his snout and slipped through. The door opened to reveal a staircase leading upwards into the gloom. Tobias had already disappeared up the stairs and Ben hesitated for only a moment before setting off after him.

It was pleasantly warm inside the tower, growing warmer the higher he climbed. At the top of the stairs was a closed door. Tobias stood in front of it, wagging his tail and looking expectantly over his shoulder at Ben. Trying the handle, Ben found the door unlocked. It opened to reveal a crimson velvet curtain, which he pushed aside.

Brother Bernard spun round as he entered the room. "It's you again!" he cried. "How did you find me?"

Without answering, Ben looked past him into the room. It was comfortably furnished with thick rugs on the floor and armchairs placed either side of a roaring log fire. On the far side was a table piled high with platters of fruit and assorted meats. Beside the table stood a cot. Ben immediately hurried over to it.

"If Mayor Ponsonby finds out that you were here –" continued the monk.

"Ponsonby's dead," interrupted Ben, peering into the cot.

Brother Bernard went pale and slumped down into one of the armchairs. "Dead? How? *When?* What am I supposed to do now?"

Ignoring his questions, Ben stared down at the baby in the cot who gazed back up at him with big blue eyes. Tentatively, Ben reached into the cot and pushed back the baby's sleepsuit. There on the baby's shoulder was the coronet birthmark. While Brother Bernard watched open-mouthed from the armchair, Ben wet his finger and rubbed gently at the birthmark.

The baby immediately let out a gurgle and began to wave his arms in the air, then he grabbed Ben's finger and tried to pull it towards his mouth. Ben pulled his finger away and stared at the birthmark. It was intact; it hadn't smudged a single bit.

He looked over his shoulder at the monk. "You have to help me; Lord Damien is on his way. He killed the king and now he wants Prince Alexander. I have to get the prince off the island before he gets here."

Brother Bernard leapt out of the armchair. "Off the island? You mean to say you have a boat? Will you take me with you?"

When Ben nodded, the monk immediately went over to the cot and lifted out the baby, who began swatting his face with his chubby hand.

"Lead the way," said Brother Bernard.

Ben pushed back the curtain and hurried down the stairs with the monk close behind. Tobias was the first to reach the door at the bottom. He slipped through the narrow gap and Ben opened the door wider for Brother Bernard, then stood back to let him pass. He was about to follow when he heard an angry bark.

Ben froze. Through the open doorway he could see Tobias standing stiff-legged with his back to the door. The dog's hackles were raised and Ben could hear a low growl rumbling in his throat. Very slowly, Ben stepped through the doorway and out into the open.

Now he could see Brother Bernard cowering against a pillar, still cradling the infant prince against his shoulder. Then he turned his head and saw, standing in the middle of the paved courtyard with a rock held loosely in his hand, a pale man in a white suit.

"Hello Ben," said Lord Damien.

20

The rowing boat lay low in the water, weighed down by the combined weight of Arrowbright, Gretilda and the cardinal. Murgatroyd flew low overhead, staying close to the boat and occasionally landing on the prow to rest, while Arrowbright peered anxiously forward. His jaw was set as he tried to be patient while Tremelia pulled the boat slowly through the maze of rocks. There was no sign of Ben and the others on the shoreline. Finally, they reached the jetty and Arrowbright jumped ashore. Murgatroyd landed beside him, while Cardinal Bolt hung back.

"Why don't I stay behind and look after the boat?" he suggested. Murgatroyd gave him a long, hard stare until the cardinal dropped his eyes and busied himself with rearranging his robes. "Perhaps not," he muttered as he stepped onto the jetty. "No, of course not, I should pay my respects to my brethren . . ."

"Tremelia, take the boat and wait for us a little way offshore," said Arrowbright. "Stay alert; we may have to leave in a hurry."

Tremelia disappeared beneath the surface and a moment later the rowing boat began to move away. Arrowbright turned to see Gretilda standing completely still. Her face was as pale as ever, but her eyes burned fiercely.

"He's here," she whispered. "I can feel his presence; I can sense my Stone." She suddenly set off over the rocks, stepping quickly and lightly without once looking down.

"Come on," said Murgatroyd, prodding the cardinal in the back with his claw.

Reluctantly, the cardinal began to clamber awkwardly across the rocks, following the shaman towards the archway set into the wall. But before any of them could reach it, a line of monks appeared. They brushed past Gretilda without acknowledging her presence and silently surrounded the cardinal, ignoring Murgatroyd who took a quick step out of their circle. Cardinal Bolt shot a panicked look at Arrowbright, but the soldier simply frowned and waited to see what they would do.

A whimper escaped the cardinal's lips as one of the monks slipped a hand inside his coarse brown habit. Arrowbright stepped forward and reached for the hunting knife at his belt, but before he could draw his weapon the monk brought out a gold chain on which hung a heavy cross, studded with precious gems. He held it out for the cardinal to inspect.

The cardinal immediately relaxed. "Ah, so you're the welcoming committee! How nice," he said, bending his head so the monk could place the cross around his neck. "I would have come to visit sooner, but my duties in Quadrivium have kept me away. Now, a bath and a hot meal would be much appreciated before I view the abbey's no doubt impressive collection of rare books." He looked over his shoulder with a smug grin as he was escorted away.

Only once the procession had made its way through the archway did Arrowbright notice that Gretilda had vanished. He turned to speak to Murgatroyd, but the eagle, too, had disappeared. The fog was drawing in from the sea, hiding any sign of the fishing boat, and Arrowbright found himself all alone on the rocky shoreline.

* * *

Ben stared at the rock resting on the pale man's palm.

"I think you know what this is, don't you Ben?" said Lord Damien, taking a step towards him. Tobias gave a warning growl, drawing his lips back to show his teeth. Lord Damien didn't take his eyes off Ben. "Call off your beast or I'll be forced to destroy him."

A flickering light shot round the circumference of the Stone.

"Tobias, heel."

Silent now, but still showing his teeth, Tobias moved slowly backwards until he was sitting at Ben's feet.

"Thank you, Ben." Lord Damien turned towards Brother Bernard who was still holding the baby. "And this must be my nephew, Prince Alexander."

The monk shrank back against the pillar and wrapped both arms protectively around the prince.

"Come now, Brother," said the pale man. "You can either give me Alexander of your own free will, or I'll simply take him from you – an experience which won't be quite as pleasant."

He held up the Sacred Stone and Brother Bernard glanced at Ben who gave a quick nod. Reluctantly, the monk lifted the prince from his shoulder and held him out to Lord Damien. Alexander raised his head and blinked sleepily. A triumphant expression spread across the pale man's face as he moved forward to take the baby, then he paused and looked down at the rock in his hand.

Abruptly he turned to Ben. "Back away slowly," he said, making shooing gestures with his free hand. "Go on, and take the dog with you."

Ben grabbed a handful of thick fur at the scruff of Tobias's neck and began to walk slowly backwards through the archway and into the courtyard.

"That's far enough!" called the pale man. "Stay where I can see you."

Ben watched him slip the Sacred Stone into the pocket of his suit jacket and take the baby from Brother Bernard. Prince Alexander began to whimper as soon as he left the monk's familiar grasp. Holding the baby at arm's length, Lord Damien stepped into the courtyard.

"Not so great now, are you, Deliverer?" he sneered as he sidled past Ben. "The Book of Prophecies hasn't helped you this time, has it? Prince Alexander – or should I say *King* Alexander? – will be brought up in *my* custody, which means *I* shall be the one who rules the kingdom!"

"Only until he comes of age," said Ben. He stared at Lord Damien, trying to decide whether he could reach him before he had time to draw the Stone from his pocket.

"By that time, Alexander will do whatever I tell him," said Lord Damien with a contemptuous smile. "He shall be my puppet king and *I* shall rule all of Ballitor!"

By this time he was halfway across the courtyard,

moving quickly now towards the steps which led to the passageway. Ben glanced over the pale man's shoulder towards the steps, wondering whether to make a last desperate attempt to stop him. Then he froze. In the shadows behind Lord Damien stood a familiar figure, and the pale man was backing straight towards it.

As Ben watched, Gretilda stepped into the courtyard. Lord Damien sensed movement and looked over his shoulder, then stopped dead. The shaman took a step towards him and he stepped back, turning his head quickly from side to side as he tried to keep both Ben and the shaman in sight.

"Stay back," he cried. "Both of you, stay back. I'm not afraid to use the Stone."

Ben's eyes went to the pale man's suit pocket. Lord Damien caught his glance and awkwardly tried to balance the prince on one hip so that he could reach into his pocket for the Stone, but Alexander was now fully awake and not used to being manhandled by a stranger. He began to writhe and scream.

Gretilda took another step forward. On Lord Damien's other side, so did Ben and Tobias.

"Stay back," warned the pale man. He clutched the prince to his chest with one arm and finally managed to get the other hand into his pocket. But Prince Alexander suddenly went rigid and thrust his body away from him, screaming hysterically. Lord Damien yanked his empty hand out of his pocket to steady the prince, and Gretilda, Ben and Tobias edged forward again.

"Give me the child, Damien."

From behind one of the pillars, Bella appeared. Ben watched in disbelief as the pale man handed her the screaming baby. With both hands now free, he drew the Sacred Stone from his pocket with a flourish and brandished it in front of them. But before he could say anything, Bella spoke again. "Damien, put down the Stone. This ends here."

He turned to her in surprise. "But Mother –"

"It's too late, Damien. I trusted you – despite everything Murgatroyd told me, I still trusted you – but you are no longer my son."

"What are you talking about?"

"I first had my suspicions when you were in such a hurry to leave Quadrivium. You didn't seem at all shocked or surprised that the king was dead, you just wanted to leave the city as quickly as possible! But I allowed myself to believe you when you said you needed to earn the trust of the council by returning Alexander to Quadrivium. Even when I figured out your plan on our first night away from the city, I still chose not to believe it; even then I was willing to give you the benefit of the doubt. But you took me for a fool, Damien, and that is something I am not. You thought I was beyond caring when you plotted with that merman who told you Ben was nearby –"

"Trenorsen!" gasped Ben, putting the pieces together.

"– you thought I was too weak to listen – on the verge of death perhaps – yet you didn't seem to care. It was my good fortune that Gertie – a true friend despite the way I treated her – had packed extra supplies with my laundry; that's what kept me alive in the face of your indifference. So I'm afraid this is the end, Damien."

Ben watched the pale man's face carefully as Bella spoke. Lord Damien's initial expression of shock was replaced first by fury and then a calmness that drove a chill to Ben's core.

Still holding the Stone in his hand, Lord Damien looked at each of them in turn. "You think you can beat me: an old woman, a child and his mutt, and a shaman without her magic?" At that moment, Brother Bernard appeared from the shadows and Lord Damien began to laugh. "Oh, I'm sorry, I forgot about the *monk!*"

While he was facing Brother Bernard, Gretilda seized the opportunity to edge closer. He spun back to face her, holding the Sacred Stone on his outstretched palm for all to see. His expression was suddenly serious.

"I wonder," he began, "whether a Sacred Stone has ever been used against its former owner? Perhaps it's an experiment worth carrying out."

Gretilda stopped dead. Her face was impassive, but Ben could see the fury in her eyes. A restless light shimmered on the surface of the Stone, casting an eerie reflection on both Gretilda's and the pale man's faces. Ben was so close that he could see the tiny letters that glittered around the circumference of the Sacred Stone. Slowly, the pale man raised his hand and the light grew more intense, as though a brilliant sun was held captive inside the Stone and was forcing its way out.

Suddenly a voice as high and clear as a bell rang out, "Look away from the light!"

Ben obeyed the voice without thinking, wrenching his gaze from the Stone and covering his eyes. He heard a soft whine and peered through his fingers to see Tobias with his head buried in his paws. A moment later there was a sound like an immense crack of thunder and he was thrown to the ground by the shockwaves that ripped through the air. He lay there for a few moments, stunned, before cautiously opening his eyes.

The first thing he saw was Gretilda, her eyes closed and her already pale skin drained of colour. He sat up slowly and felt Tobias stir beside him. Brother Bernard was leaning against one of the pillars, rubbing his head and looking dazed. Nearby, Bella struggled to her feet with Prince Alexander still clasped to her chest. She gave a cry and staggered towards a crumpled heap of white. It was Lord Damien. As Ben watched, the pale man's hand fell open and the Sacred Stone rolled out and came to rest at Ben's feet.

Ben sensed a presence behind him and turned slowly. Before him stood a hooded figure in a long robe. His heart began to thud painfully in his chest as the figure moved towards him with outstretched arms. Like a sleepwalker, he took a step forwards, and then another. The figure pushed back its hood and a cascade of golden hair tumbled out, falling over slim shoulders to frame the most beautiful face that Ben had ever seen, the face he saw every day in his locket.

It was his mother.

21

Bella trailed after the solemn procession of monks. They walked slowly, carrying between them a long wooden board on which lay the motionless body of her son. The monks had appeared almost immediately after the incident with the Sacred Stone and had loaded Lord Damien onto the board. Everything had happened in silence. Bella hadn't intervened. She had simply watched and then followed the monks, lost in her own thoughts.

Eventually the monks came to a stop outside a stout wooden door and lowered Lord Damien to the ground. One of them drew a key from his habit and unlocked the padlock that hung from a rusted chain around the door handle. Inside was a small cell, bare apart from a narrow bed and a barred window. Picking up the board, the monks entered the room and unceremoniously rolled Lord Damien off it and onto the bed. Bella watched from the doorway. Her face was expressionless, as though she barely knew the unconscious man in the crumpled white suit.

Lord Damien suddenly let out a groan. The monks immediately turned and shuffled quickly out of the room one after the other, slamming the door shut behind them. There was a shout from within, and a moment later the door shook on its hinges. Two of the monks threw their weight against it while a third, after fumbling and almost dropping it, finally managed to wrap the chain around the door handle and snap the padlock shut. Then, still without saying a word, they turned and filed away.

Bella was left alone in the corridor. All was quiet behind the locked door. Drawing closer, she noticed a letterbox-sized hatch with a sliding shutter at eye level. Bella reached up and slid the shutter open. Immediately Damien's eyes appeared, staring wildly through the gap.

"Mother! Is that you?"

"Yes," said Bella.

"Can you open the door . . . please?"

"No," said Bella, quietly but firmly.

"Open this door immediately, or I'll . . . I'll . . ." The door rattled but the chain held firm.

"Save your strength, Damien, I couldn't open the door even if I wanted to; the monks have the key. I'm here to say goodbye."

There was a long pause, then, "What do you mean: goodbye?"

"I'm taking Alexander back to Quadrivium, back to his mother where he belongs."

"But what about me?"

"You're staying here."

"No, Mother, don't leave me! I'm sorry for everything!"

"I have to go now, Damien, the others are waiting for me."

"Don't go! Take me with you! I promise I won't try to take Alexander! I'm sorry – you have to believe me, Mother. Mother? *Mother?* MOTHER!"

There was no reply. Damien leant his back against the door and slid down until he was sitting on the cold stone floor. He rested his head in his hands and massaged his temples with his long, pale fingers. Then a noise outside his cell made him look up.

"Mother?" He scrambled to his feet and rested his hand on the wall for support. "Mother, is that you?" He peered through the narrow hatch and groaned at the sight of the robed figure standing outside his cell. "What do you want? Come to gloat, have you?"

"No, Damien, I've come to lay my eyes on the man I feared for so long."

Damien's eyes widened at the sound of the voice,

and he pressed his face to the opening. "Teah, is that you? Teah?"

"Yes, it is I."

"At long last! I've been looking for you for so long, Teah. Open the door so I can see you!"

"I'm afraid that's not going to happen, Damien."

"Oh, of course not, it's locked . . . but one of the monks has the key! Run and fetch it, quickly!"

"I came to talk to you."

Damien closed his eyes. "Oh Teah, I've waited years to hear your voice! Where have you been? I looked everywhere for you, but not even the Book of Prophecies could reveal your whereabouts."

"I was here, Damien, in the Abbey of the Ancients. It was my last safe haven; the one place you could never find me. I've lived here undisturbed for many years, but when Brother Bernard arrived with the prince I knew my refuge had been compromised. But it has all turned out for the best –"

"Yes," breathed Damien, "and now we will be together!"

"– and now I can finally come out of hiding," continued Teah. "You will be kept in this room until nightfall, by which time we'll have departed, and then you will be released."

"What?" Damien peered through the hatch, desperately trying to get a glimpse of Teah's face, but she drew away from the door.

"You will find that there is no way off the island, so do not try or you will perish."

"But you can't leave now, not when I've just found you again!"

Teah's voice grew faint as she walked away. "Goodbye, Damien."

* * *

Arrowbright carried Gretilda down to the jetty where Tremelia waited with the rowing boat. The shaman lay limp in his arms, her long, golden hair falling almost to the ground. She hadn't moved since the explosion of light from the Sacred Stone. Ben walked behind them, carrying the Stone wrapped in a piece of sacking. They had almost reached the boat when Murgatroyd suddenly appeared, dropping out of the sky to land on the side of the jetty.

"Murgatroyd!" cried Ben. "Where have you been?"

"I had an errand to run," he answered distractedly, watching as Arrowbright laid Gretilda in the boat. "Is she . . ?"

"She's still alive," replied Arrowbright, "but her pulse is very faint." He leant down and brushed a strand of hair from the shaman's face.

Ben wanted to question Murgatroyd further, but

the eagle would not meet his eye, and was instead staring past Ben, back towards the abbey. Ben turned to see Bella hurrying across the rocks towards them.

"Where's my mother?" he asked when he saw that she was alone.

"I thought she was with you," replied Bella. She nodded a quick greeting to Murgatroyd, then took Alexander from Brother Bernard who was hovering close to Ben, anxiously eyeing the huge eagle and the mermaid.

"But she went after you," said Ben. "She said she had some last minute business to take care of." He looked back at the abbey. "I can't leave without her! Come on, Tobias, let's find my mother!"

He handed the Sacred Stone to Brother Bernard, who took it gingerly in both hands, then he turned and began to pick his way over the rocks.

"Hurry, Ben!" called Tremelia. "The tide has already turned; if we wait much longer we won't be able to leave."

Ben lifted his hand to show that he had heard, then disappeared through the archway and into the abbey. Tobias bounded up the dark passageway and Ben hurried after him. He spied daylight ahead and at the same time heard a commotion. Coming out into the grassy quadrangle, he saw Cardinal Bolt standing in a nearby doorway. The cardinal's crimson robes hung open to reveal his white undergarments, and he was tugging on the end of a rope. As Ben came closer, he realised it was the belt made of plaited gold thread that was usually wrapped around the cardinal's slender waist.

"Give me back my belt!" cried the cardinal. "I've told you already, I am *not* wearing that awful sackcloth!" He gave the belt an almighty tug, then spotted Ben and suddenly let go. There was a thud and a clatter from inside the room. Glancing through the doorway, the cardinal said, "Well, it serves you right; I told you I wasn't going to dress like some novice!" He reached down and picked the belt up off the floor. "Now leave me in peace!" he said, knotting it firmly around his waist before turning to Ben and opening his arms wide. "Ben, I've been looking all over for you. Is it time to go?"

Ben took a few steps backwards. "I'm looking for my mother. The others are by the jetty, I'll meet you there."

He was about to run off when the cardinal grabbed his arm. "Oh no, I'm not letting you out of my sight! What, and risk being left behind? This place is a cultural desert: no books, no wine, and *terrible* clothes . . ."

Ben looked at the cardinal. "Fine, just don't slow me down or we might *both* get left behind."

Cardinal Bolt released Ben's arm and together they hurried across the quadrangle to join Tobias who was waiting for them on the far side. The dog led them down another passageway and it wasn't long before Ben realised he was taking them to where they had last seen his mother.

They entered the paved courtyard beneath the tower to find the stones cracked and blackened from the earlier blast. Ben looked around. There was no sign of Teah, but the door to the tower stood ajar and through the open doorway he could see the stairs that led to the room at the top. He hurried over and entered the tower, followed closely by Tobias and the cardinal. Taking the stairs two at a time he soon reached the top and pushed back the velvet curtain.

Behind him, Cardinal Bolt gasped. "Now this is more like it," he said, pushing Ben aside and entering the room. He turned full circle, taking in the huge fireplace and fine furnishings. With a happy sigh, he sank into one of the fireside armchairs and plucked a plump, red apple from the bowl of fruit on the table beside it.

Ignoring him, Ben ran over to the nearest window and looked out. From this vantage point he could see a garden with a greenhouse and a small orchard. A monk was on his knees tending to the plants, but he couldn't see Teah. He moved to the next window. This one looked down into a kitchen yard where a couple of novices sat on their haunches peeling potatoes – but still no Teah. The third window gave a fine view of the sea, dotted with the long, low islands that made up the drumlins. Ben spotted the fishing boat lying at anchor a little way out. It looked tiny from this distance. He drew his gaze towards the shoreline and finally spied Teah's slender figure on the jetty.

"There she is! We must have just missed her!" He tore down the stairs and across the courtyard. Reaching the far side, he skidded on the damp stone floor and almost collided with some monks coming the other way. He managed to avoid them at the last minute and ducked into the passageway. Tobias overtook him, his tail wagging quickly with excitement. More monks were gathered in the grassy quadrangle and Ben caught a glimpse of the abbot in their midst. The old man waved at him as he passed and Ben grinned back. Then he was hurtling down the final passageway that led to the shore.

"Mother!" he cried as he came out into daylight, and then stopped in dismay. The waterline had fallen dramatically in the short space of time he had been gone, and the jetty now rose up from a bed of rocks draped with slimy, evil-smelling kelp. Lying low in the water some distance from the shore and drawing further away as Ben watched, was the rowing boat.

"NOOOoooooo!"

Ben jumped as Cardinal Bolt cried out next to him, right in Ben's ear. Beside him, the cardinal fell to his knees and stared after the departing boat. One of the figures on board had heard his cry and turned to look back. A moment later Ben heard Arrowbright's faint voice, "Farewell, Ben, and good luck!"

"Good luck with what?" Ben wondered out loud.

"With your next task."

Ben turned. Behind him stood his mother, still dressed in the monk's robes but with the hood thrown back to reveal shining blonde hair exactly the same shade as his own.

"Come back!" screamed the cardinal. He turned to Teah and held out his hands pleadingly. "Can't you make them come back?"

"I cannot," answered Teah. "They must return to Quadrivium with the tide. Now it has turned, it will not turn again for a century or more. They cannot return."

"But what about us?" asked Ben. "How do we get back?"

Teah turned to face him. "We go forwards, Ben, not back."

"I don't understand."

"Neither do I," interrupted the cardinal. "I want to go *back*, back to my books and my wine and my palace. I want to go *home!*"

"This is your home now," said Teah. She looked towards the abbey and the cardinal followed her gaze. His face paled and Ben turned to see what they were both looking at. A procession of monks had emerged from the abbey. They approached without a word and surrounded the cardinal.

Teah continued, "I have been the abbess for many years, but now it's time for me to leave. Your coming here was no coincidence, Cardinal Bolt; you are to take over from me as abbot."

The cardinal's mouth opened and closed a few times, but no sound came out. He stood as though rooted to the spot while the monks removed his crimson robes and replaced them with a plain brown habit, but when they took his arms to lead him back towards the abbey he finally began to struggle. "No! I don't belong here! There's been some mistake! Ben, tell them I don't belong here!"

Ben looked at Teah who shook her head. They watched as the cardinal was escorted through the archway and waited until the echoes of his cries had died away. Then Teah took Ben's hand in hers. "Come," she said, "we must be gone before nightfall."

Ben didn't move. He had suddenly turned very pale and his eyes were wide and staring. "The Book," he said, in a voice not much more than a whisper.

He turned slowly and looked out to sea. The fishing boat was still visible in the distance, but as he watched it began to move, turning away from the abbey and slipping towards the horizon.

"Come, Ben, it's time to go."

"But the *Book* . . ."

"Trust me."

Still holding Ben's hand in hers, she led him away from the jetty. He stumbled after her, looking over his shoulder until the fishing boat had disappeared entirely from view. When he faced forward again, he realised they had passed the archway which led back inside the abbey. Instead, his mother was leading him around the outer wall of the abbey, over the rocks exposed by the receding tide, until eventually they came to a door set into the wall. Standing beside it was Murgatroyd.

Ben looked from his mother to the eagle and then back again. Teah didn't seem surprised by Murgatroyd's appearance.

"Do you have it?" she asked him, to which Murgatroyd gave a brief nod and pushed open the door with his wing. Teah ushered Ben through.

It was dark inside and Ben hesitated on the threshold, waiting for his eyes to adjust to the dim light. Gradually, a shape in front of him resolved itself into the form of a large wicker basket. Teah entered behind him and went over to the wall opposite, where a wheel was fixed. As she spun the wheel, there came a loud creaking sound from above and the room was flooded with light as the ceiling was winched back.

"Ben, get into the basket."

Ben did as his mother said, throwing one leg over the side and levering himself over. Something shifted beneath his feet and he bent down to have a closer look. In the bottom of the basket was a large object covered with a piece of oilskin. Heart pounding, he pulled the oilskin aside and gasped as he recognised the leather and bronze cover of the Book of Prophecies.

"I had a feeling we might need that," said Teah, climbing in beside him and dropping a coil of rope on the floor. "So I had Murgatroyd fetch it from the boat and bring it here while everyone else was otherwise occupied."

Ben hugged the Book to his chest and looked around for the eagle.

"He'll be waiting for us outside." As she spoke, Teah attached a hose to a tall, narrow box in the centre of the basket and turned a knob. There was a hissing sound and a bright blue flame leapt from a funnel at the top of the box. Something shifted above Ben's head. Tobias looked up and began to growl.

"Here, Tobias," called Teah, patting the side of the basket. The large, yellow dog backed away, still growling.

Ben raised his head. Suspended on a shelf of thin wooden struts, and attached to the basket with ropes, were layers and folds of silvery-white silk. As Ben watched, the silk began to billow upwards and he felt the basket move beneath his feet.

"Quickly, Tobias," called Teah, more insistently now.

Ben's stomach lurched as the basket lifted off the floor, then thumped back down again. "Come on, Tobias," he called urgently.

With one last anxious glance upwards, the dog took a running leap towards Ben. He got his front paws over the side, but it was too high and he fell back as the basket lifted off the ground. This time it continued to rise, slowly gathering speed as it headed towards the opening in the ceiling. The wooden struts broke away and fell to the ground as the folds of silk filled out to become a huge balloon.

"Tobias!" shouted Ben, leaning out over the side and looking down at the forlorn dog staring back up at him.

Then Tobias began to move. He leapt onto a wooden packing crate and from there onto more crates stacked haphazardly against the wall. The stack teetered but Tobias kept going, jumping from crate to crate, keeping pace with the basket which was still rising. Finally, with one almighty leap, he flung himself into the air, legs splayed, and landed half inside the basket, his back paws scrabbling against the wickerwork. Ben leant over the side and quickly hauled him in.

At that moment there was a scraping sound and the basket tilted to one side. Teah turned back to the controls, tapping dials and looking anxiously at the balloon as she pushed buttons and adjusted knobs. Finally, the basket righted itself, and then they were free and soaring up into the open sky.

Ben peered over the side to see the tiled roofs of the abbey falling away. The balloon began to drift sideways, dragging its shadow over a high wall and into the garden with its long greenhouse, then across the paved courtyard – narrowly missing the tower as it gained height – and finally the grassy quadrangle. There was still a crowd of monks huddled in the quadrangle, but only one looked up as they passed overhead. Ben heard a faint cry, but by now they were too high for him to make out the words, and still they were rising. Now he could see the whole abbey laid out beneath them, surrounded by a ring of rocks and the flat sea. The drumlins protruded from the water like the humps of a sea monster, encircling the island on which the Abbey of the Ancients stood. Then Ben caught sight of the fishing boat far below, looking like a child's toy.

"Arrowbright!" he shouted, then turned to Teah.

"Can we go down?"

She nodded and pulled one of the knobs. The basket began to sink slowly and eventually Ben made out three tiny figures standing on deck, waving. As they sank closer, he identified the figures as Arrowbright, Bella and Brother Bernard, and then suddenly they were past. He turned to the other side of the basket and waved until the boat was no more than a speck on the calm, grey sea.

Ben looked up to see Murgatroyd gliding effortlessly alongside the basket. Tobias was curled up on his feet, his tail tucked firmly between his legs and his furry eyebrows raised anxiously as he watched Ben's every move. Ben bent down to give him a reassuring pat, then looked up at his mother. She was still turning knobs and checking the glass dials containing tiny needles that spun round and round.

"Murgatroyd," she called, "we need to turn due north, towards the pole."

Without a word, Murgatroyd began to spiral upwards. Ben watched him soar higher and higher until his neck hurt from looking up. Then abruptly the eagle turned and swooped back towards them, flattening out as he came level with the basket.

"There's a thermal stream a little higher. With a bit of luck, it will take us most of the way there."

Teah made a few more adjustments to the dials and

then finally turned to Ben.

"Well done, Ben," she said. "You've done everything I expected of you, but there is one last thing that we must do together."

Without realising he was doing it, Ben reached up to touch the locket around his neck. "What is it? Where are we going?"

"To the northernmost point of the meridian," answered his mother. "We are going to find your father."

Book Three
MERIDIAN OBSIDIAN

In this final instalment of the Prophecies of Ballitor series, Ben must defeat his nemesis, the pale man, once and for all.

According to the Book of Prophecies, the pale man has only one weakness: his obsession for Ben's mother. If Ben is to save the Kingdom of Ballitor and successfully reunite his own family, he must locate the mythical Cave of All Souls and exploit this weakness in the pale man's soul.

But no one knows if the Cave really exists.

The Book of Prophecies offers up a single clue: Meridian Obsidian, a hard, glasslike substance believed to line the walls of the Cave of All Souls. When Ben accidentally comes across it in the most dangerous place he's ever been, he wonders whether the price for defeating the pale man is simply too high.

About the Author

Kirsty Riddiford was born in Lancashire but moved with her family to South Africa at the age of nine. She left South Africa after university to see the world, and finally settled in South West London where she lives with her husband, Matt.

Most of her time is spent writing, visiting schools and walking their two Labradors, Toby and Megan.

You can discover more about Kirsty, her books and her school visits at:

www.kirstyriddifordbooks.com.

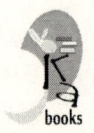